Dieppe

Book 4 in the

Combined Operations Series

By

Griff Hosker

Published by Sword Books Ltd 2015
Copyright © Griff Hosker First Edition

A CIP catalogue record for this title is available from the British Library.
Cover by Design for Writers

Dedicated to my little sister, Barb, and in memory of my dad who served in Combined Operations from 1941-1945

Part 1

Dieppe

Chapter 1

Falmouth June 1942

The dog bite I had suffered on the reconnaissance patrol to Dieppe did not take long to heal. That was more than fortunate for we had to prepare for Operation Rutter, the attack on Dieppe. This would be a sterner test of the defences of Occupied Europe than St. Nazaire had been. That had been a hit and run attack. This would be an attempt to capture a port. The captured German E-Boat we used would need to be repaired and adapted for, once again, we would be going in before the main Canadian attack. Our unit was to be used as a scalpel to prepare the way for the major surgery that would be the two Canadian Infantry Brigades, the 4th and the 6th along with the Calgary Tanks. The British element would be commandos from Number 2, Number 3 and Royal Marine A Commando. The British section was well prepared but for the Canadians it would be their first combat. We just did not know how they would cope with it.

Now, a week after our return from Dieppe and with our intelligence assessed and evaluated, we awaited orders. Sergeant Major Reg Dean had managed to acquire the staff car which the officers of Number 4 Commando had left at our base. No one questioned the formidable Sergeant Major's right to use the vehicle. How he got petrol I have no idea but he was a most resourceful Commando. He drove me down to Carrick Roads where the *'Lucky Lady'* was moored. He nodded to my hand as we negotiated the twisting and narrow roads. "Healing nicely, sir."

"It is Sarn't Major. With luck it will be ready when we embark."

"That is a week or so off isn't it, sir?"

"First week in July. I have to pop over to the Isle of Wight and meet with Major Foster before then. Apparently there is some sort of problem with the operation and they need us to explain a few things to them."

"Will you be taking the E-Boat, sir?"

I shook my head, "The less she is seen the better. She is our ace in the hole. No we shall be going by train."

"You and the pirate eh sir?"

I laughed, "I am not certain that Lieutenant Jorgenson would appreciate that particular title, Sarn't Major."

"But you have to admit he does look like one. And he plays a good Jerry too, sir."

"Oh he does that. I can speak German but he sounds German, you know what I mean?" We had turned the last bend in the road and we saw the anchorage. The E-Boat bobbed up and down beneath the camouflage net. Her crew were still making good the damage we had suffered when we had been extracted from the beach. Sergeant 'Polly' Poulson was working with my section on the jetty. They were making charges. As Commandos we had to improvise. We had discovered that preparation gave us more opportunities to do so. Whatever we were asked to do in this operation we knew we would have to buy ourselves time to escape. Charges and booby traps did that. We were very good at making booby traps.

I climbed out. Sergeant Major Dean put it into reverse, "What time shall I pick you up, sir?"

I shook my head, "Don't bother, Reg. I will go back with the lads. I need the exercise!"

We prided ourselves on our fitness and doubling back with the section would help us all. When you ran together you got into each other's rhythm. Somehow, and I didn't know how, that translated to a better understanding when you were in action. We had to be as one when we worked behind enemy lines.

We were informal and no one leapt to their feet to salute me as I wandered up. Sergeant Poulson nodded as he helped Private Groves with the charge. "Young Groves here is becoming quite good at making charges, sir."

"Good!"

I ducked under the netting and found Lieutenant Alan Jorgenson, the captain of the boat.

"Good timing Tom, we are all ship shape and Bristol fashion!"

It always seemed odd to hear such phrases coming from someone who looked like a German. With a monocle in his eye he would look every inch the caricature German the press used to deride the enemy. "Good, we have to pop down to the Isle of Wight tomorrow. I will get the travel warrants from the Quartermaster later today."

"Shame we can't take the *'Lady'*. It would be faster and more comfortable."

I doubted the comfort side of it but it would be quicker. "Every time we take her out we risk a German spy or an aeroplane seeing her and giving the game away. Besides I like trains."

He shrugged, he did not agree, "Anyway come and see the improvements we have made." He led me along the side. He pointed to the torpedo tube. "We would never have used it as a torpedo tube. It just added weight to the bows. We have cut away half of it. With one of your chaps or one of mine lying in it we could use it as a machine gun position. The half of the tube we have left will give a metal shield and we still look like a German ship.

3

I knelt down to inspect the work. The edge had been smoothed. It curved over at the top and would protect the machine gunner. "You did the same on the other side?"

"Yes; we now have two forward facing guns."

"Excellent. I will see if I can get a couple of Bren guns."

"German ones would be better. The sound of a German machine gun would confuse them eh?"

"We will need to capture them. Until we do, we will use Bren guns."

We went to the area between the tubes. Here were where the rubber dinghies were stored. I saw that they had fitted an Oerlikon. He patted it affectionately, "Jerry uses these too so it won't seem odd here. Damned good against aircraft and ships. The Killick has been training the men. This give us a bit more bite at the sharp end!"

There were other changes which had been made. We had learned through experience what needed to be done to make it a home for almost forty men. Below decks they had rigged up more hammocks to make the sleeping arrangements more comfortable.

"With the metal we saved on the torpedo tubes and the chief's modifications to the engines we reckon we can get five more knots out of her. If we meet one of her sisters we can out run them."

"That is good news. Well I will leave you lads to your tasks and I will see what my boys have been up to."

They were just finishing up making their charges. Sergeant Poulson stood, "The Killick says we can store these in the *'Lady Luck's'* magazine, sir. It will save us lugging them back to the camp."

"Excellent. I am afraid, however, that we will need to get to the camp tonight anyway. We need a couple of machine guns for the forward tubes. Get everything squared away and we will double time up there."

Had this been almost any other unit in the British Army there would have been complaints and moans. These, however, were Commandos. They just got on with it and viewed it as extra and therefore worthwhile training. We had done the run so many times that no one took the slightest notices as we donned Bergens and ran up to the headland above the town. The camp was now a transit camp. There was a skeleton staff who were responsible for specialist training. The cliffs were perfect for rock work and the old abandoned tin mine could be used for the testing of explosives. My first sergeant, Daddy Grant, was Quarter Master and Sergeant Major Dean took charge of all else.

When we arrived, slightly out of breath, I saw that the camp was almost deserted. For ordinary soldiers being a little out of breath was nothing but I deemed to be acceptable. We had had a few days off and were out of the habit of running. I would remedy that. I took the section to the QM stores. Daddy Grant, tapped his pipe out as we entered. "Now then, sir, what we can we do for you today?"

"We are after a couple of Brens."

Daddy frowned, "But why, sir? They use .303 ammo and you use .45."

"I know but we need a couple of light machine guns which can be fitted into the torpedo tube of an E-Boat."

He stroked his chin, "Well if you aren't bothered about carrying two types of ammo I have a couple of machine guns which might suit. Hang on a minute. They are out the back." He disappeared into the rabbit warren that was his stores.

His two clerks eyed us suspiciously as though we were going to steal everything that wasn't nailed down. I kept the smile from my face for, if we chose, we could have stolen everything in the stores without them even knowing. If any of my lads chose to go down the criminal route once the war was over they would be very successful.

I heard the Quartermaster shout, "Hey Charlie, Jack get out here."

"But Quartermaster, that will leave the stores empty!"

I heard an exasperated snort and then a shout, "Get your arses out here! Lieutenant Harsker can have anything he likes! Unlike you shower these lads are proper soldiers!" They hurried out to help my former sergeant when I had been just a corporal.

5

The two clerks struggled in with two packing cases. Daddy followed them, "Sorry about that sir. These two dozy buggers are new to the base. They will learn."

"And you will, no doubt, teach them."

"That I will, sir." He took a crowbar and lifted the lid. There was straw within. I was intrigued. Like a magician producing a rabbit from a hat he pulled out what looked like a brand new German MG 42. He put a hand up to theatrically flourish.

"Where on earth did you get this?"

"Remember when the '*Cossack*' caught the '*Altmark*'? The one with the prisoners from the '*Graf Spee*'?" I nodded. It had been good publicity for the Navy. "They found these and about six others in the hold. It isn't the latest MG 42. It is the prototype. I think I was told it was the MG39/41. It works the same as the newer one. It takes the same ammo as your Luger and it is belt fed."

"That is fantastic but just a couple of questions. How did you get hold of one and what about ammo?"

"When I went to a depot in Pompey I saw them there. The Quartermaster didn't know what to do with them and he had a bit of a storage problem. I said I would take a couple off his hands."

"A couple?"

He laughed, "Well four to be exact and he had a few cases of ammo. That is the real reason I got them. I remembered as how you liked the Luger. I was thinking of the ammo more than anything else."

"Thanks Daddy. It is perfect." I picked it up. It still had the grease on it. This had never been fired. "Much as I want to husband the ammunition I think we will take one to the range and try it out. We might as well find out the problems here rather than at sea. Keep your eye on that one until we come back. Lowe and Groves, pick it up. Hewitt, fetch the ammo."

When we reached the range we were all like children with a new Christmas toy. We crowded around as Polly worked out how to feed the ammunition through. It was a gun you fired lying down. That too would suit the new role we had in mind. Polly stood and gestured, "There you go, sir, do you want to do the honours?"

"Much as I would love to I suspect that one of you will be firing it. You can have the first burst, Sergeant."

I could see that he was desperate to try. He nestled the stock into his shoulder and then squeezed the trigger. I have never heard such a rapid rate of fire. It sounded like piece of cloth being torn.

Poulson took his hand off the trigger. "Bloody hell, sir! I thought the Thompson had a good rate of fire but this one..."

George Lowe said, "Aye, Sarge, but you have fired almost two hundred rounds." He held up the belt to show him the fifty or so bullets that were left.

Scouse Fletcher had been looking through the ranging telescope at the target. "And another thing Sarge. The last few bullets were high. The barrel must have a tendency to rise when you are firing."

That decided me. "Well we won't waste any more of our ammo. Not until we manage to get some more, at least. We just have to remember to use it like the Tommy guns. Short bursts."

He nodded and stroked the gun, almost affectionately, "Well at least it has a good range. That target is a thousand yards away. I reckon it could fire another thousand and still be accurate. With short bursts."

"Right, let's take these back to the digs. When the Sergeant Major comes for me in the morning we will take them down in the car. Put it back in its packing case."

Fortunately there were no markings on the wood. It could have been anything we were carrying. With the two guns and two cases of ammo and my overnight bag we were laden down as we headed back to the bed and breakfast we used as our lodgings. It would not do to tell Mrs Bailey, our landlady, what lay within the boxes. She would only upset herself. What she didn't know wouldn't upset her.

When I told Reg Dean what we carried he chuckled, "I am glad you didn't tell Mrs Bailey. She would not have been happy!"

"Are you two still courting, Reg?"

He laughed, "We are a bit old to be courting sir. Walking out is more what we do. We are comfortable with each other. It is just company. I have been married to the army for eighteen years and she has been married to the boarding house. We are just finding out about each other. There's lots of time and we are, well, both a bit shy."

I heard a warmth in his voice I had not heard before. "Well if she is half as happy as you, Reg, then it is no bad thing."

He nodded, sagely.

Alan Jorgenson was delighted with the guns. His engineer rigged the bipod so that it would not move. He bolted it to the bottom of the tube. We had spare barrels for the guns; they had been in the packing cases and the new emplacement meant we could easily change them.

"Sergeant you take charge of the men. We should be back tomorrow."

"Right, sir!"

"Are you ready, Alan?"

"I'd like to see the guns fitted and tested properly but yes. Our masters call and like good hounds we respond! I'll sling my bag in the back eh?"

Reg took us to Truro to catch the mainline and we had a carriage largely to ourselves. We were able to chat in a way we normally could not. It was a long journey but there was a buffet car. I enjoyed the train journey. It was late afternoon when we reached the huge camp which was filled with Canadian troops. Major Foster was acting as an adviser to Lord Lovat and he met us at the Headquarters building. As the Major walked us to our quarters for the night he said, "Keen as mustard these Canadians but very green."

"We were too, sir. Remember the Loyal Lancashires?"

He laughed and said to Alan, "That was where we first met. I was a gung ho captain and young Harsker here was a private with more guts than was good for him. It seems a million years and a lifetime ago. You are right, Tom, we were naive and we were green. The difference is the Germans have also improved since we fought them. They have decent tanks now with guns that are better than ours."

As if to make the point a couple of tanks drove by making us step off the road. "They are new sir. What kind are they?"

"Churchills. Hopefully they will stand up to the German armour a little better than the ones we had in France."

Alan asked, "I can see why Tom is here to answer all these questions; he landed and reconnoitred but all we did was drop them off. We have no idea what the landing zone will be like."

"No, Alan, you know the waters. You were handpicked to be the captain of, what is it you lads call her? *'Lucky Lady'* because of your experience in the Channel. The destroyers will lie offshore but the landing craft and the launches will have to close in with the shore. You know those waters better than any."

"It will be like St. Nazaire all over again, sir."

"Yes Tom and that is the danger. The Germans have learned lessons. The RAF and Coastal Command tell us that they have beefed up their defences. It will not be as easy and we have more men going in this time." We stopped at a hut. "You two are in here, first room on the right. Just dump your bags and then come with me. We have lots of people to meet and all of them want to pick your brains. Tonight is informal; you will just chat. Tomorrow will be harder. It will be like Whitehall all over again."

After we had dropped our bags Alan and I were taken around like a pair of candidates for Parliament. The Canadians quizzed us about everything. Many of the questions we could not answer and I, for one, felt foolish. By the time it was time for dinner I was exhausted.

Major Foster came back to our quarters with us. His room was opposite ours. "You did well chaps."

"What about those questions we couldn't answer?"

He smiled, "That was the purpose of this informal chat. We now know what further intelligence we need."

I groaned, "You mean we go back?"

"Exactly, old son. We need to reassure our Canadian friends."

"And when does the operation begin?"

"The troops will embark on the second of July and it starts five days later."

"That doesn't give us long then does it, sir?"

"No. To be frank I have made a bit of a cock up. We really needed you to leave within the next day or so to be able to return with the information. We have to have their questions answered before they embark."

"But what information, sir? I thought we completed our last mission. What didn't we do?"

"Nothing Tom. You did all that we asked of you." He sighed, "We need you to get to the beaches close to the port. You need to reconnoitre the places where the Canadians will actually land."

I looked at Lieutenant Jorgenson and laughed, "Well that should be easy enough!"

Alan shook his head, "Sir, with due respect, after the last time they will be on edge. Won't this make them even more suspicious?"

"Perhaps but what you two discovered helps the paratroopers and the Commandos. They are going to take out the two batteries. The information we have about Dieppe is based upon aerial photographs and your reports. You didn't get to the beaches did you?" We shook our heads. "The Canadians have complained that they don't know what to expect. They need to know what the beach will be like. What defences are there, at sea level. We need samples of sand. What are the exits of the beaches like? Aerial photography can tell us only so much. We need to know how steep the beaches are. Which ones will be easier than others. So we need you back as soon as possible."

This was a fait accompli. No matter what we said we would have to go and the sooner the better, "Well sir if you radio the camp Sergeant Major Dean could tell the men to get here. If they leave tonight they could be here by morning."

He nodded, "I can do that."

"And have you an idea how you can get us what we need?"

"Not yet sir but if there is a bar here then Alan and I can try to work something out."

During dinner I watched rather than talked. I wanted to know about these Canadians from the west of that huge country. The Canadians were not impressed by the food which was being served. Apparently they had better at home. The beer was also too warm. In fact everything they had before them was not right. I saw some of the younger officers glancing over at the fruit salad on my battledress. None asked me about them but I knew they would.

After dinner Alan and I found a quiet corner where we sat with the one whisky each we had been allowed and we talked. I had found that the best way to deal with a problem was not to see it as such. We looked at what we could do. We worked out what we needed to do and then discussed the various options available to us.

It was Alan who came up with a solution. We were just talking and he spirited it out of the air. "It is a pity that we don't have any of those experimental frogmen on board. They would make it easy."

"Frogmen?"

"Yes, in March I was in Portsmouth and saw them beginning their training. They have these rubber suits, big flippers, a face mask and something they called rebreathers to help them swim underwater and stay hidden. I think they use them to attack enemy ships at anchor and to check our ships for explosives too."

"That sounds like science fiction to me."

"Oh it works. I saw them underwater for half an hour or so. In daylight you can see bubbles but I am guessing that, after dark, they would be invisible."

An idea began to form. "Alan, we are going to have to go in at night, aren't we?"

"Of course."

"We risk grounding as we don't know the shape of the beach and the Germans would be suspicious of any boat being that close to their beach." He nodded. "So the best idea would be for you to be out of sight, say four hundred yards off the beach. If it was a cloudy night then we could manage that."

"I suppose so. But how does that help? That is a long way to go in a dinghy and you would risk being seen by the patrols they have."

"If I had a pair of those flippers and a mask I could swim in and test the beach and the sand. I would be able to check out the beach defences too."

"You would freeze!"

I shook my head, "It is July. I used to swim all the time when I was younger and that was in England where the waters are colder." I saw him beginning to see how we might do it. "The thing is you and the E-Boat might still be spotted; you would need to say you had engine trouble or something."

"We could do that. But that would mean we would have to get you the flippers and the mask." He swallowed his whisky, "And you would need someone with you. It is too risky to have you go alone."

"We ask your crew and my lads. A volunteer is better than a pressed man. But this plan ends here if we can't get the equipment. The only alternative is to land as close to the beach as possible and make it a ground reconnaissance."

"And that could end in disaster."

"I know."

I saw Major Foster speaking with Lord Lovat and the commander of the operation, Major-General Roberts; we approached them. They looked up. Lord Lovat nodded when he recognised me. Major Foster stood and said, "These are two of my chaps, Lieutenant Jorgenson and Lieutenant Harsker. They are the ones who will reconnoitre the beach." He looked at me expectantly.

"Could we have a word, sir? We have a plan."

He was about to take us away when the Major-General said, "I'd like to hear it; if you don't mind, Major. The lives of my men may depend on these two young men."

Inwardly I groaned. I didn't mind the Major thinking I was a fool but not two senior officers. "Well, sir, if we are to do this without arousing the German's suspicions then we have to do it without landing."

The Canadian snorted, "Impossible!"

I saw Lord Lovat begin to smile, "Go on Harsker. I always enjoy the way your inventive mind works."

"We swim ashore and collect the information from the shoreline."

Both the Major and Lord Lovat nodded but Major-General Roberts said, "Swim! Impossible!"

Impossible appeared to be his favourite word. Alan said, "No sir, the navy have been using divers equipped with flippers and a face mask. They make swimming easier. If Tom was given two sets of flippers and masks then he and another of the team could easily swim ashore, collect samples and test the shelving of the beach. We would lie offshore and feign damage."

Lord Lovat turned to the Canadian. "It might work, John. I have seen these flippers in use and the sailors who use them move like fish."

"We would need samples from the whole of the beach, you know." The Major General was like a dog with a bone. He would not let it go.

"Yes sir. We have done this before."

His eyes narrowed at the implied impertinence. Major Foster added, hurriedly, "These officers were the ones who provided all the information upon which we have based Operation Rutter. They are the best we have."

"Well I should damned well hope so!"

Major Foster said, "I will get you two sets and the boat and your team will be here by morning. Well done."

He nodded for us to leave. We saluted and left. Alan said, "Nice of our allies to have such confidence in us eh?"

"They are new to it, Alan. They will learn."

The questions we had to endure the next morning were even more searching. Luckily the RAF had taken some excellent aerial photographs and the fact that we only had sketchy knowledge of the actual buildings in the town was overlooked. They were, however, quite worried and daunted by the prospect of the guns in the massive batteries wreaking havoc on their ships as they approached. By the time we had finished answering the barrage of questions I was exhausted.

Lord Lovat and Major Foster escorted us out. Major Foster put a hand on our shoulders, "Well done chaps."

Lord Lovat nodded, "You did well and don't worry about the batteries, the Canadians won't have to worry about them. The Airborne Commandos will deal with them."

Major Foster smiled, "Your gear has come and your boat is in a small cover on the west of the island. There is a car outside to take you. It has your diving equipment in the boot. Leave as soon as you deem it practical. It is just five days before we launch. Your information will determine what red and white beaches are like." We now knew the code names for the beaches. They were colour coded and red and white were the ones closest to the Germans.

"Yes sir." We saluted and left. I much preferred doing than talking. We would soon be back in our element; the front line.

Chapter 2

The cove the crew had found for us was truly out of the way. We had to walk the last four hundred yards after the car dropped us off and negotiate a small path which led to the beach. The crew had rigged a camouflage net over her. She was not completely hidden but could not be identified as German. We struggled down the path until Sergeant Poulson saw us and sent Crowe and Fletcher to help us carry our new gear.

Fletcher said, "What you got in here sir? The kitchen sink!"

"It could be worse, Scouse. We didn't bring everything we could have!"

We paddled out to the E-Boat in the rubber dinghy. Anticipation was written all over the faces of the crew and my section. Alan said, "I had better go and get the charts sorted. I will ask if any of my lads can swim well enough to do the job."

"Righto." As he wandered off I said, "Right lads, to the foredeck and gather around." When they were seated at my feet I told them what we would be doing. None of them looked very happy about the task I had suggested. I smiled, "I take it none of you are that good at swimming? I know you can all swim but I am talking up to a mile of swimming at night."

Poulson looked around at the section, "You are right, sir, we can all swim sir. I mean you have to be able to swim be in the Commandos but I am not certain that any of us could swim as far as you want us to. It will be a quarter of a mile to the beach and then we have to swim along it. I will have a go, sir but..."

"No, Sergeant, I want honesty. There is no point saying you will do it and then have to be rescued. It could be a one man job.

If I have to I will do this alone. Perhaps one of the Navy lads can swim longer distances. Anyway unpack the gear. I need to try it out." While they took out the flippers and mask I went to the cabin I shared with Alan, undressed and donned my swimming trunks.

I had just put on the flippers when Bill Leslie and Alan Jorgenson appeared, "Well Lieutenant, you are lucky. We have a good swimmer here. Bill won medals in the St. Helens Swimming Championship of nineteen thirty six."

I smiled, "Are you sure, Bill?"

He nodded, "Aye sir, but I am not certain about that gear."

"I have never used it either. Let's give it a go eh? I'll go first."

Putting on the face mask I stepped to the side of the boat and threw myself backwards. I deduced that would be the easiest way to immerse myself in the sea. Once in the water I found it easy to almost walk around as though I was on land. There was little effort involved but I noticed, after a moment or two, that my face mask fogged up. I took it off and rinsed it. That seemed to clear it. Bill copied me and jumped in. When he came up I said, "Rinse out the face mask and then put it on again."

He did so and then gave me the thumbs up. "Let's just try to swim around the '*Lady*'."

I lay face forward and put my hands by my side. I was going for the streamlined approach. I could not believe how easy it was to move. Just a flick of each foot propelled me a lot further than I would have expected. Soon we were all the way around the boat.

I lifted up my mask as Bill trod water next to me. "Bloody hell sir! I would have won every race with these buggers on!"

"Hang on here I am going to try something." I put the mask on, took a deep breath and dived down to the bottom. It was easy. I came up slowly and bobbed next to Bill. "Well I am happy. If we are spotted we can dive to the bottom. Although that should be unlikely given that we are doing this at night." He nodded, "Are you sure about this? You aren't a Commando. You don't need to come with me."

"I wasn't certain before but I am now, sir. The flippers make swimming easier."

"Then let's get back aboard. We need to organise how we do this."

As we were drying off Bill said, "You know sir, it will be cold in the sea at night. How about getting some goose grease?"

I nodded, "A good idea. "

Sergeant Poulson said, ""George, nip ashore and get some."

"But Sarge the nearest shop might be miles away."

"There is a farm at the end of the lane. I can see it from here! They should have some goose grease."

He nodded, "Right Sarge."

I took two pound notes from my wallet, "Give these to the farmer."

"But it's for the war effort, sir!"

"Just give it to him, eh!"

The cold soon went, especially when we were handed a mug of cocoa. Alan joined us, his inevitable cheroot in his mouth. I had no idea where he got them from but he always managed to have one to hand. I gestured with the mug to the east. "We need a pair of chinograph pencils and acetate. We will have to mark what we find."

"I have those, Tom."

"And something to keep the sand in. Best have them marked with an indelible pencil so that we know where each sample comes from. There may be differences along the beach."

Bill said, "We have some hessian bags. I think they were from the time it was German. They smell like they had charges in them."

"Good. We will use them." I smiled, "I reckon that is it. We know what we are doing. We swim ashore. Crawl up the beach and see what the sea wall defences are like, collect some sand. We go back in the water swim another forty or fifty yards or so and repeat. When we meet back in the middle we swim back to the boat."

Alan finished his cheroot and threw it over the side. "Not quite. What if something happens to you and Bill? There may be sentries.

17

You might get lost. I know it is unlikely but we ought to prepare for the worst."

He was right and I had not thought of that. "Well, you give us an hour or an hour and a half to do the job and if we are not back then you will have to land the sergeant and the section. They will have to do it the hard way."

Sergeant Poulson nodded, "Don't worry, sir. We will finish the operation."

"But hopefully you won't have to and the Lieutenant's pessimism will not be justified.

As we prepared for sea I sat with Alan and checked out the charts. The beach at Dieppe was about three quarters of a mile across. I waved Bill over, "You can begin your swim here, on the west side of the beach. I will begin at the harbour mouth."

"That is more dangerous isn't it, sir?"

"It doesn't matter, Bill. This is my idea and one of us has to examine that side of the beach. I am quite willing to take the risk. We both swim inshore, fill a bag with sand and mark the shelving of the beach. The bigger landing craft shouldn't have a problem but we have a few of the smaller ones with us. They might struggle if it is too steep."

"Do you want me to go on to the beach to get the sand or just take it from the surf?"

"That would be best but don't take risks. Keep your eyes peeled for defences. We each have four bags. We will meet in the middle and then swim back out to the boat."

"Seems straightforward enough, sir."

"I know and these things seldom are. Something we haven't foreseen will happen and we will have to make it up as we go along."

Alan said, "You had better get your head down, Killick."
"Right sir."

After he had gone Alan said, "I will try to get in as close as I can for you."

"Not too close though, eh? We don't want to alert Jerry."

18

I did as I had ordered Bill to do and I slept while the *'Lucky Lady'* sped east across the Channel. This would be a dangerous passage as the nights were so short that we could be observed for most of our journey across. We would only have four hours of darkness in which to carry out our task. The RAF would attack us first and ask questions later and the Germans would ask for codes we could not supply.

When Hewitt brought me the cup of tea the sky was darker although not the black night we had hoped for, "Lieutenant Jorgenson says we will be on station in an hour. He thought you might want something to drink and a bit of food inside you."

"Thanks Hewitt. I needed this!"

Lowe had managed to get some goose grease and a dozen eggs from the farmer. I wolfed down the fried egg sandwich and washed it down with the hot sweet tea. "Another cup, Hewitt and I will get this goose grease slapped on."

While he scurried off I began to smear the goose grease on my chest, arms and legs. It was really a way to slow down the effects of the cold once we were in the sea. I had almost finished when he returned. "You look like a cold greasy chip, sir!" He realised what he had said, "Sorry sir!"

"Don't worry, son." I drank the tea and draped a blanket around my shoulders. I padded my way up to the bridge, the flippers slapping on the deck. Ahead of us the coast was dark while to the west the last vestiges of the sun could be seen glinting in the west.

"Half an hour to go. It seems fairly quiet. I heard some bombers but they were high up and heading north west. Someone is in for a pasting." He pointed ahead, "You can just make out the shadows of the cliffs. I will cut the motors soon so that we are barely making way. Wacker is on the radio in case Jerry asks us any questions."

Bill appeared similarly smeared and with a blanket around his shoulders. I nodded to him, "This is the hard bit, just before we go in. Once it all starts you have no time to think. Now all you can do is worry and think about what can go wrong."

He nodded and I saw he was nervous. He was used to action but Bill never left the ship. He knew the ship and he was comfortable there. This was foreign to him, quite literally. I felt guilty. I was certain he had volunteered because of our friendship. If anything happened to him I would not be able to forgive myself.

"Fifteen minutes. You had best get yourselves ready."

We slipped out of the bridge and went to the stern. The transom was lower than the bow and we did not want to make a splash when we entered the water. Sergeant Poulson and the section waited with our masks and flippers. I saw that they had already immersed them in the sea. Our chinograph markers and acetates were ready with the empty bags. We draped them around our necks and sat with our flippers trailing in the water.

I said quietly to Sergeant Poulson, "Give us ninety minutes; no more. If we haven't done it by then we are probably in the bag. You will have to do it the hard way."

He shook his head, "No sir, this is the hard way."

I noticed we were barely moving. I looked to my right and saw the cliffs rising as a dark shadow ahead. A seaman came and said, "Captain says we are here, sir!"

"Ready Bill?"

"Aye sir."

I slipped into the waters which felt like ice; they weren't, it was an illusion. I put my head down and began to kick. Bill had been on the other side of the boat. The next time I saw him we would be meeting in the middle and the job would be done. I just kept going at ninety degrees to the shore. Every so often I stopped to take my bearings and when I saw the breakwater and the entrance to the harbour I knew where I was. I corrected my direction and closed with the beach. To my great relief it shelved slowly. It would not be an obstacle to the small landing craft. I crept through the surf and lay on the beach. It was sand and shingle. I put a good handful into the bag marked with the number one.

After scanning the sand I began to creep forward. I wanted to take the opportunity of seeing the town from the sea. We had not managed to do so the first time. I took off my flippers. It was easier moving that way. The beach seemed quiet and I did not see anyone. I risked raising my head a little. I saw that there was no barbed wire on the beach. That was a good thing. I moved up the beach. The shingle would help to disguise my prints although the morning tide would remove them completely. Although there was no barbed wire and no mines there was a five feet high wall. I knew that behind that was an open esplanade area but the five feet high wall would be an obstacle. If a tank tried to climb the obstacle then the vulnerable underneath would be exposed for German gunners. I looked beyond the esplanade and the roads into the town; I saw that there was a huge concrete wall; it looked to be more than six feet high. Tanks would not get into the town that way. They had, effectively, blocked in the beach. I wondered what it would be like further away from the port.

I had seen enough and I crept back into the sea. I sat in the surf and put on my flippers. Before I slipped back into the surf I marked a number one at the left side of my map. Once I started to float I kicked hard and moved about a hundred and eighty yards to my right. I repeated my action. I collected my second sample and I crept up the beach to check that the defences were continuous. The goose grease was working. I was not as cold as I thought I would have been. I was about to slither on the beach for the last time when a movement caught my eye and I froze. It was a German sentry. Even as I stopped I heard him talking. There were two of them. The other had approached from the opposite direction. I lay with my face down in the surf and did not move.

"I do not know why they have us patrolling this beach. Why in God's name would the Tommies want this shithole?"

"It was those attacks we had not long ago. Perhaps they were preparing for another raid."

I heard a match being struck but I kept my face down in the sand. "This is not St. Nazaire. We have no dock here. It is a little port with a few fishing boats. They would not come here."

"Someone in Berlin thinks it is worth protecting. Perhaps they think the Tommies will invade here."

"Perhaps."

"Come, General Haase will have our balls if he finds out we have not walked the length of this beach. Let us get this leg finished and then have coffee."

The cigarette stub glowed as he threw it in the air and it hissed just five feet from my head. "It is not proper coffee. It is roast acorns."

"Better than nothing and it will warm us up."

I noticed the voices receding as they headed up the beach towards the harbour wall and the mole. "Now when I was a student in Vienna then we had real coffee."

I risked looking and saw that they were disappearing into the dark. I quickly filled my last bag with the same shingle and sand which covered the whole beach. I then slipped back into the sea. It was time for my rendezvous with Bill. I had seen enough. The concrete blocks stood at every road which led from the esplanade. The bags around my neck suddenly seemed heavy. Perhaps I was tiring or the cold was getting to me. I felt cramp begin to kick in. I moved my legs economically. There was little point in rushing until I had found Bill. I reached where I thought he should be and I trod water as I rotated to find him. I heard splashing to my left. I kicked in that direction. A white face loomed up out of the dark. It was Bill. He looked to be in distress.

"Are you all right?"

He turned at the sound of my voice. "Sorry sir. I have cramp. I have it bad. I can barely move my legs. And I can barely get my breath. I haven't got the lungs I had a few years back."

"Lie on your back and I will tow you."

"Leave me sir...I..."

"If I leave you they will find you and the game will be up. We don't want them to know we have been here. Just lie back and try to move your feet. Even a little will help. We will both get back Bill. A Commando never leaves a comrade behind. Even a sailor!"

He chuckled and rolled on to his back.

I put my right arm under his arms and across his chest. I began to kick my legs as I swam out to sea. I had to work them harder than I had done before but we began to move out to sea. We were moving slowly. I realised that the tide was coming in and I was having to fight that too. When a wave splashed over our heads I realised that the waves were getting higher. Either I was further out than I thought or the sea was getting up. The beach was almost invisibly black and I risked speaking.

"*Lady Luck*'!" I did not shout but whispered loudly.

There was silence. I expected to hear the diesel engines but there was nothing.

"Don't worry, sir. The lads'll be keeping a weather eye for us." Bill sounded confident but I was not too sure.

"But I am not certain if we are in the right place." I risked speaking a little louder, "*Lady Luck*'!"

There was nothing and I began to feel both the cold and the cramps. I had not swum for as long as this since I had been a young lad. It was only the Commando training which had kept me going as long as I had.

"I am going to tread water for a bit, Bill. Let's turn around and look out to sea."

We rotated through a hundred and eighty degrees. "*Lady Luck*'!"

"There sir! I saw a whitecap. It might be the bow wave!"

"*Lady Luck*'!"

This time I saw it and caught the diesel throb of her engines. I raised my white arm and saw the faces lining the bow of our boat. It was *'Lady Luck'.* We had not been abandoned. Lines were thrown and we were soon hauled aboard.

The crew threw blankets about our shoulders. I felt my teeth begin to chatter. Sergeant Poulson said, "Sorry about the delay, sir. The Lieutenant heard a pair of armed trawlers leaving the harbour. We drifted without engines for a while. We weren't on station." He sounded critical of the Lieutenant but Alan had done the right thing.

"You got here and that's what counts. Groves take the gear from Bill. Hewitt get him down to the SBA. He has cramp."

One of the hands put a mug of cocoa into my shivering shaking palms. "Here y'are sir. Stoker's cocoa! That'll put hair on your chest!"

"Thanks." He was right. The double tot of rum coursed through me. I found that I had finally stopped my teeth chattering. I made my way to the bridge.

"Sorry, Tom. I daren't risk starting the engines with Jerry so close."

"No problem. Leslie did well. He got cramp quite badly but he did his job."

"Good. I'll write him up. He deserves another promotion. Well?"

"The good news is there are no mines and the beach is just shingle. It has a shallow shelf."

"That sounds all good to me."

I shook my head, "They have barbed wire at the sea wall and the sea wall is about five feet high. The roads are all blocked with huge concrete pillars. The tanks will struggle to get off. I can't see them being able to get any further than the esplanade."

"It is all good news then." I cocked my head to one side. His words made no sense. He shrugged, "This way they know what they have to face."

"I suppose." I was not convinced. I could not see how they would be able to overcome such obstacles. I perched in the corner of the bridge with the blanket still draped around me.

Symons, the radar operator popped his head out from his cubby hole. "Trouble sir. Those two trawlers are out there again. Look like they are making a sweep right across our course."

"Damn."

I put my empty mug down. "Do you think they are looking for us?"

"Not unless they have radar too. I think we are just unlucky." He pointed to the east. False dawn could be seen. The true dawn was not long off. Late June meant the shortest of nights. "Middy, have all the guns manned. It might get a bit lively soon."

Midshipman Rowe raced around the crew checking that they were ready for action

"And I will get dressed. It would be rude to face Jerry half naked eh?"

As I passed Sergeant Poulson I said, "You had best man the two guns in the torpedo tubes. There may be trouble."

"Righto sir."

It did not take me long to dress. The goose grease which still remained after the towelling would have to stay until we reached Blighty. I would, at least, be warm when we went into action. I checked that both the Colt and the Luger were loaded and that I had spare magazines. I returned to the deck. Already the sky was visibly lighter in the east.

Alan had his head in the radar cubby hole. He stood as I approached. I noticed that Bill Leslie was on the wheel. He was a hard man to keep down.

"They will see us soon. They are patrolling about a mile apart. I think I will try to use my speed and get around their southern side. They won't be able to catch us but they will radio our position. We can't outrun aeroplanes." He shook his head. "I prefer winter. It might be cold and the weather awful but at least we have night's cloak to hide us!" He turned to Bill Leslie, "Right Killick. Let's head due west and give her some juice!"

"Right sir!"

The *'Lady Luck'* leapt out of the water like a greyhound from the stalls. It was lucky that I was leaning against the bridge else I might have fallen. Symon's disembodied voice came from his cubby hole. "We are starting to lose them, sir! It looks like they are sailing a box pattern."

"Good. Our luck might have held! They must be hunting submarines."

Five minutes later our hopes were dashed. I heard Symons say, "Bugger!"

"What is it Symons?"

"A small convoy ahead of us. It looks like it is on a course to meet the trawlers."

25

"And I am guessing that it is German." We had been told that there were no British ships in the area. By now the dawn was most definitely in the east. I could see the thin smudge that was the French coast behind us. Alan ducked down to the radar set. His face was grim when he emerged. "Five ships. One looks to be a destroyer and there is an E-Boat too. The other five look to be coasters."

"Can we avoid them?"

He shook his head. "We will see them soon and the destroyer is bigger than us; they will spot us." He chewed his lip.

"Look, Alan, it is your boat. You know what she can do. What do you reckon is our best move?"

He grinned, "We will try to bluff our way through them. Head straight for the Isle of Wight. Have your chaps ready with their guns. Wacker get on to base and report the convoy. Tell them we need aerial support."

"All right sir." Wacker's comforting and cheeky Liverpool accent was somehow reassuring.

"Sarn't Poulson, have the men find defensive positions. We are going to be in action soon!"

"Righto sir."

I went down to the mess to retrieve my Thompson. If we could put up a wall of bullets we might just get through the enemy ships. As I came up I heard a lookout shout, "German convoy directly ahead, sir!"

Alan shouted, "No one fire until I say so. They might take us for one of their own E-Boats."

I went towards the bow and lay down next to George Lowe who was manning the starboard MG 39/41. He patted it and grinned, "Be good to see how this works sir, in action, so to speak." He nodded towards the half of the tube which remained, "Nice and cosy down here, sir."

"Well if it gets too hot up here I may well join you."

I saw the five ships. They were going at the speed of the slowest coaster. We were travelling almost at full speed. I knew that Alan had a couple of knots in hand if he needed them. The E-Boat was leading the convoy and the destroyer was at the rear of the line. I could see that Alan was aiming between the E-Boat and the leading coaster. The E Boat just had a machine gun in the bows. We had the new Oerlikon as well as the two MG 39/41s. It might be enough.

Wacker said, "Sir, Jerry is calling. They are asking for a code."

"Pretend you are dozy. Just keep them talking."

I heard Wacker as he tried to convince the Germans that we had lost our code books. It bought us some precious minutes while we closed with them.

They were not fooled. I saw puffs of smoke from the German coasters. Each had a small deck gun. The calibre was not very big and they were trying to hit a rapidly moving target. All that they did was send waterspouts up which obscured us from the destroyer. The bigger warship had better and more accurate guns. As long as we were not struck by the destroyer's guns we had a chance.

Alan shouted, "It looks like it is a Zerstörer 34 class destroyer. She is almost as fast as us and has five guns. They are the same as our five inch. If she turns to face us we have a chance as she can only bring two to bear."

I watched as the E-Boat began to turn. She had been travelling at the sedate pace of the coasters and it was taking time for her to turn. The coasters did the same. I realised why; they thought we had torpedoes. The destroyer captain must have thought we were attacking his convoy. They were making us take a bow shot; always the hardest.

"Oerlikon crew, you can start to fire whenever you have a target."

As the E-Boat picked up speed we began to close really rapidly. I shouted to my men. "Those on the port side target the coaster. Don't waste ammunition!"

The German secondary armament began to fire but we were travelling so fast that most were missing. I heard the ping of bullets as they struck the metal torpedo tubes. We were less than five hundred yards apart and closing rapidly. I waited for a moment or two and then shouted, "Commandos, open fire!" Our combined speed would meant we would be together in seconds rather than minutes.

I leaned my Thompson on the torpedo tube and aimed at the open bridge of the E-Boat. I fired short bursts. I felt the vibration from the tube as Lowe let rip with the MG 39/41. With so many of my men firing we had to hit something and I saw three men fall from the bridge of the E-Boat. The machine gun crew at the bow were also scythed down. We must have hit the helmsman for it began to lurch towards us. Suddenly Sergeant Poulson and Private Hewitt hurled two grenades towards the approaching E-Boat. It would be close enough for the shrapnel to hit and they could both throw a long way.

"Grenade!"

Lieutenant Jorgensen threw us to port to avoid the careering German. The grenades went up and the shrapnel cleared the decks. It became a charnel house. It would not be a threat. My men on the port side had managed to kill the gun crew on the coaster.

I fired the last of my magazine at the coaster's bridge and then we were in open water. The destroyer would have to turn to catch us and we had the speed to escape. I heard Lieutenant Jorgenson shout, "Hang on to something. We will use everything we have got!"

It felt like being in a fighter which was diving. The speed was so great that we almost felt out of control. We sped across the water while the wounded were tended by the SBA and Private Hewitt, our section medic.

The sun appeared behind us. The sea looked grey. The lookout at the stern shouted, an hour after we had passed through the convoy, "German aircraft sir. 110's!"

Whilst not the greatest of fighters in aerial combat, as ground attack aeroplanes these twin engined beasts were a problem; they were deadly. "I hope the RAF have scrambled fighters or all your efforts will have been in vain, Tom!"

"Don't worry! They will get here." I was less confident than I sounded. I knew just how stretched the RAF were. The German machine guns in the two tubes were fixed and of little use to us. "Commandos, to the stern. Let's give them a hail storm they will remember!"

I went with my men and sat with my back to the bridge, my Thompson resting on a ventilator. The three black crosses drew closer remarkably quickly. They stood out against the rising sun. They came three abreast. I saw hope for that was a mistake. Line astern would have enabled them to bring all of their guns to bear in succession. They were anticipating that Alan would turn to port or starboard and they would have a beam on shot. Alan did not oblige. Our disadvantage was our speed. We were bouncing over the waves so much that aiming was almost impossible. Any hit would be pure luck. Sometimes luck favoured the brave. I hoped so.

Each of the fighters had four machine guns at the front. Wherever they aimed the aeroplane was their target. It was our stern. The Hotchkiss began to pump out shells and then the first of the Messerschmitts began to fire. We were lucky. The bouncing E-Boat upset his aim and the shells whizzed overhead.

"Fire!" We all let loose with our Thomson's and the Lewis guns by the bridge joined in. As soon as it passed the bow the Oerlikon added more firepower. Something must have hit for smoke began to pour from its fuselage. The other two banked to port and starboard. I saw now that their plan was to attack us at the same time across our beam. We would be the nut in the nutcrackers.

I heard Alan yell, "Hang on!" He threw the boat around so that we were racing towards the starboard 110. This time the Oerlikon gunner had more of a target and he pounded the nose of the 110. Its guns stopped but before we could cheer his back was torn open by the second 110. We turned to port. As we did so I saw the flight of Hurricanes dive down to attack the enemy. They had come too late for Jackson, the gunner, but they had saved us. As the three Hurricanes chased the fighters back to France Alan slowed us down to a speed which was not as hazardous to our safety. We had survived.

Chapter 3

Wacker's head popped up from the radio, "Sir, we are to go to Weymouth and report to Lord Lovat."

"Righto."

I handed my Thompson to Lance Sergeant Gowland, "Here, Harry, stow this for me will you?"

"Right sir."

"Any casualties?"

"A couple of lads were hit by flying splinters. Nowt to worry about, sir."

I saw that Bill had his pipe going while his relief steered the boat. I shook my head, "That is why you haven't got the lungs you used to have."

He grinned, "I know sir and next time you need a volunteer to get his bits frozen, with respect, I will leave that to someone else. Mrs Leslie's lad has done his bit!"

I nodded, "And he has that. You did well. I hope that the information is worthwhile."

Alan Jorgenson sucked on his cheroot, "If it isn't Tom it is not your fault. You both did what they asked."

I nodded, "It might be they weren't asking the right questions. There seemed to be more gun emplacements along that sea wall than the last time we were there."

The three Hurricanes had returned and were nursemaiding us back to Weymouth. They waggled their wings and sped off home as we entered the harbour. We had told the base of our injuries and ambulances were there as well as a car ready to whisk me off to see Lord Lovat.

"I'll get the '*Lady*' sorted out Tom. God knows when they will want us back out again! I will take her back to Falmouth."

I gathered the samples and the two maps. "Sergeant Poulson, take care of the lads. I will get back as soon as I can."

The driver was a Commando sergeant. I vaguely recognised him from our training at Oswestry. He looked at me in the mirror. Grinning he said, "I thought I recognised the name, sir when his lordship asked me to pick you up. Didn't we train together at Oswestry? I am Jack Jones. You were the one had that run in with those instructors."

"Yes, sergeant. I thought your face was familiar."

"You have done well for yourself. A nice bit of fruit salad too."

"I think I have been lucky."

We chatted about our careers. Both of us avoided specifics. It was better that way. When we reached headquarters he helped me carry my gear inside. I was whisked away before I could say more and I found myself in an office with Lord Lovat and three Canadian Lieutenant Colonels. Lord Lovat was a dour man. He spoke economically, "Harsker. Get it done all right?"

"Yes sir." I laid out the bags of sand in order and the chinograph maps. "This is the sand in order from east to west. It is pretty much the same all the way along; mainly shingle and soft sand. The beach is shallow. Your LCP won't have a problem."

They all looked relieved but Lord Lovat knew me. "There is more isn't there, Harsker?"

I nodded, "Yes sir."

"Go on, elaborate. I am sure these gentlemen would like to hear from someone who has been there."

"The beach is a death trap sir. There are no mines and there is no barbed wire but there is a wall about five or six feet high at the end, just before the esplanade. I am no tank man sir but I am a Commando. If I was a German defender I would have a field day when the Churchill tanks tried to climb them. You wouldn't even need an anti-tank gun; a grenade would do it. Then there is the barbed wire on top of the wall. It is backed by machine guns. Even if you did get off the beach and over the wall there is a wide esplanade and the guns on the cliffs and in the Chateau could fire right down on you. And just supposing, by some miracle, you did get the tanks off the esplanade, they have blocked all of the streets with six feet high blocks of concrete."

There was silence when I had finished. Then Lieutenant Colonel Merritt began to chuckle and shook his head, "You don't pull your punches do you, Lieutenant?"

"No sir, I was not brought up that way. *Tell the truth and shame the devil'*, my grandmother used to say."

"Mine too and yet Lord Lovat here tells me this is the second time you have been to Dieppe. You got in and out both times. How hard can it be?"

"The difference is, sir, we were dropped in quietly by boat, at night and we were sneaking around. We were able to lie up during the day. Even so we were nearly caught and I left good men over there. When your lads go in there will be naval bombardment and aeroplanes will drop bombs. Jerry will know you are coming. You won't be sneaking."

Lieutenant Colonel Menard said, "Are you saying we can't do it?" I sensed that he did not like the implications of what I had said.

"No sir. I think you could do it. My question is, is it worth leaving half of your men on the beaches just to prove you have brave lads who can wade through machine gun bullets? What would be achieved?"

Silence filled the room. My words were not what they wanted to hear. Lord Lovat rose and went to the coffee pot, "Coffee, Lieutenant?"

"Yes please, sir."

As Lord Lovat poured the coffee he said, "What you gentlemen should know is that the Lieutenant here swam ashore last night to find out what the beach was like. On the way back they encountered a German convoy and were attacked by German aeroplanes. I tell you this because this is a professional. He is giving you the truth; no matter how unpalatable." He shrugged. "When Number three and Number four Commando attack we will take casualties. Of that I have no doubt but we are on the periphery of the attack. We will be the side show. We can, as the Lieutenant so eloquently says, sneak around. You cannot."

"Any advice, son?" Lieutenant Colonel Merritt seemed to be the one who wanted answers.

"When your men land they use as much of the limited cover as they can. Use the groynes for example."

"What the hell is a groyne?"

Lord Lovat smiled, "A long wooden barrier in the sea which stops the shingle shifting."

I nodded, "Keep moving and fire in short bursts but keep firing. You might be lucky. Find those men who can throw a grenade a long way."

"We have grenade launchers."

"They are fine Colonel but I can throw three or four grenades in the time it takes to fire one."

Lieutenant Colonel Merritt said, "Pretty much what your chaps have been telling us."

Lord Lovat said, "We have learned through experience and the blood of dead men."

"How about having the Lieutenant and his chaps come and tell my men how to do it?"

Lord Lovat said, "You will all be embarking in two days. I am not certain we have time." They nodded and looked glum. "Well Lieutenant, we will have this sand analysed. Thank you for your efforts. My driver will take you back to Falmouth. Have some rest. You look like you need it."

"Sir."

The three Canadians all stood. Lieutenant Colonel Merritt shook my hand, "Thank you, son, both for what you did and the fact that you had the guts to tell us the truth. I hope we meet again."

"Thank you, sir, and I do wish you all the success in the world."

Lord Lovat took me to the car, "Thanks for that honesty, Harsker. I agree with you and think this is a beach too far. Still some good may come of it but for the life of me I can't see what." We reached the car. "Jones, drive the Lieutenant back to Falmouth eh. You might as well stay overnight. I shan't need you again until tomorrow."

"Right sir." As we headed west he said, "Any chance of a billet, sir?"

"There is a half empty camp, Jack."

"Thanks sir." I saw him look at me through the rear view mirror. "You best get some shut eye sir. You look all in."

He was right and soon the motion of the car sent me to sleep. It felt like being in Dad's car before the war when we would drive overnight to get to our cottage in France. Happier days and much simpler then.

Sergeant Jones woke me. "Sir, sorry to wake you but we are approaching Falmouth. Any chance of directions?"

"Of course." I directed him to the sea front and Mrs Bailey's guesthouse.

Reg Dean was just coming out of the front door. He opened my door. "That was quick. The lads only beat you back by an hour or so. Mrs B has a nice rabbit stew on the go."

"Good oh! Oh this is Sergeant Jack Jones. He needs a billet for the night. I said there were plenty up at the camp."

Reg shook his head, "No need to trek up there. Mrs B has a spare room and the food is better here. Come with me, Sergeant, and I will introduce you."

I picked up my Bergen from the back and followed them in. They went into the kitchen to see Mrs Bailey and I trudged up the stairs. I heard noises from the bathroom. I would have to join the queue for the bath.

As I was the last to bathe I was the last to join them all for supper. It had taken some time to rid my body of the last vestiges of goose grease. They had all waited for me and stood to attention when I entered. I laughed, "Don't start with all that. Sit down and eat!"

They all looked up at Mrs Bailey she said, "They wait Lieutenant Harsker because I told them to. You have had a rougher time of it than they have." She nodded towards Reg, her source of information. "You get the choice bits." She dolloped a

34

huge amount of mashed potatoes and a ladleful of saddle of rabbit on my plate. "There you go, sir. Now for the rest of you!"

Of course no one went short. Mrs Bailey had cooked four rabbits. I suspected that they were courtesy of Sergeant Major Dean. He was a good shot and there were plenty of bunnies close to the camp. It was good; it rivalled Mum's. There could be no higher praise.

I gave the lads a day off and then, on July 1st we went to help the Lieutenant to repair our boat and make her shipshape again. We had been lucky. The strafing runs of the German fighters had not badly damaged our vessel but she still needed repairs. Hobson, the dead gunner, had been buried already by his mess mates. He had been popular but we were in a dangerous game. The stakes were high and if you lost you paid with your life.

One thing you could guarantee in England was that you could not guarantee the weather. It might be summer but that didn't stop foul, almost autumnal weather from sweeping in. It wasn't just the rain, it was the wind. Half of the Canadians had tents ruined by the unseasonal gales. The storms began the day the Canadian troops embarked on their transports and did not relent for more than a week. Of course we were many miles from the isle of Wight and knew little of Operation Rutter. Our part had finished and we were too concerned with ensuring that *'Lady Luck'* did not get pounded on to the rocks of her anchorage. We learned all of this later on.

Once the boat was secured from the worst of the weather I took the section on a cross country march. We might have to operate behind enemy lines during such weather. The war did not stop because of a storm, no matter how bad! As we double timed across the rain and wind swept headlands with visibility down to a few yards Harry Gowland asked, "Do you reckon those Canadian lads stand any sort of chance sir? I mean Dieppe is a hard nut to crack."

"Ironically, Harry, I think the weather will help. The ships and men will be harder to see. If they are attacking now then they have a chance. Of course they will have no air support but neither will the Germans."

"Are they attacking now, sir?"

"I don't have the exact date but it is sometime around now."

Major Foster returned at the start of the second week in July. His face was as black as thunder. "Tom, Sarn't Major join me in the office would you?"

When the Major closed the door he waved us to our seats. "Operation Rutter has had to be cancelled." There was little to say and we just looked at him as he told us the reasons. The Germans bombed the convoy when it was assembling in the Solent. That, and the bad weather, meant it was a no go.

"Were many men killed in the raid sir?"

"Thankfully there were not as many as there might have been. They are going to have to tighten up the air defences." He smiled, "They have dispersed the troops along the south coast. I am not certain if the operation will take place but they are keeping the troops handy in case they do. You impressed Colonel Merritt, Tom. He is sending a company of the South Saskatchewan Regiment here for you to train. They are his best company. He wants them, as he put it, *'to be as good as the Commandos*'!"

Reg rolled his eyes, "How long have we got sir, six months?"

"No, Reg, two weeks."

"Then it is purely cosmetic sir?"

"Not really, Tom. Whatever skills you give them will be a help. He sees it as a rolling programme. In a fortnight another company will come and so on. They will never be Commandos but they should become better soldiers. You would agree wouldn't you?"

"Yes sir." I looked at Reg, "We won't bother with all the strangleholds, laying charges and that sort of thing. Just get them fit and show them how to fight in small groups."

Reg nodded, "Aye sir, that would work. That is manageable."

"So the operation is definitely off then, sir?"

"In its present form? Yes. Lord Lovat and Colonel Durnford Slater are at Whitehall with the Major General looking to see what they can salvage from Rutter but Operation Rutter is dead and buried. At least the information you brought back is not wasted, Tom. They are setting up a department of boffins to evaluate things like the quality of sand and so forth. Other units are slipping ashore at different parts of Occupied France to bring back samples. When we do finally go back then we will have more information and make a better job of it."

Reg looked surprised, "So we will be going back then sir?"

"Back?"

"Invading France. I heard that things are looking bleak in the desert." We had heard reports that the desert campaign was not going as well as it had been and the 8th Army was perilously close to Cairo.

Major Foster smiled, "Defeatist talk, Sergeant Major? That doesn't sound like you."

"And it isn't sir. We'll beat these buggers. I just didn't think we were quite ready yet."

"Between you and me neither do I but with the Americans in the war Mr Churchill is keen for us to fight back."

I said nothing but I could now see the attack on Dieppe for what it was; a chance to bloody Herr Hitler's nose. I was pleased it had been cancelled. I had seen the beach and knew that it would have been a disaster. "Right Reg, let's go and get this organised eh? I'll get my lads and we will go to the tin mine." I looked at Major Foster, "When do they arrive?"

"They will be here by tonight."

"Good then that gives us a day to make the tin mine into a defensive position. I'll go and see Daddy Grant and get some smoke bombs."

Reg was always happier when he had something to do and he lost his scowl and smiled. "I'll get the PTIs organised."

"Good. I'll get some paperwork done and catch up with you this afternoon."

The section were in the armoury cleaning their guns. Operating at sea, as we often did, meant that we had to be vigilant in our maintenance of our weapons. We knew that they gave us an edge in battle.

"Right lads we are training Canadians for the next two weeks. We start tomorrow. Sergeant Poulson, take the lads up to the tin mine. We will make it a fortress for them to attack. They have done beach work. Let's show them that attacking a defensive position is harder."

"Yes sir."

"Gowland and Groves, you stay with me. We have to pick up some gear from the QM."

"Sir!"

I could smell the smoke from Daddy's pipe as soon as we opened the door to escape the sudden downpour which had descended upon us. He grinned as we hurried in to escape the deluge. "Ah three drowned rats. How can I be of service, gentlemen?"

"We need smoke bombs, blank ammo, and rope, Daddy." He nodded. "Any barbed wire?"

"I can let you have a few rolls why, sir?"

"Some Canadians are coming tomorrow for us to train. We are going up to the tin mine."

One of his assistants said, "In this?"

Daddy shook his head, "Oh I wish I had real soldiers sir. This lot have their basic training and that is it." He rounded on the unfortunate private, "Listen, Blair, war doesn't stop because it is pissing down with rain. You can't go and get dried off with a Panzer rumbling towards you. Go and get the wire for Lieutenant Harsker!" He grinned when his men had disappeared. "Mind you he is right; you have to be mad to train in this!"

Harry said, "You know what they say, Quarter Master, you shouldn't volunteer if you can't take a joke!"

Daddy sent his privates with us to carry the barbed wire. They struggled to keep up with us in their trench coats. We wore the oilskin capes which gave us more freedom of movement. We reached the mine five minutes before they did. As they dumped the bales on the ground and prepared to descend I heard Private Blair say to Groves, "You lot must be mad as a bucketful of frogs!"

Peter Groves laughed, "Of course we are! We are proper Commandos!"

After they left, eager to be back in the shelter of their stores I gathered the men around. "They were expecting to attack Dieppe.

Let's make this like it. Find as many logs as you can. I want a rampart five feet high with barbed wire in front and on the top." The mine had a natural crown and we would use that. "Hewitt and Fletcher, use the wheelbarrow and collect as many bits of stone as you can. I want the area in front of the barbed wire covering in them. Make it as much like a shingle beach as you can. Use big stones, small stones, anything. Harry I want a machine gun emplacement over there on the flank. Make it well hidden. We will give them a surprise when they think they have the site sussed out!"

My men had attacked such places enough times to think like a German. If they made it hard for the Canadians then more would have a chance of survival when they met the real enemy.

I waved Sergeant Poulson over, "Make up a few small charges. Let's make this realistic for them."

He grinned, "I'll give it to George. He likes messing on with this new explosive."

I took off my battledress and joined in. We would all be soaking wet when we finished but it would be worth it. We had completed everything by five thirty and we trudged, sodden, down the hill.

As we descended, too tired to double time, Corporal Lowe asked, "Why are we training the Canadians if they aren't going to attack Dieppe, sir?"

"Their Colonel thinks they need the skills, Lowe. I suppose you can blame me. I told them what they would need to do to succeed and he wanted us to train them."

He shook his head, "I wasn't complaining sir. I am quite looking forward to the challenge. I might get some sympathy for the instructors who trained us."

George said, "I wouldn't waste it. They were bastards! They were a bunch of sadists."

Polly Poulson said, quietly, "We didn't turn out so bad though did we? Perhaps we have lasted this long because they did such a good job!"

"Mebbe!"

I laughed, my Lance Sergeant was not convinced.

"We are due a replacement aren't we sir. I mean we are one short."

"I daresay we will get one when the next batch arrives. That just means more work for you Sergeant. Whoever it is they will need the edges knocking off."

Scouse Fletcher hung his head, "I guess you are talking about me there, sir."

"I am talking about all of us, me included."

We decided we would all go to the shower block when we reached the camp to warm up and then dry off. We were all due new uniforms anyway and we made it to the stores before Daddy had locked up. I knew he would be working late preparing for the Canadians the next day. "What now then, sir?"

"We are due new uniforms, Daddy."

"Yes sir, you should have had them a week ago. You didn't come for them."

I laughed, "We were a bit busy a week ago. Could we have them now, Quarter Master?" He nodded, "Blair put that ciggie out and bring me number one section's uniforms. They are on the top shelf." I heard grumbling, "And stop moaning or you will be on a fizzer!"

The hot shower, shave and clean uniforms made all the difference. None had their rank or medals on. We would all have to sew them on. We looked like recruits. We went to the mess to get a brew of tea before we headed down to the boarding house. I said, "I'll see if I can get us some transport, Poulson. I'll meet you here."

Reg was just locking up the office, "You still here sir? I thought you would have been away on your toes by now."

"Just finished."

"New uniforms I see. You lads don't half get through them."

"They keep sending us where Jerry can make them mucky. Any chance of transport back to Mrs. B's?"

"Sorry sir, I sent the lorries off to the station to meet the Canadians. They should arrive here in the next half hour or so ago."

Just then we heard the grind of a labouring engine as the lorries struggled up the hill.

Reg grinned, "We are in luck! I'll get one of the RASC drivers to drop us off." He opened the office door again, "I'd best get the paperwork sorted out."

I stood under the shelter of the lean to roof and watched the lorries pull up and the men disgorge. They were loud. And they were unhappy.

"I thought it was supposed to be summer in this cockamamie country?"

"I heard it rains all year!"

"And it comes from every direction. How does it do that?"

"I hope they have some decent food here. I am fed up of corned beef!"

Their sergeants began to shout out orders and then men formed themselves, reluctantly, into lines. A staff car pulled up and Lieutenant Colonel Merritt got out and stood next to me. "Good to see you Lieutenant Harsker. Filthy day!" The Canadian Major General got out when the driver put up the umbrella.

"Yes sir."

Sergeant Major Dean saluted, "Major Foster has just gone into town. He will be back shortly sir. I have your barracks here."

He nodded, "Captain Friedmann is in command. Major Wallowitz was taken to sick bay this morning. Something he ate, I think. Wally! A moment if you please."

The Captain was a huge man who had, as far as I could see neither neck nor eyes. I do not know what I had expected but it was not this.

"Yes sir?"

"This is Lieutenant Harsker, I told you about him."

He grinned and his slits of eyes disappeared into rolls of fat. "Yes indeed. I am looking forward to this." I must have glanced

41

down at his waistline. "Don't worry about this. I can keep up with the fellahs."

Reg Dean kept a straight face, "Sir, I have the barrack assignments here. I have done three copies. One for you, one for you senior NCO and one as a spare."

"Very efficient. Sergeant Hutchinson!"

A tree trunk with arms and eyes lumbered over to us, "Sir?"

"Here are the barrack assignments." The Captain looked at Reg. "Does the mess have food for us? We were on the train a long time. The men are hungry."

"Yes sir and you are, largely, the only ones left in camp at the moment." The Captain cocked an eye.

"Our men stay in the town. They get their own accommodation. The Corps believes it breeds independence."

The General said, "Damned good idea."

Sergeant Hutchinson shook his head, "We wouldn't get most of them back if we let them loose sir. No, a barracks suits me."

I saluted, "Well sir, we will get off. We will pinch one of your lorries and send it straight back. We will be here at six thirty a.m.. We begin training at six forty five. You can have a lie in tomorrow!"

Lieutenant Colonel Merritt laughed, "I told you it was going to be tough, Wally!"

I shouted, "Sergeant Poulson!"

My men ran towards me. I heard comments from the Canadians, "Look at the new uniforms!"

" They must be raw recruits!"

"Don't rush back, girls!"

Captain Friedmann said, "Sorry about that, Lieutenant. They have had a long day and they are a little tetchy."

I laughed, "Oh don't worry. They will be saying much worse tomorrow."

The next morning we ran, along with Reg Dean, to the camp and arrived by six o'clock. I sent Lance Sergeant Gowland and the rest to the tin mine to prepare it. The three of us were ready at six thirty on the parade ground. There was a drizzle, it was the fine

42

rain which was insidious as it seeped into your clothes. The Colonel and Captain Friedman were there at six thirty five. The captain looked towards the gate. The barrier was still down. "Where is the truck you guys used?"

I smiled, "We ran, sir, We do it every morning. It keeps you fit. We only used the lorry last night because we had been working since six preparing for you."

The Colonel chuckled, "Told you!"

The Company Sergeant Major joined us next. I had sewn on my fruit salad as did Poulson who now had his stripes. I saw his look. He knew that we were veterans. We were not just blokes who trained them and then sent them out. He shook his head as his men shambled up to us. When it reached six fifty Captain Friedmann said, "Go get them Jake; this is embarrassing!" The NCO raced off and I heard him yelling at the stragglers to join us.

When they were lined up the Captain was going to speak. The Colonel said, "We are guests here Wally, let our hosts take charge." He nodded to me.

I stepped forward, "Not a good start gentlemen. You are now five minutes late. The Germans are never late! They always come early! Ask their wives!" I received a laugh for that. "That laugh will be the last you have this morning. In fact during the whole time you are with us I doubt that your faces will crack into a smile of any description. I make no apologies for that. You need to be fitter and more battle ready than you are. We have two weeks to do that. It will not be easy." I pointed to Sergeant Poulson, "The Sergeant and my section have just run all the way from Falmouth and we will run you all the way to the training ground. Sergeant Poulson will bring up the rear. Any man who slows up the Sergeant will be on jankers tonight."

I saw the looks of confusion. The Colonel said, "Jankers?"

"Fatigues? Punishment detail? Washing the pans?"

The Colonel nodded, "Understood."

I smiled, "And that includes officers and NCO's."

The two lieutenants and the Captain shot me a look of disbelief but Colonel Merritt nodded, "Bring it on son! I love a challenge!"

43

"You need to return to your barracks and bring your pack and coat as well as your blanket. You need your weapons but not your ammunition. You have three minutes. I will begin my run three minutes from... now!"

I had their attention and they sprinted. Even the officers went. The Colonel just stood there, "I don't have a bag."

"Sergeant, go and get him the new man's Bergen."

When Poulson returned with the Bergen it was two minutes and forty seconds. Many of the men were back. By the time the Colonel had slipped his on it was time to go. I blew my whistle and began to run up the steep track which led from the camp. I smiled as the Canadian Company Sergeant Major ran next to me, "Well done, Sarn't. It is a tricky route. Just keep this speed."

I settled into the easy, ground eating rhythm which would mean I would arrive at the tin mine able to speak. I did not look behind me that would be the task of the sergeant. I didn't even turn when I heard someone vomiting up their breakfast behind me. Just before the top of the run, some four miles from the camp, there was a really steep part. I began to stretch my legs. The Canadian sergeant tried to match me but he couldn't. He began to fall back. Part of me knew that I was showing off but I still did it anyway. I reached the barrier and turned with my Thompson slung across my chest. I cocked it and pointed it into the air.

The first twenty men who had kept close to me collapsed behind me. I fired my gun in the air. Right on cue Sergeant Poulson did that at the rear. I heard shouts and expletives as the men from Saskatchewan threw themselves to the ground. As the cordite drifted in the drizzle I shouted, "Men of Saskatchewan, welcome to the war! You should be dead but you are alive. Welcome to hell!"

Chapter 4

Captain Friedmann stood and shouted, "Come on boys. We look like asses this morning. Let's see if we can change the Lieutenant's opinion of us!" His men stood and struggled up the hill. As he passed me he said, quietly, "Point made, son. Let's make these boys into real soldiers!"

I saw that Lieutenant Colonel Merritt was not at the rear as I had expected. He was with the leading group. He gave a mock salute and a grin as he passed me.

Sergeant Poulson grinned and shouted. "We have eight men, sir, for dishwashing duties." He gestured with his thumb as seven Canadians passed us, "Number eight will be along just as soon as he has finished bringing up his breakfast."

My men were standing in a half circle, their bodies obscuring the target. The Canadians were seated on the ground. The officers and NCOs stood and sucked in air. Sergeant Poulson and I joined my men and faced them. We were breathing normally.

"Gentlemen, if it is any consolation to you, all of the men you see before you would be as you are now before we began training. We do this run most days and we run back. Double time is our normal speed. If you would like to be as fit then it is in your own hands. When we finish here Sergeant major Dean has PTIs waiting for you." I saw the Captain nodding. It was a strategy he would implement. "Today we are going to give you the opportunity to experience attacking a German defensive emplacement." I swept a hand around the site. "This is where we train. Your object is to capture the flag." I pointed to the Commando flag which hung limply in the drizzle filled air.

There were targets off to one side, away from where the men were seated. I cocked the Thompson. I fired a burst at three of the targets which were shredded. The men on the ground jumped. "We use Thompsons. They fire a big bullet; it is also a noisy bullet. My men have placed explosive charges around the site. We want this to be as realistic as possible. You should be all right." I saw nervous looks. "We are being slightly unfair in that you have not had the chance to reconnoitre. However had you gone in at Dieppe then the intelligence you would have had had would have come from us. I will brief you now." I turned and pointed behind me. "In a moment my men will go behind a defensive barricade. There is barbed wire all around and there are hidden gun emplacements. I will give you chaps fifteen minutes to plan your assault. My lads will pass amongst you and give you the blank ammunition you will use. When I blow my whistle then do your best. The exercise is over when I blow my whistle three times."

One of the Sergeants asked, "Sir, you have live ammo in your gun. Are you using blanks too?"

I smiled, "That would spoil the surprise wouldn't it, Sergeant? Suffice it to say that all of my men are expert shots. They only hit what they want to hit." Of course we would be firing blanks but I wanted that edge of fear within them.

When my men returned they took up their positions. The Canadians could now see, through the murk, the target. I had Gowland and Groves guarding the rear. If the Canadian Company had any sense they would send some men around that way. In theory it should have been over really quickly. There were over a hundred and twenty of them against just eight of us. The ace in the hole was Fletcher who was hidden half way down the slope in a hidden gun position.

Three of my men were ready to set off charges as soon as I blew my whistle. Three others would throw smoke bombs. I peered down the hill and then checked my watch. They had wasted five minutes talking amongst themselves. Another five passed by before I saw them descend to their men. I hoped the Colonel had taken my advice. Small groups advancing slowly might stand a chance a frontal charge would not.

When I blew my whistle they were still not ready for the attack and when the explosives were set off they threw themselves onto the ground. I heard Captain Friedmann yelling for his men to attack. The smoke grenades soon filled the slope. The drizzle made visibility poor, the grenades made it almost like night. As soon as I heard their shouts as they charged I said, "Ready!" When the first of them slipped on the shingle I shouted, "Fire!"

There were shouts as they slipped and fell. I heard men falling down the slope The drizzle had made the stones both slick and treacherous. Men fell into each other's way. The sudden gunfire had shocked them and the smoke had disorientated. None, it appeared, had gone around our rear and I shouted, "Lance Sergeant, get round here."

Sergeant Poulson set off the next charges. They were off to the flanks. I wanted them herding in the middle. They obliged. Suddenly three Canadians made it to the barrier. George Lowe stood and put his Thompson to their heads, "Bang, bang, bang, You three are dead!"

Suddenly Fletcher's Bren began to fire from the flank. "Right lads, over the top." There would be confusion amongst the attackers; we would use that to our advantage.

We slipped over the barrier and began to make our way down. We knew the way through the wire. It was our own maze we were negotiating. The Canadians' heads were down and they were too busy trying to get up the slope to be aware of our move. My men held guns to their heads and said , "Bang, you are dead!" Once I cleared the smoke I ran directly for the Colonel who was standing with his aide watching the attack. Both of them stared at me as I ran up and pointing my Colt at them I said, in German, "I think your war is over!"

I blew my whistle three times.

Lieutenant Colonel Merritt shook his head, "A shambles, Lieutenant, a shambles."

"Commandos have made the same mistakes, sir. It is why we use it. It is a realistic test for them. Three of your men made the top. The rest were defeated by the terrain, the wire and the tricks we used. The Germans can't control the weather but everything else they can."

Captain Friedmann joined us. He was breathing heavily, "Those damned stones made us slip and fall."

I nodded, "That is the same shingle that is on the beach at Dieppe."

He nodded, "And the smoke; I wasn't certain of which direction to take. When that damned gun fired on our flank...."

The Colonel finished his sentence for him, "We would have been slaughtered." He nodded, "Perhaps the postponement was a good thing. We can learn lessons here."

Both the Captain and myself picked up on his words. Captain Friedmann said, "Postponement?"

"Yes Wally, we are going in. This is real training for the real thing." He turned to me and said, "Right Lieutenant, you have made us see we aren't ready. Now show us how to do it."

While some of the men were not happy about the humiliation of being beaten by a handful of Commandos, the NCOs and officers took everything we had to say and made a note of it. We showed them how to move in small groups, one man covering the others. Sergeant Poulson said, "I didn't hear many rifles. Why weren't you firing at us? When you attack you keep firing. Even if you are attacking a strong point you might be lucky and get a bullet through the slit. Believe me when bits of concrete start zipping around you are more likely to duck."

I held a Mills bomb in my hand. "These can save the day more times than enough. Two things to remember: throw them as high as you can and get down as flat as you can." I pointed to the nearest sergeant, "Get to know which of your men can throw the furthest and make sure they have more of these than the others. If you hear the shout, '*grenade*' then get down."

I took out a German grenade from my Bergen. "This is the German equivalent. It has a five second fuse."

48

I had already primed Harry Gowland who stood at the top of the emplacement and knew what to expect. I smashed the porcelain top and threw it towards Harry. He picked it up and threw it on the other side of the emplacement, "Grenade!"

We all threw ourselves to the ground. The concussion was greater than our tiny charges and pieces of wood fell with the drizzle. When the Canadians rose they all looked for Harry. He strode down, smiling.

"We can adjust our fuses, the Germans can't. Five seconds is longer than you think."

Company Sergeant Major Hutchinson said, "Jesus, Lieutenant, your men sure trust you."

I nodded, "And I trust them. This is not our usual job. Normally we are behind enemy lines. If we can't rely on each other then we are dead men." I saw him take that information in.

We double timed down to the camp. They were all tired but Company Sergeant Major Hutchinson joined Sergeant Poulson at the rear to chivvy on any laggards. The Colonel and the Captain ran next to me. "Impressive, Lieutenant. I can see that our time here will not be wasted."

"To be honest Colonel I would spend just half a day training to assault and the rest getting your men fit and working together." I explained how the Commandos worked.

"So you are like a family?"

"Yes, imagine a family of eight brothers. That is us. When we have a big family gathering then we work with the rest of the family but the eight of us can work by ourselves and we are not put off when we are alone. That can happen on the battlefield. When we retreated through Belgium we had no officers. It was just NCOs trying to keep together a handful of men. Lots gave up. The ones who didn't, well they are better soldiers for it."

I knew I had hit the mark and the two of them exchanged ideas as we headed for the camp. The Canadians paraded before they were allowed to go for their meal. I saluted the Colonel. "We will see you in the morning sir."

"And this time we will be ready!"

"Right lads, double time!"

As we headed down the road I heard Company Sergeant Major Hutchinson shout, "And that, you apologies for Canadians, is what we will be doing by the time we have finished training! They are real soldiers!"

The next week flew by as the men from Saskatchewan threw themselves into the training. The officers and the NCOs had had their pride hurt and they worked harder than anyone. I liked the Colonel and Wally. They loved their regiment and it showed. Wally even began to lose some weight. I am not certain if it was the food or the training but he physically changed over that week.

Our training was ended when we returned one night, actually singing, as we came down the road, to see Major Foster waiting for us. He had not returned when we had expected and his presence was ominous. He saluted and said, "Colonel, if you and Captain Friedmann would join me in the office." As they turned he said, "You too, Tom."

Reg left the office and said, "I'll watch the door, sir."

"This looks serious, Major Foster."

"The operation is back on, sir. It has been adjusted in light of our experience. It is now called Operation Jubilee. Your trucks are here to take you to your new base at Southampton. You embark on the eighteenth and the attack is on the nineteenth."

Captain Friedmann whistled and said, "No hanging around in the Solent then? My boys will appreciate that."

The Colonel said, "And will Lieutenant Harsker's section be part of this?"

The Major nodded, "He will sir but his part is top secret. You understand?"

"I didn't but I do know. Me and my boys are the sledge hammer. Lieutenant Harsker here is the lock pick." He held out his hand, "I'd just like to say, Lieutenant, that no matter what happens in this operation more of my boys will survive and that is down to you and your, what do call them? *'Lads'*. Thank them for me."

50

"I will sir and good luck. You have a fine regiment. They will do you proud."

Captain Friedmann said, "When all this is over, Tom, I shall buy you a pint."

I patted his middle, "Not too many, eh sir? We don't want the baby back!"

He laughed, "No indeedy."

The two saluted and left. Reg came back in, "Well sir, what is our job?"

"You and your section are going back behind enemy lines. You are being parachuted in."

"No *'Lucky Lady'* then sir?"

"She will pick you up after it is all over. She has a separate mission." He looked up at the map on the wall. "It has been decided to do away with the airborne element. Number three and number four Commando will be going their job along with the Marines." He smiled, "I am going in again too! You impressed the other Canadian colonels. They said they wanted Commandos. And they have them."

"When do we leave, sir?"

"You have four days to prepare. You will go in three days before Operation Jubilee begins. You need to be behind the lines, alone, for two days."

I saw Reg's face. He knew the dangers now. "The new man is here sir, will he be going on the operation?"

"Has he had parachute training?"

"Yes sir."

"Then he might as well come."

"Report here tomorrow at eight, Tom, with your men and I will brief you. I want you all fresh."

"Yes sir."

As I left with Reg he said, "I took the liberty of telling him to go to Mrs Bailey's, sir. He should be there now."

"Thanks Sarn't Major." The drizzle had finally stopped and my men sat waiting for me. "I thought you lot would have gone back by now."

Sergeant Poulson said, "We knew something was up, sir."

"You will all find out tomorrow. We have an eight o'clock start. You can have a few pints tonight if you like."

Harry said, "That means we are off again soon eh sir?"

I nodded, "It does, Harry, it most certainly does."

Ken Shepherd was sitting outside Mrs Bailey's, smoking, when we arrived. He leapt to his feet and almost fell over as he tried to put out the cigarette and salute all at the same time. "Private Shepherd, sir, reporting for duty!"

I smiled, "At ease, Private. We will get to know each other over one of Mrs Bailey's famous meals." He nodded, "Did you give her your ration book?"

His face fell, "No sir. I forgot."

Sergeant Poulson chuckled, "Well I would do it now before she divvies up the food!"

He was joking, of course, but Private Shepherd raced back inside. Harry Gowland said, "He looks about fourteen, sir! I bet he hasn't even started shaving yet!"

Scouse said, "Well I am happy! I am no longer the baby of the section!"

It was a stew made with a cow heel and shin beef. I suspected that Mrs Bailey had used some homemade elderberry wine in the sauce. Whatever she had done it was delicious. I let the rest of the section grill the private. They elicited all the information I needed. He was eighteen and had volunteered for the Commandos. He had just travelled all the way from the Commando training school in Scotland. He was an only child and was, unlike most of the section, a country boy. He came from a farm up near Middleham in North Yorkshire. He was quiet and I saw that he was embarrassed by some of the questions. He had to fight with these men; better to get any discomfort out of the way.

When the pudding dishes were taken away and the lads whose turn it was for dishes had left I spoke with Ken. "Don't let them get to you. They are all good lads and they have been together for a few months and completed a couple of missions."

He nodded, "I know sir. Everyone said this was the best section. The instructor told me I was chosen especially for it."

That was intriguing. "There must be a good reason for it. What special skills do you have?"

"I came top in shooting sir and I seem to have an affinity for explosives. The shooting I can understand. Dad is a farmer and I grew up with a twelve bore in the crook of my arm but explosives." He shrugged.

I tried a stab in the dark, "I am also betting that you score highly in the field craft section."

He grinned, "Yes sir. They gave up looking for me on our final test."

"Well you will fit in well. Just to let you know that we have a big operation coming up. I am afraid you will be thrown in at the deep end."

"That is fine with me, sir. I want to do my bit for the war."

The dishwashers returned. Scouse said, "Mr Harsker said we could go to the pub! Who is up for it?"

They all cheered. I nodded surreptitiously to Shepherd who said, "Could I come with you chaps?" I saw the looks from my section at the sound of his voice. He sounded a little like me and I knew they would think that posh.

Harry would be with them and he said, "Aye son."

When they had gone I said to Sergeant Poulson, "Come on we will go and see if Reg is in the pub eh? It will be our last one for a while."

We frequented different pubs. Officers and NOCOs used one, other ranks the other. The main reason was to give each other space. I knew my lads would behave themselves but they would be uncomfortable with Polly and me looking over their shoulders.

Now that the rain had finally stopped it was a pleasant evening. Dusk was falling and there were people taking constitutionals along the prom. It was a way of bring normality to the war.

"Have you any idea what they want us to do, sir?"

"No, but we are going in by air and coming out by sea. We have to lie up behind the lines."

"That is a bit rough on the new lad isn't it sir? He seems, well a little young."

"We all were once. Don't worry about him. Apparently he was selected for our section. Someone at the training camp thought he had skills we could use."

"Really?"

"Top in shooting and field craft and handy with explosives. I'll check his field record tomorrow but I can't see why he would lie."

"Then he sounds like just what we need."

Reg was in the pub and we joined him when we had paid for our beer. We had a corner in the snug which we used. The locals gave us space and we were always able to talk, albeit quietly. Reg lit up and we drank a third of our pints. The first swallow was always the best. We would savour the rest. Two pints would be our limit.

"You have a good' un there sir."

"Who, Shepherd?"

"Aye, I was checking his service record. Top in almost everything. The only critical comment was that he was a bit of a loner. Captain Marsden is up there now and he recommended him."

I nodded, now it made sense. "I think once he gets over his shyness he will fit in."

Polly said, "The lads are just loud sir, you know Scouse, got a gob on him like the Mersey Tunnel but he is all right underneath."

"You are right. It is a funny old war throwing us all together."

Reg shook his head, "There's no way the likes of us would have been able to talk to a bloke like you sir. Not without the war."

"Are you certain? I mean I know that was true in my Dad's day but I thought things had changed since the Great War."

"Don't get me wrong sir but you are the exception. You have come through the ranks and you are, well let's call a spade a spade, you are posh but you are all right. Now there are too many like Captain Grenville. Too many full of themselves. That Canadian colonel and captain; they were all right too. They both had a sense of humour and their lads like them. That can make all the difference you know."

"Major Foster is a good bloke."

"He is sir and that proves my point. We are the best brigade in the Commandos and we have the best officers. That Sergeant you knew, Jack Jones, he told me about some of the officers he had served under." He shook his head, "Wouldn't work here. Anyway enough shop. This will be your last night out for a while eh? Let's talk about more pleasant things."

We chatted about this and that: the latest George Formby film, Mrs Bailey's cooking, the price of beer, shortages, queuing. Everything was inconsequential and by the time we left the pub I felt as relaxed as I had in months. I was ready for the next challenge. Being dropped behind enemy lines.

Chapter 5

"You have two missions: first you have to destroy the rail junction just outside Dieppe and then isolate the German Headquarters. Your target is two miles from Dieppe. The Hampden will drop you some way inland and you will make your way to Arques-la-Bataille. It is a swampy area and you should be able to lay up during the day. Aerial photographs show plenty of woods."

Scouse asked, "Can't the RAF knock out the junction and HQ, sir?"

"They could, Fletcher, but it would alert Jerry. It would tell him that something was up. You will strike the night before the dawn assault. It will be too late by then for the Germans to react as the Canadians and other Commandos will have landed."

Fletcher had been right to bring it up but the fact that we had been chosen meant that they must have considered that alternative. I was more worried about other issues. "Sir, blowing the railway line will not be a problem but how do you mean *'isolate the Headquarters'*?"

"Just that. Cut the telephone lines and disrupt their radio. Damage their vehicles. Stop them getting information."

"Bring the full force of the Germans on to us, sir."

"In a nutshell, yes, Tom. It will buy the attacking forces time. That might make all the difference. Your eight men can lead them a merry dance."

I nodded. I had had clarification at least. "And where do we rendezvous with Lieutenant Jorgenson?"

"Along the coast, east of Graincourt."

I knew it. We had been there before. "That is a good five or six miles, sir. Won't Number 3 Commando be in the area attacking the batteries there?"

"That is part of the thinking, Tom. Hopefully you will be able to slip through in the confusion."

I looked him in the eye, "Just like St. Nazaire again, sir."

He frowned, "We learned our lesson that day. The RAF will be heavily involved. There will be air support. I am certain it will all go swimmingly"

I realised that I was spitting in the wind. It was a done deal. "Right sir, here is what we need to enable us to pull off this conjuring trick. I want to see a similar set of points over here and I would like to be able to talk to a railway engineer. I take it there is no railway we can blow up?"

He brightened, "That is a damned good idea. You know there might be. There are disused railway lines all over Cornwall. Leave that with me. Anything else?"

"An idea of how many men we can expect at the Headquarters?"

He picked up a couple of sheets of paper and settled on one, "It looks like a Headquarters Company and a Communications unit. Probably no more than a hundred and twenty men all told."

Scouse said, "Doesn't sound like many if you say it quick." He saw the frown and added, "Sorry, sir."

I ignored Scouse's comments. They were understandable. "We will need plenty of explosives and timers, ammunition sir and more of those silencers."

Major Foster looked unhappy. "I can get you five but they are like gold dust."

I still had mine. That would give us six. It would have to do. "And camouflage nets."

"Right." He made a note and then said, "Look chaps. This is important. I know that it is a risky venture but things are not going too well for us in the Med. We have just lost a crucial convoy which was heading for Malta and we are barely holding the Germans in the desert. We need the Germans to move units to the

coast and to halt the flow of reinforcements to Africa. If we lose
Egypt we lose our oil and that would mean we would lose the war.
An attack on Dieppe will make them think this is a precursor to an
invasion."

I realised that he had breached numerous rules by confiding in
us. It was a measure of the mutual trust.

"Don't worry, sir we will do our best and get the job done but
we can't guarantee anything."

"I know, Tom, I know. Here are the dates and times. You and
your men will be picked up from your camp on the fourteenth of
the month. You will leave England on the fifteenth and parachute
into Occupied France. You have the sixteenth and the seventeenth
to reconnoitre the railway line and you attack on the night of the
eighteenth."

"And if the attack is postponed again, sir?"

"Go ahead with your mission and make your own way out. You
and Lieutenant Jorgenson can work out the exact location of your
pick up and your own codes." He smiled at Scouse, "I daresay it
will be unintelligible Scouse that you use!"

Scouse grinned, "As me da says, *'if it ain't broke, don't fix it'*!"

"Right sir. We will go and begin training. If you could find us
an engineer, some points and a line to blow up that would be
perfect."

Once away from the Major and when we had assembled our
supplies we went up to the tin mine. It was quiet there and easy to
think. George Lowe and Ken Shepherd would be the explosive
experts and they practised using explosives to blow up the rusted
track lines at the mine. The rest practised cutting telegraph and
telephone wires. There were quick ways to do these things which
did not compromise efficiency. They did the same things over and
over again until it was almost second nature. I sat with Polly and
studied the aerial photographs of the Headquarters.

"Well, sir, at least it isn't a fortress. There is a barrier on either
side of the road and a bit of barbed wire. Those anti aircraft
machine guns won't worry us and I can see the barracks block. It is

far enough away from the communications set up so that we won't be disturbed."

"You make it sound easy, Sergeant."

"We know it won't be, sir but we can do nothing about the problems we know nothing about can we?"

I shook my head, "No. And we need somewhere to lay up." I looked at the map and photographs. I laughed.

"Something funny sir?"

"Look here. They have a large area of water and swamp at the back of the radio building and there is a small wood. It is surrounded by swamps and water too. If we made that our camp...."

"Then we would be almost in the camp and it would be the last place they would look. We would be in their back yard."

"And the German dogs would not be able to smell us either."

"That is a risk sir but I think you are right. We camp on their doorstep."

A few days later Major Foster made good on his promise. "I have a retired engineer and I have an old railway line. The two are not far from each other. He lives in Truro and the railway line is just a mile or so from where he lives. It is an old line; it hasn't been used in thirty years but it has points. He is keen to help. I said you would pick him up in the morning. Don't tell him where you are going, just that you need to know how to do this. Time is getting on."

"I know sir."

"Sergeant Major Dean has a lorry waiting for you."

Albert Harris was seventy five years old. He looked more like a retired sea captain than a railway engineer. He had a neatly trimmed goatee beard. His waistline showed that he liked food and beer but he was sharp as a tack. His eyes were bright and sparkled at the thought of being involved in the war effort. As we drove up to the railway line he said, "I was too valuable in the Great War. I couldn't do my bit. I am glad to be helping you chaps. I hope that this railway line you are going to blow up is in Occupied Europe."

"I'm afraid that is classified information sir."

He laughed, "I am old but not stupid. It has to be in Europe. Never mind. I have a fertile imagination. I will have to make up where it is. Can you tell me what you have to do?"

I was on safer ground, "There are two railway lines and they merge before heading to an important town. We have to stop trains getting in or out."

"For how long?"

The question confused me, "Is that important?"

"If you have to stop trains using it for a day or so then you won't need much of a charge. A pound or two of dynamite strategically placed should do it but if you want a more permanent destruction then you would have to use a bigger charge or blow up a bridge. That would do the trick."

"The more damage the better sir."

He rubbed his hands, "Excellent!"

He peered out of the windscreen, "I did work on this line when I was a young man. That was in the last century. I helped to build it. Strange to think I am going to blow it up now."

When we reached the site I had the driver light a fire to make a brew. Albert, as he told us to call him, led us to the rusted points. "If you set a small charge here underneath the rail and a second one in the actual points it would damage them sufficiently so that they would need to replace the whole unit. That is a day's work. Trains are funny creatures. They like smooth running. If they don't get it then they jump the rails. They might be big but they can be delicate."

I nodded, "And if we want to make a bigger repair job?"

"Firstly you make a bigger charge and you make sure you bury them beneath both rails as well as on the points. Get them underneath the ballast; concentrate the explosion. Then you go here." He walked down the line. "This is where two rails join. You blow up here too. That means they have to replace all four lengths of rail and level the ballast as well. If you do the same on the other side then it will take a few days to repair." He rubbed his hands. "Well that is enough talk. How about a bit of blowing up!"

He had an infectious smile and I saw that my section were smiling too. "Shepherd and Lowe this is your show but you others watch. If anything happens to these before we go into action then you have to be able to do what they are doing."

Albert lost his smile, "What do you mean, *'anything happens'*?"

"People shoot at us, sir and we have lost men before."

"Dear me. I suppose I am lucky." He looked at Ken and shook his head, "You young men need to come back. We shall need chaps like you after the war."

Under his keen eye and sage advice Ken and George laid the charges. When we were all happy George said, "We will set the timers now. You had better take cover, sir."

"Of course. This is exciting!"

We all retired a suitably safe distance. Ken and George shouted, "Ready to fire!"and they hurtled towards us. "We set it for five minutes."

Ken looked at Albert, "I should cover your ears, sir!" The old man nodded.

We waited. Suddenly there was a flash of flames, a concussion and then the explosion. It was a good job we had retired a long way away. Ballast clattered down as well as some of the bolts which held the rails together.

Albert stood, "My goodness me! That was noisy."

I headed back towards the rails. They were totally demolished.

Scouse said, "That is great sir! It works!"

Albert said, with his finger in his ear, "How many points and lines are there?"

I almost slapped myself in the head. "There are two lines coming from each direction, going into two." I saw the looks on my men's faces.

Albert said, "You will need four charges!"

Ken proved that day just how much of a thinker he was, "Sir, we have it wrong."

George Lowe shook his head, "You are still wet behind the ears. The Lieutenant doesn't make mistakes!"

"Hang on Lowe, let Shepherd speak. Go on, what have I got wrong?"

"The number of lines. There are four coming in and two heading for... er the target. That means we have eight rails to destroy on one side of the points and four on the other."

I nodded, "You are right, Shepherd." I looked at Albert.

"The small charges would still close the junction for a day but the lad is right you would need more explosives to do a proper job." He swept his hand around the site. "This isn't big enough "Then what we need to do is to use enough explosive to totally destroy the rails there." I pointed further down the line where a spur ran from the central line.

Most of the men stared at me as though I had made another mistake but Ken and Albert nodded, "Aye that would work."

Ken became animated, "We measure the blast crater and that will tell us if that amount of explosive is enough to destroy the whole junction."

George finally got it, "So instead of smaller charges we use one bigger one."

We began to walk towards the spur. Albert took out a pipe and began to fill it. I smiled, he was thinking. It was just like Dad. He finally got it going and then he spoke. We had reached the spur and the rusted points. "It is not as easy as that." He pointed to the ballast which lay beneath the rails. "You will have to clear all of that out and then repack it back on top."

Ken said, "That's right you need to direct the explosion to the rails and the points."

"Let's get on with it then!" Sergeant Poulson liked to be doing things and he had stood around flapping his gums long enough.

"Fletcher, you go half a mile west and Crowe half a mile east. We don't want any civilians blundering into us."

"Yes sir."

I used my watch to time them as they toiled away. It had taken twenty minutes to set charges under the rails. Some of my men could do that while Shepherd and Lowe made the more important bomb. Even with many spare hands helping it still took forty minutes to complete the task. As we headed for safety so that it could be set off I began to run through the problems the timing might create. The most obvious one was German sentries. We were not far from German Headquarters. It would be easy for them to regularly check the security of the points. The second problem was noise.

As we hunkered down I mentally allocated jobs. Sergeant Poulson and Lance Sergeant Gowland would have to be the security. They could not do it alone. That would leave me and Fletcher. The rest would be setting charges. It was fortunate we had had our replacement. Otherwise we would not be able to do the job.

"Ready to fire!"

This time the shower of debris covered a much wider area. We would wake the Germans up, that was for sure. As we headed back to the crater and Fletcher and Crowe ran to join us, I realised the other implications of my plan, we could not afford to lose any men in the drop. I needed every one of my section.

Albert chuckled when he saw the crater. "That is a grand hole." He tapped his pipe on the rusted rail which twisted up into the air. He pointed his pipe at the rail some ten feet away. "If you were to put the charge yonder on the further rail the odds are it would mean they would have to replace at least twenty four rails. That is a lot of steel! And if you loosen the ballast it will have more of an impact."

Ken's nod told me he had understood the implications of Albert's words.

I patted Albert on the back. "Well Mr Harris, we had better be getting you home. Thank you for your advice. We couldn't have done it without you."

He looked crestfallen, "Oh, you don't need me anymore." He shook his head and berated himself, "Of course they don't, Albert, you dozy old bugger!" He shook my hand, "Thank you for inviting me Lieutenant Harsker. I felt like a vegetable without any purpose. I feel like I am part of the war effort now."

"You are Albert, you are. You watch the newspapers over the next few weeks. You will know when have done our little job."

"It will be that big?"

"We are all little cogs in a big machine. We are one part of a bigger team."

He nodded, "I shall scour the newspapers and look for references to Commandos. It will be better than just reading the obituaries."

After we had dropped him off we returned to camp. I left Ken and George to tell Daddy Grant the exact quantities of explosive we would need. I reported to Major Foster and gave him a full report. "I think you are right, Tom, your numbers are tight. Do you want some men from another section?"

"I would say yes but I am guessing that the ones I want, Gordy's section and the like, will be involved anyway?"

"I am afraid so. It would have to be outsiders."

I shook my head, "It might upset the balance of my team. I will stick with what I have."

"Shepherd is working out then?"

"Today was the day he found his feet and his position. Even George Lowe defers to him on some matters. We will go tomorrow and see Lieutenant Jorgenson and then we will just have to practice our unarmed combat. I think we will need it."

The E-boat had been repaired. As we approached I saw Bill Leslie with a huge grin on his face. Alan Jorgenson shook his head, "If Mr Leslie looks like a dog with two... it is because he is now Petty Officer Leslie."

"Well done Bill. Promotion eh?"

"Yes sir. It was worth getting a soaking for the stripes."

"I am pleased for you." I turned to Alan, "We have to arrange a rendezvous."

"You are going in by air I hear? The *'Lady'* not good enough for you these days?"

"Believe me I would rather go by boat but we are going to be well behind enemy lines. I think they do not want to give away the fact that we will be attacking Dieppe."

He nodded, "We are being used as well. We go in with Number 3 Commando as support. At least we fly British colours this time. Let's go and check the charts."

Alan had already marked Yellow 1 and Yellow 2; the beaches Number 3 Commando would be using for their landing. He jabbed a finger at the map, "I think Yellow beach will be hot. You don't want to risk that. We could pick you up east of Yellow beach. In fact that is what I have been told is the best pick up point."

"The problem is that leaves us with a long hike. The further we have to travel the more chance we have of being spotted. I am guessing the hornets will be well and truly awake when we are heading back. How about here?"

"That is Blue beach. It has a good beach but the Canadians are landing there."

That ruled that one out. We needed one where there was no fighting. I peered at the map. "There, not far from Belleville, that is a beach!"

He looked down and then up at me. "That is tiny and there are cliffs!"

"There are only a handful of us. We need a tiny beach. We are Commandos. We abseil down the cliffs. We have been along the coast there. The Germans don't have any garrisons. Just the regular sentries. They will be busy fighting the Canadians. That looks perfect."

He nodded, "We are just the taxi, you are the customer. I will have Wacker work out call signs with Scouse."

"And we will practise coming down cliffs!"

We had not trained at the cliffs for some time and it proved useful. Putting your life in the hands of a comrade made for closer ties. For Ken this was the first time he had had to do this. I could see why he had been recommended. He had high skill levels and was totally confident with a rope. By the time came for us to head for the aerodrome we were as ready as we ever would be. The extra weight of the ropes was a problem. I wrestled with it all the way to the airfield.

When we arrived a Flight Sergeant greeted us, "I am Flight Sergeant Richardson and I will be looking after you on the jump. The Hampden is on its way down from Ringway sir. Lieutenant Rogers is the pilot. He said for you and your lads to wait in the hangar."

"Right. "Bring the gear, Sergeant."

"Right Lieutenant Harsker."

"Sir, are you related to Group Captain Harsker?"

"He is my Dad. Do you know him?"

"My Dad served with him in the Great War in France. He was the armourer. He speaks highly of him."

"You must be Percy Richardson's son then. My father rated your Dad too."

"Things have changed since then eh sir?"

"They have indeed." An idea came to me. "We have a problem Flight and you might be able to help. We have to take explosives and ropes with us. Normally we carry them in the Bergens but I worry that will make us too heavy. We can't afford any broken limbs when we land. The extra weight increases that risk. Any ideas?"

We had reached the hangar and Sergeant Poulson and the men were making themselves comfortable. The Flight Sergeant looked around and pounced on a large kit bag. "We have some of these spare. If you put explosives in one and ropes in the other that might work. We attach a static line just like yours and drop them out. They would land in the same area as your lads. You will have to unpack them once you land."

"That is not a problem. Well done Flight. I'll get the gear. Sergeant Poulson, have the ropes and explosives taken out of the Bergens. We will pack them in the kit bags the Flight Sergeant will provide."

I could tell that the section was relieved to have lighter Bergens. Hurtling towards the ground was bad enough without pounds of extra weight. Once the kit bags were filled I was happier. The bags were robust canvas.

The Flight Sergeant said, "What you could do, sir, if you wanted the kit bags to land close to you would be to tether them to two of your men."

I shook my head, "We will put the kit bags in the middle of the stick. We should find them. It will be safer for my lads that way."

"You are probably right."

We heard the unmistakeable sound of the flying coffin, the Hamden, as it came in to land. Flight Sergeant Richardson said, "It will take some time to refuel and the crew will need a break. I think there is food for you in the mess if you wait until the crew arrive."

"Will our gear be safe here?"

"I'll keep an eye on it. The ground crew know better than to cross me!"

They taxied the bomber right up to the doors of the hangar. The crew came down to join us,

The pilot held out his hand, " Lieutenant Rogers, I am your taxi driver tonight. Weather forecast is good. Let's go and get something to eat and we can chat about the drop zone. Apparently you know it better than we do."

I nodded, "We have been there before."

We left the hangar and headed towards the mess, "That is what I heard. You are a cloak and dagger specialist eh?"

I laughed, "If that means spending longer behind enemy lines than is healthy, then yes."

"We just swan in, drop you off and then head on home."

The memory of the crew who had dropped us at St. Nazaire and then went up in a fireball filled my head but I said nothing. Pilots were a superstitious bunch. It would not do to jinx the mission.

The smell of frying bacon greeted us. Lieutenant Rogers rubbed his hands. "One advantage of being on Ops is bacon and egg. With any luck there will be a few sausages too!"

I must confess the smell of frying bacon always had the same effect on me, it made me hungry and I began to anticipate the taste. The plates were brought to us in double quick time. I saw the men's eyes light up at the filled plates. The waitress said, "You lads enjoy it! The eggs were still inside the chickens this morning!"

There was even a bottle of HP sauce on the table. This was luxury indeed! When we had cleared our plates, and it did not take long, the air crew lit up. "So, we are heading east of Dieppe?"

"That's right but you need to come in from the north." I took out my map. "Here is the drop zone, Dampierre-Saint-Nicholas. Here is the German Headquarters of the 302nd Division. They have anti-aircraft around there and that is one wasp's nest we do not want to disturb."

He nodded and stubbed out his cigarette, "You do know the area. Well we shall carry on south and do a loop. We will avoid the area completely."

"I would keep going almost to Fecamp. There are some big guns here and here." I pointed at the map. "There is a gap close to Saint-Valery-en-Caux. Not as many AA there."

"Thanks for the tip." He stood, "We will just use the facilities and then see if the ground crew have finished. Take off in ninety minutes if all goes well."

"Right, see you on board." I turned to the men, "We have ninety minutes. Use it wisely. Check weapons and remember this will the last chance to use a toilet for some days."

Once back in the hangar I went through my routine. I took out all my magazines and checked they were filled. I replaced them. I checked my grenades and then my tool kit: wire cutters, toggle rope, blackjack, knuckledusters. They were all there. I repacked the bag so that the balance was right.

"Sergeant Poulson check that no one has any papers on them."

"Sir."

I knew they wouldn't but you could bet the one time I didn't have Polly check would be the day someone did take an incriminating letter or photograph.

The aeroplane was familiar. It smelled of aviation fuel and, when the engines started speech became impossible. Flight Sergeant Richardson had done as I had asked. The two bags were in the middle of the stick. Lance Sergeant Harry Gowland had them before him and behind. Sergeant Poulson was the last man in the stick and I would be first. I had young Ken Shepherd just behind me. I had no doubt he had been trained but this was his first drop over enemy territory. I wanted him close.

The flight would take less than two hours. We could have done it even quicker but Lieutenant Rogers want to have as much altitude as possible when we crossed the French coast. We had to use hand signals. Flight Sergeant Richardson pointed to the static lines. I nodded, stood and hooked on. He checked my chute and I turned and checked Shepherd's. When the Flight Sergeant was satisfied he pushed Polly in the back and we shuffled up to the bomb bay. As soon as it was removed there was a cold wind and a roar. We waited. The Flight Sergeant was looking in at the cockpit. Lieutenant Rogers would give him the signal when we were to jump. As we had had no flak I knew that we had crossed unobserved. I prayed that would continue.

Chapter 6

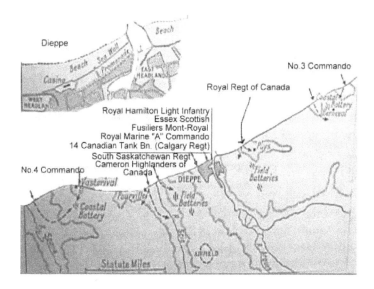

The Flight Sergeant pointed and gave me the thumbs up. I crossed my hands over my straps and took that leap of faith into the dark. It was always the same. You waited for that jerk and then the billowing chute. You hoped it would not be a flare and a Roman candle which would mean a messy death two thousand feet below you on the ground. When I saw the chute open I breathed again and looked down. I grabbed the cords. We did not want to land in Dampierre-Saint-Nicholas. I wanted to be west of the village. There was a wood there and an ancient track way. I scanned the blackness below me for a sign that we were close.

I saw the snake that was the River Béthune. The wood was just half a mile to the south. I pulled on one side of the chute and I began to move south. I kept my eye on the ground. Ken would have to follow. I kept adjusting my cords as I descended. I was looking for an area clear of trees. When I saw the ground I began to flex my knees. By pulling on the chute I managed to land upright. I quickly gathered the parachute in before it lifted me up again. To my great relief I saw Shepherd and Fletcher on the ground, rolling up their chutes. I had my radio operator and one of my demolition experts.

I ran to them. "Keep hold of the chutes!" They naturally followed me as we headed back down the line to make sure that everyone was down. "Grab the kitbags."

It was with some relief that I saw they had all landed. "Empty the kitbags and disperse the ropes and the explosives. Put your chutes in the kitbags. Cut off some of the cords as you do so. They will come in handy." I said that for the benefit of Shepherd, the rest of us were aware of the uses for the cord. " George and Harry you take one and Crowe and Hewitt take the other. Polly, you are tail end Charlie. I will lead."

The men worked quickly and the ropes and explosives were shared out equitably. With the kit bags filled I pointed north and west.

We moved quickly. I had no idea who might or might not have seen us land. I wanted to be away as speedily as we could. Lieutenant Rogers had done well. We were just a mile or so from where we would camp. The greenway was an ancient path. Those who were here before the Romans would have used it. Henry V and his men might have used it. It had overhanging trees and was well worn. We were able to move swiftly and unseen. We reached the first of the patches of water. I was not sure if they were fish farms or fishing holes but they were water. I stopped. "Find stones and put them in the kitbags. Throw the kitbags as far into the ponds as you can."

When I had seen the patches of water, back in England, I had seen the potential. Digging holes and burying parachutes was not only time consuming, it told the enemy you had landed. This way we were invisible. They might find the kitbags eventually but we would be long gone, or dead, by then. After the two bags had sunk I led the section forward. I was acutely aware that we were drawing close to the German Headquarters but we had to have a camp before dawn. I kept the water to my left. I knew the river was some two hundred yards to my right,

It was the noise from the German Headquarters which alerted me to its proximity. I held up my hand. Turning I made the signal to wait and, dropping my Bergen I moved along the green way. I saw that the river was now just thirty yards away. I knew where we were. German Headquarters was four hundred yards to my left. We needed to cross the River Béthune or as it became the River Arques. The woods were just to the north of the river. Making my way back to the section I picked up my Bergen and waved them north. When we reached the river I signalled for Groves to ford it. The river came up to his chest but it was not fast flowing. Once across we had the tricky job of negotiating the road which ran into Dieppe, the D1. As it was still dark of night and we were darkened it would not be a problem to cross it but I was glad when we all made it across. Groves and I led the way and we disappeared into the woods.

The aerial photographs had suggested that there was no one within a mile of the woods. We would discover that soon enough. We headed deeper within the wood. I was looking for somewhere with high trees and enough cover to hide us. We had not gone more than two hundred yards when I found it. The trees thinned out; someone had copsed them. I dropped my Bergen next to an elm and signalled for the others to do the same. They were all grateful to have the weight off their shoulders.

I pointed to Groves and Hewitt. They nodded and, taking out their Thompsons became sentries. I waved my right arm in a circle and the rest of the section took off to scout the vicinity. "Scouse, check that the radio works but do not transmit!"

"Right, sir."

"Crowe, take out the camouflage nets and make us disappear."

Out greatest danger lay in enemy aircraft. The nets would hide us. Part one had been successful. We had landed, found a camp site and done so unobserved. We had two days to find out as much as we could about the area without being seen. We had yet to do the hard part!

Forty minutes later and they had all returned. We now spoke in the hushed voices of those in church. "All clear sir."

Handing him my binoculars I said, "Sergeant Poulson, your team has the first watch. Wake me in three hours."

"Sir!"

I drank some water from my canteen. The nearby river meant we could be profligate with our water. Then I wrapped myself in my camouflage net and rolled under a young elm. The thin branches and leaves would disguise my outline even more. I slept. Sleep was as valuable as rations. A tired man made mistakes.

Polly woke me. He put his mouth to my ear, "All quiet. The Germans are up and about; eight hundred yards west of us." He gave me my glasses and moved to find the others in his team.

I nodded and rolled out of my net. I went to Shepherd and shook him awake and then did the same with Fletcher. While we were in France we would work in teams of three. There was a balance in each of them. When we moved we would do so in our teams so that if anything happened to us we had a chance of continuing with the job. Polly's team, now relieved, found their own beds. Before we ate or drank anything we secured our perimeter. I waved my hand in a circle and the two others disappeared.

I went to the western end of the woods. When I reached the eaves I lay down and took out my binoculars. The road was coming to life. The ferns, bracken and undergrowth hid me but I kept perfectly still as I scanned the German Headquarters. There were the ubiquitous Kubelwagens as well as two lorries. As we had been told there were just barriers guarding the building although I spied rolls of barbed wire close to the road. Two sandbagged machine gun emplacements were on either side of the only road in and out of the buildings. It looked like they had just taken over an existing building. I raised the glasses and spied the telephone wires which entered the building. I followed them and saw that they came to the road. There was a pole not forty yards from me and the line ran along the road. The telephone could be cut easily. The railway line ran between the river and the camp. There were two lines.

I then scanned the buildings for signs of the aerial which would tell me where the transmitter was housed. It was not in the main building. There was an outbuilding close to the river. It looked to me likely to be the radio room. The headquarters company looked to be in tents which were around the barrack building we had spied on the aerial photographs. The tents were new and that should have alerted me but it did not. They had been reinforced. They were close to the large patches of water. I smiled. They would be a haven for midges and mosquitoes. I was betting that the soldiers would not be happy.

It looked satisfactory although there were German soldiers guarding the bridge which crossed the Béthune. I suspected the river might be a little deeper there. I counted six sentries. There was no barrier but, even as I watched, they stopped an old French van. It looked like the bread delivery van. They checked papers and opened the back. I had seen enough and I slid back into the woods on my belly. Once I had gone far enough I stood and went back to the camp. Fletcher and Shepherd waited for me.

I waved them to me. "Eat, then report."

I took my hard rations from my Bergen. I had already divided them into the meals we would need for the operation. They had nutritional value and that was all. We ate to survive. There was little to be enjoyed about the taste. I smiled when I saw Ken Shepherd's face. If he had been brought up on a farm then he would be used to good, wholesome food. I washed it down with water from my canteen. We have to remember to refill them from the river and use the water purification tablets.

Once they had finished I told them what I had seen. That was important. If anything happened to me then two others would know what I had seen. From the other two I discovered that the road which led to the bridge was just three hundred yards to the north and the woods extended to the south and east for at least a

74

mile. Neither had seen signs of anyone although Fletcher, who had scouted the northern road had seen vehicles on the road.

I set them at their posts and I sat with my back against an elm on the western side of our camp where I could hear the noise of the traffic on the road. When I heard the sound of the aeroplane engine I moved back to my observation post on the edge of the woods. The sound came from beyond the Headquarters. I took out my glasses and scanned the skies. I saw a Fieseler Fi 156 Storch rise slowly into the sky. That must be the airfield. The aerial photographs had not identified any fighters there but it was obvious now that the Germans were using it. It did not head over in our direction but flew towards Dieppe. I moved back to the camp.

Lance Sergeant Gowland and his team took over after a further two hours and we managed another three hours sleep. When I awoke the whole team was awake. We prepared for our night time reconnaissance. I detailed Lance Sergeant Gowland's team to watch the camp. We would not need Bergens, nor Tommy guns. As soon as dusk fell I led the other five north to find the railway line. If we encountered an enemy we would have to use silent methods to eliminate them. I had my silencer fitted to my Colt.

We went across the road in pairs. It was quiet and we would have heard the noise of any approaching vehicles. We moved north, through the woods for four hundred yards. I used Ken Shepherd's young ears and eyes to be the scout. He held up his hand and we dropped to our knees. I heard nothing at first and then, to our left I heard German. I could not see them but I could tell, from the sound of their voices that they were moving in the opposite direction to us. Maddeningly I could not make out any words. When the voices receded Ken looked at me and I nodded. We reached the edge of the wood and I heard a train to our left. It told me where the line was. We had to negotiate the D1 once more. Once across we descended into the low lying ground which ran along the river and the ponds. It was hard going. I sank up to my knees at one point but when we heard a train, just two hundred yards away I took heart. We were close.

I spied the line coming from the north east. It crossed the River Arques. We would have to do the same. There was no road near to the railway line and I took a chance. We needed to cross the river anyway and rather than getting wet we would risk the bridge. My hopes were dashed when we found the small river, L'Eaulne which ran into the Arques. Fortunately we could ford it and the water only came to our thighs. I waved everyone to the ground when we reached the bridge. It was barely six feet above the water. I crawled up and put my ear to the rail. I heard and felt nothing. There was no train approaching. I looked down the line. There was no sign of German soldiers and I waved my men to join me.

We ran across the bridge and followed the railway line. I felt quite exposed as we made our way along it but I knew it was an illusion. We were invisible. There was no one to see us. When I heard a car to our left I threw myself to the ground. There was a road ahead. When it had passed I moved slowly and saw the other railway line. We had found the junction. Having had Albert explain about such junctions I had a better idea of how they worked. I found the first point. We kept moving down the line and I looked ahead. There was a second junction fifty yards away. We would have to use two charges! When we examined the second one we found that it was larger. We spent just ten minutes exploring the site and then I waved my hands for us to move back. Our return was easier as we knew which places to avoid.

We crept into the camp. When Lance Sergeant Gowland's Colt appeared before me I smiled and nodded. They had done their job well. I gathered them around me and spoke quietly. "We have three targets now."

George Lowe said, "Three?"

"There are two junctions. One is smaller and will need a smaller charge but we crossed a bridge. If we could blow that then it would take longer for them to repair it."

He nodded, "We will have to use all the explosives then."

Polly shook his head, "Were you intending to take some home with you?"

George smiled, "Fair point but I just meant we have no spare left for the Headquarters."

"That doesn't matter. The priority is the railway line. We improvise with grenades for the Headquarters. Tomorrow we make up the charges. That is your job George and you Ken. There will be three. Harry, your team will go tomorrow night and lay the charges. I will take the other two to the Headquarters. We will rendezvous on the north side of the bridge. I will give you the timings tomorrow when I have worked them out. Now get some sleep."

I took the first watch. This new problem was in my mind and I would get no sleep. Ken sidled over to me, "Sir, I thought you wanted me with the explosives?"

"I did but the fact that we have no explosives left for the Headquarters means I need to use two teams for that. Just make sure that the charges are well made and you will have done your job."

He nodded and went off to his patrol. The attack by the Canadians was scheduled for four o'clock in the morning. We could not set off our charges before then. My two teams needed to have isolated the headquarters by four o'clock at the latest. I hoped to do what we had to and be away without anyone being the wiser. That meant killing the sentries, cutting the telephone lines and disabling the radio. A tall order but if we were to stand any chance of escaping that was what we would have to do. By the time I woke Sergeant Poulson I had my plan in my head.

By five o'clock in the afternoon all of the charges had been organised and were in the three Bergens of the demolition team. That meant the ropes to descend the cliffs were in our Bergens. It was not satisfactory. If we didn't make the rendezvous then the others would have to work out another way to get down the cliffs. Harry made light of it, "We'll work something out, sir but you and the lads will be there. It just means we will have empty bags!"

"Only use the Thompsons as a last resort. Once Jerry hears them he will be roused and after us. That is not just bad for us but the poor lads who will be coming ashore. We leave at midnight.

We will rendezvous at the north side of the bridge by five at the latest."

"The charges will have gone off by then, sir."

"I know. George, you will wait half a mile to the north of the bridge. There is a small village off to the side, close to the road. We will meet you there. If we aren't there by five thirty set off the charges make your own way to the cliffs."

"You have the radio, sir."

"I know George. You will have to use your torches to signal. Scouse what is the call sign?"

"Scotty Road, sir."

"And the response?"

"New Brighton Ferry."

I shook my head, as a code it was unbreakable. Only two Liverpudlians would have worked them out. "Okay? Now get some rest and make sure you fill up your canteens when we cross the river."

I watched as Scouse helped Ken to organise his bag. There had been a time when our radio operator had been the baby of the section. He was helping Ken. All the training in the world couldn't totally prepare you for an operation behind enemy lines. I went through my own routine. I used my webbing to secure my Mills bombs. I slipped my knuckle duster into one trouser pocket and my sap into the other. I slid my dagger in and out of its scabbard to make sure it would be there when I needed it. I secured my Thompson to my Bergen and I was almost ready. The last task was what Gordy, my old corporal had called, *'Al Jolson'* time. I blacked up my face and hands. We needed to be invisible.

At midnight we departed. We moved together until we reached the edge of the woods. Then I led my sections down to the river. Before we crossed the road I had Crowe shinny up the telephone pole and cut the wires. We would need to do it on the other side of the camp too but part of our job was completed at any rate. There were two sentries on the bridge and we would need to eliminate them. Our observations had told us that they were changed at eleven and then at three. Poulson and Hewitt crept quietly along the bank towards the Germans. I had my silenced Colt ready as we moved behind them. Our rubber soled shoes meant we were silent. Crowe also had a silencer on his Colt and he had a bead on the far sentry.

The two Germans had obliged us by standing together and looking north towards Dieppe. I knew that at this moment the flotilla of ships would be negotiating the German minefield which lay just off shore. An explosion now would mean that all attempts at secrecy were gone. The silence was reassuring. Poulson and Hewitt were now shadows. It was bizarre watching shadows end the lives of two Germans. One moment the sentries were standing by the bridge and the next moment they had gone. We quickly ascended the bank and crossed the bridge. As I passed the sentries I took two grenades from their belts. Fletcher took the other two. The Headquarters was silent.

Sergeant Poulson and his section covered our backs as we covered the open ground to the radio room. Fletcher and Shepherd watched as I put my ear to the door. I could hear little. I holstered my Colt and took out my sap. I slowly opened the door. Thankfully it had been recently oiled and it did so without a sound. I saw the radio operator. He had his back to me and headphones on. I heard the muted sound of music. In two strides I was behind him and had rendered him unconscious with a blow to the back of the head. My sap was a very efficient weapon. While we did this Crowe climbed up the next telephone pole and cut that one too.

I went to the door and waved my men in. Sergeant Poulson and his section took over the duties of sentries. I pointed to the radio operator and the two of them began to tie him up. I went to the radio and turned it around. Taking my wire cutters I cut every wire and then removed every valve I could. I put them in my battle dress. The sentry was secured. I pointed outside and they carried him there. I broke the cap on the grenade and carefully positioned it between the door and the jam. When the door was opened the grenade would go off and ensure that the radio could not be used.

I went to the river and threw the valves into its water. They were swept towards the sea. The radio operator was tied to a stanchion on the bridge. I led the section towards the vehicle park. Taking our daggers we punctured every tyre. I held up the grenade and nodded to Fletcher. He scurried off to use them as booby traps. I used mine on the Kubelwagen which was closest to the back door of the building. I looked at my watch. It was one thirty. We were on schedule.

It was a risk but I took my section along the side of the Headquarters building. I saw that there were four sentries at the two machine guns which guarded that entrance. They were watching the road. I took out my Colt. Crowe and Poulson also had silenced pistols. We moved towards the four men. It was eerie moving silently towards them as they chatted with each other. We got to within eight feet before one of them turned. I hissed, "Hands up and you will not be hurt!" This was the moment when a false move by one of the Germans would have resulted in a fire fight with but one outcome, their death. I think it was the three Thompsons aimed at them which made three of them comply but as one moved a hand to his rifle I fired a round into the sandbag. The '*phut*' sound it made seemed more sinister somehow. Their hands flew into the air. While Shepherd and I covered them the rest took off their helmets and tied them up. I nodded and each of them was sapped on the back of the head. While they were taken to the bridge to be secured with the radio operator Fletcher and I began to take the ammunition from the machine guns. We would take it back for our boat. We took the two machine guns and lowered them in the river.

Looking at my watch I saw that it was two thirty. My deviation from my own plan had made us slightly late. I signalled for them to follow me and led them across the road towards the railway line. I would risk using the line as the most direct route to our rendezvous. Of course it was inevitable that we would run into a train. We had heard none the night before but this night there was one. It was heading along our line towards Dieppe. Sound travels a long way at night and we had plenty of opportunity to hide in the culvert which ran alongside the line. We lay face down and I doubted that we would be seen. It seemed a long train. Part of me wished that it had come along a couple of hours later. It might have been blown up along with the tracks.

When I was certain it had passed I rose and we continued along the line. The delay had cost us. It was three thirty and we seemed to be nowhere near the rendezvous. I was loath to move any faster for that might attract attention. Dawn would be upon us by five at the latest. I wanted to be heading towards the cliffs by then. When, fifteen minutes later, I saw the bridge to our right, I began to hope that we might make it safely. My hopes were dashed as we stepped on to the bridge. There was a crack behind us in the direction of the Headquarters. The first of the booby traps had been triggered. We kept moving towards the bridge.

Harry and George rose like wraiths as we reached the far side of the bridge. "We wondered if that was you, sir?"

"No, Harry, just our calling card." A moment later there was a much bigger explosion followed by a couple more.

Scouse said, "And there goes the lorry park, sir. I reckon they will be a bit annoyed when they find what we have done to their tyres!"

Just then I heard the sound of gunfire. It was to the west. That had to be the flotilla. It was before they were due to land and that meant they had run into trouble at sea. "Harry, set the charges to go off in fifteen minutes."

"Are you certain sir? It will draw Jerry like flies."

I pointed to the east, "I reckon the show has begun." As if to echo that we heard klaxons from the headquarters and a more distant one from the aerodrome.

George, Harry and Ken went back to the charges to set the timers. We waited by the bridge. This would be the last one to go. It took fifteen minutes for them to reach the junction and set the timer. They raced towards us and I set the timer on the bridge explosives for ten minutes. As soon as it was light they would have the spotters up looking for us. My demolition team reached us. "Right, let's move. See how far we can get in eight minutes."

We ran. Once we stopped we would have to reorganise the Bergens. We had all the ropes and all of the captured German ammunition. The other three had empty bags. We stopped near to the village of Martin-Église, The railway crossed the D1 at this point and would be a good place to wait. We slid down the bank. I opened my Bergen and handed some of the ammunition I had taken from the German machine guns to Harry. "Rearrange your bags. " I took the opportunity of unfastening my Thompson from the Bergen. I would need it soon.

Right on time the junction exploded. We were more than a mile away but we felt the concussion. A few minutes later the bridge went up. This time some of the debris and dust showered us. Suddenly there was the sound of a naval bombardment from the west. The attack proper had begun. Within the next hour the Canadians would be pouring ashore. We had done all that we could and now it was time to get to safety; if we could.

Chapter 7

Although we had less than five miles to go the land was already filled with the sound of vehicles and men being moved to the front. The Germans now knew of the allied attack and were responding. While the Headquarters might have been temporarily disabled there were many more men in Dieppe and in camps around the coast. I led and Sergeant Poulson brought up the rear. We avoided the road and headed across country. I counted on the fact that we were going in the same direction as the Germans. They might mistake us for their own troops.

Our first problem came close to Grèges; although it was just a small village it had a camp around it. Luckily we spied it before we stumbled in to it. We ducked into the hedge which surrounded the field. Inside I heard orders being shouted. Engines were being started as they organised their response. The naval bombardment was still crashing away to the west. Occasionally a random shell would burst nearby and shower us with earth. Then the aerial battle began. Eyes in the German camp were either on the skies or the sea.

"We will have to go around. We head along this field and go east. Ken, you have sharp ears. You stay close by me."

"Sir!"

I cocked my Thompson. This was dangerous. Germans were all around us and if we met any then we would have no warning. We came to the end of the hedge and found ourselves close to the main road. I peered down, towards the east. It appeared to be empty. I stepped into the road and waved the section across, "Hurry!"

We almost made it. The two motorcycles appeared from nowhere. I barely had time to fire a burst from my Tommy gun. They were so close that every bullet found a mark, either flesh or the cycles themselves. Both men were down but the damage was done. The gunfire would draw the Germans. We had to get away. My men had not waited for me. Sergeant Poulson led them through the narrow streets of the village. The French were inside. I kept turning to see if we were being pursued. I saw no one.

I heard a burst from Sergeant Poulson's Thompson. German rifles responded. As I ran towards the gunfire I heard two more Thompsons fire. I almost stumbled into German bullets. We had been held at the edge of the village. I saw the coal scuttle helmets on the other side of the wall some thirty feet away. Three dead Germans lay before the wall.

I turned to Fletcher and Crowe. "Grenades on my shout. Throw them high. I want them to go off in the air. You know what to do."

"Sir." We would all release the handle and count to three. It was risky but the effect would be devastating.

Sergeant Poulson and Lance Sergeant Gowland both stepped out and fired long bursts. Stone chips flew from the wall. I pulled the pin and realised the handle. I counted to three and threw, shouting, "Grenade!"

The three grenades went off almost together. I did not see the effect for I had my face buried in the wall. Pieces of stone ricocheted off the wall. I stood and shouted, "At them!"

I knew that if they were not wounded or dead they would be concussed. I used the two dead bodies to springboard over the wall. As I landed I fired a burst at the ones who survived. "Keep going!"

We had the advantage now. We had cleared our path. We could not halt. The wall surrounded part of a field and I ran along the right hand side. We were heading parallel with the coast but we would be sheltered from attack by the wall. There was a hedge ahead and I ran hard. This was where our fitness would pay off. I did not look around. That was a luxury I could not afford. I relied on the fact that Sergeant Poulson would ensure that no one was left behind.

When we reached the safety of the canopy of branches and leaves I stopped. "Fletcher, radio! Sergeant, defensive perimeter. Reload with fresh magazines!"

I went to the edge of the field and looked back. I saw no grey but someone would spot the dead Germans and investigate.

Fletcher had the radio and was giving the call sign, "Scotty Road, over. Scotty Road, Over."

All we heard was static. He shook his head.

"Keep trying." This was maddening for the coast was less than four miles away as the crow flies. "Lowe, go down the field and see what is on the other side, to the west."

"Sir."

"Scotty Road, over. Scotty Road, Over."

The gunfire from the beaches was now constant. I heard small arms fire as well as the sound of naval guns. Worryingly I could hear the Goebbels battery firing. Number Three Commando should have silenced them by now.

"Scotty Road, over. Scotty Road, Over."

"New Brighton, over, New Brighton, over!"

"We are three miles from you and ready for pick up."

"Negative! We are not close. We are under attack."

"Tell him we will go to the beach and wait." I shrugged, "He gets there when he can get there."

"We will go to the beach and wait. Over and out!"

"Get that packed away and let's move."

George Lowe came running back, "No go sir! There is a squad of Germans there and they are heading in this direction."

Our route to safety was blocked. "We'll head to Graincourt. We can make our way back from there."

As we started to run Sergeant Poulson said, "There was a German garrison there the last time we were here, sir."

"Hopefully they will not be there but we are running out of alternatives, Sergeant."

"Yes, sir."

I tried to remember the roads. We did not have enough time for me to check the map. Our lives were measured in minutes now. Luckily for us the fields were filled with wheat. Although it did not cover us we had somewhere in which we could dive if danger approached. It was Crowe who was in the lead. He suddenly shouted, "Track ahead!"

"Keep going!"

He leapt over the wall and was followed by Fletcher and Lowe. Polly and I had just climbed over when a knot of Germans appeared less than fifty yards away. We both turned and gave a burst from our guns. Two dropped and the rest took cover.

"Come on move yourselves!" Sergeant Poulson's voice had the desired effect and they ran. We had just cleared the wall when I heard the sound of a heavy machine gun and chips of stone flew into the air.

I saw the village ahead. There was a lane which ran parallel to the field and it had a wall too. "Over the wall!"

We dropped over the wall and I held up my hand. We waited. I heard the German officer as he shouted, "They must have gone to Graincourt. Follow me."

I heard them as they approached, their boots pounding and clattering on the stones. They were speaking to each other as soldiers do and it helped me locate them as they approached. I took out a grenade and pulled the pin. The others did the same. When I deemed they were next to us I nodded and threw the Mills bomb over the wall three seconds after releasing the handle.

One of the Germans shouted, "Grenade!" and then a wall of concussion, smoke and shrapnel showered us.

I had no hearing but I stood and sprayed, blindly, the other side. "Let's go!"

We had bought ourselves some time and I led them directly towards Belleville-sur-Mer. There was little point in hiding. Our path to the beach was marked by the German dead. We had eaten into our stock of luck. I just hoped that *'Lucky Lady'* was on station. There was a pall of smoke drifting in from the sea and the sound of small fights to our left and right. Ahead seemed remarkably quiet. Above us the air was filled with Spitfires and FW 190s. The Germans appeared to have the upper hand.

We were approaching the main road when I heard the sound of a vehicle. We ducked down. Sergeant Poulson who was nearest to the road crawled forward and peered down. He turned and held up three fingers. I nodded and took out my last grenade. I saw that some of the section had no grenades left. Sergeant Poulson held up three fingers, then two and finally one. We hurled our last five grenades high in the air. The explosions were not simultaneous but the smoke and flames told me that we had hit at least one.

Sergeant Poulson led the charge. He ran into the road, firing his Thompson from the hip. We all followed. One of the Kubelwagens had been overturned a second had crew injured and the lorry which followed was on fire but Germans were pouring from it. In these situations it was the ones who reacted first who won. Our Thompsons wreaked havoc. When mine clicked empty I drew my Colt and emptied that too.

"Run!" We climbed the wall and ran over the fields towards Belleville-sur-Mer. I remembered this part of the coast. We were less than a mile from the cliffs. I would have to risk running through Belleville-sur-Mer. We had no time for any more detours. We needed to be on the beach as soon as possible. As we neared the coast road I saw a line of German vehicles heading towards the Goebbels battery. As its guns were still belching smoke and flames I knew that the attack by Number Three Commando had failed. We dropped to the ground and disappeared in the wheat. The convoy continued on. I felt guilty as we resumed our race to the sea. Commandos were dying and we were leaving.

Belleville-sur-Mer was deserted, or at least there were no people to be seen. These houses all had cellars. I suspected they were taking cover there. Once through the hamlet we had just five hundred yards and then we were at the cliff top.

"Fletcher, radio. Sergeant Poulson, get the ropes rigged."

I took out my binoculars. From my elevated position I could see all the way along the coast. My heart sank. Towards Dieppe I could see burning tanks on the beach and sinking landing craft in the surf. Ripples of flames filled the cliff top around the beach and I could see the flames from multiple machine guns. The Canadians were trapped on the beach.

I turned my glasses towards the Goebbels Battery. I could see that Commandos were attacking the gun but to no avail. I was just considering taking my men to aid them when I saw them begin to fall back towards the beach.

"Sir, it's *'Lucky Lady'.* She is half an hour away. The Lieutenant says to get down to the beach and he promises he will be there."

"Right lads, down the ropes. Sergeant you and I will go down last. Fletcher get the radio down and keep in touch with the boat."

As the first four men descended Sergeant Poulson said, "Bit of a cock up sir." He pointed to the huge battery, "They are still firing.!"

"I know and the beach at Dieppe looks to be a shambles too. Don't be downhearted Sergeant, we did our bit. I know we can't see the results but it might have been even worse; who knows."

We were the last two and we began the descent to the beach. Our men on the ground had their guns trained on the cliff top. We had seen no Germans but this was when we were at out most vulnerable. We were half way down when a shell from the Goebbels battery crashed over our heads and barely missed the destroyer which was racing in to the beach at Dieppe. Had it been struck it would have been sunk.

"Any sign of the boat?"

"Not yet sir but there are so many launches out there it is hard to tell which is ours."

"Be ready to wade out. We don't want them to ground themselves. Shepherd, wade out and see how far you can get."

He strode into the water. I saw that he was soon up to his waist. It was a good job we had not tried to land on this beach. It would have been too steep.

"Sir, they can see us." Fletcher shouted, gleefully.

Sergeant Poulson shouted, "There it is!"

Coming at us bow on it was unmistakeable. "In the water everybody and get on those German machine guns when we board. We might have to fight our way out yet!"

Lieutenant Jorgenson threw the E-boat around in an arc. We were sprayed and soaked but it meant we could all climb up on its starboard side. He had rigged a net over the side and we raced up like monkeys. Even as I grabbed the net he had spun the boat around and was racing out to sea. I struggled to climb up, burdened by my Bergen and the force of the water. But I managed it and rolled on to the deck.

I looked up into the face of the SBA, "I don't think we require your services Johnson! But thanks anyway."

"Captain says sorry about the quick manoeuvre but launches and landing craft are being sunk if they hang around too long."

"Don't worry about it. We are off the beach and that is all that counts."

The SBA pointed to the skies. They were filled with aeroplanes and there seemed to be more Germans than RAF. "They have sunk a couple of launches sir."

I stood, "Right lads get on the guns and be ready to fire ay any Jerry that comes close."

I made my way to the bridge. Bill Leslie was on the wheel. Alan shook his head ruefully, "Bloody shambles Tom. Sorry we were late but we had to help out on Yellow beach. The whole flotilla ran into a German Convoy. Only six landing craft from the Brigade made it. We had to engage a couple of the German convoy so that the Colonel could extricate his men. Brave buggers still landed but," He pointed, "They are having to be taken off now."

"If you want to hang around...."

"It seems rude just to run. We will wait until they are safely away from the beach before we leave." He shook his head. "We have lost a lot of brave men this day."

The Lieutenant did his best. We went as close to the shore as we dared and plucked another dozen Commandos from the sea. The German defenders had become braver and had set up machine guns on the beach. They had a surprise when our German machine guns began to tear through them. George Lowe said, "There you go Fritz! Have a taste of your own medicine!"

The Commandos were all grateful to have been rescued. Most were in total shock. For many, we discovered, this was their first taste of raiding in Occupied Europe. It had been a baptism of fire. When Lieutenant Jorgenson saw that there was no one left alive on the beach he turned west and joined the landing craft as they headed home. The disaster that was Dieppe was over. My section had escaped lightly but the Canadians and Number Three Commando had been scarred for life.

The boat was crowded and so I joined Lieutenant Jorgenson on the bridge for the sombre journey home. "You did warn them Tom but they didn't listen."

"Warned them?"

"The tanks. None got off the beach. Most were stuck in the shingle and the machine guns slaughtered the men."

"What about Lord Lovat and our lads? They were attacking the Hess battery."

"I don't know. We were here on Yellow Beach. Lord Lovat is a wily old bird. He might have been lucky. You never know."

Part 2

Africa

Chapter 8

We did not return as the other ships did to Newhaven and Southampton, instead we went all the way back to Falmouth. We did not arrive back until after dark. On the journey back we heard how the disaster had unfolded. The few boats which had landed had not had sufficient men to assault the guns. The ones we had with us had been with Major Young who had come the closest to success. Lack of heavy weapons had forced him to withdraw. Wacker picked up radio traffic which suggested the large numbers of Canadians had been killed or captured. By twelve noon it was all over and those that could be rescued and recovered were heading home. It was a pitifully small number.

Alan lit a cheroot as we saw Falmouth in the distance. We had reduced speed to save fuel. "You went in twice, Tom, to recce this place do you think it was a waste?"

I shook my head, "I got a dog bite and we lost no men. No, neither patrol was a waste. We learned a great deal. What we saw on the beach was. I suppose we just keep on doing our jobs and hope that the powers that be know how to win this war. Today showed me that we are nowhere near ready to invade Europe yet. The men who went in were well trained and well led. As far as I can see we didn't even dint the German defences and we lost a whole tank battalion of brand new tanks. That was a waste."

"Well the *'Lady'* suffered a little bit of damage and one of the engines needs an overhaul. I don't think we will be going over again anytime soon."

"We will just keep on training then and be ready when we are called upon. That is one good thing to come out of this. I know that my team is as good as any out there. Even the new lad, Shepherd, fitted in well."

"We are lucky in that respect. No bad apples in our barrel."

The next day I let the section have the morning off but I went up to the camp to write my report. Sergeant Major Dean listened as I told him of the raid. "You need more silencers then. I'll have a word with Daddy. We will see what he can do. I'd look on this as half full, you know. You did everything you were asked to do and more. The Germans will have to repair the bridge and the junctions. It might have been much worse if you hadn't. There would have been a delay getting word out from the German Headquarters. You did all right, sir."

I knew that he was right.

When Major Foster and some of the brigade arrived back in the late afternoon we were just finishing stripping and cleaning our weapons. My old Corporal, Sergeant Gordy Barker, now sported a sling, "We did our bit, sir. We destroyed the guns but we were knocked about a bit. Lord Lovat is a good lad. Even though we landed in the wrong place he didn't panic and we got the job done. Me and the lads would like to thank you, sir. It was your information which helped. We appreciated it."

"I am glad, Gordy. A shame that the other battery wasn't knocked out."

Gordy sniffed, "Number Four Commando is the one you go to if you want to get the job done, sir. And if you ever need another section to go with you then you know me and my lads won't let you down."

"I know Gordy."

"Lieutenant Harsker, Major Foster would like a word."

Major Foster looked drawn, "Sit down, Tom." He poured us a glass of whisky each. "I just wanted to say well done. I came back with his lordship. He told me that the RAF said you did your job well. The delay caused stopped them reinforcing the Hess battery. Lord Lovat is pleased. He intends to mention you in his report. I have forwarded your report to him. Lord Louis also mentioned you to his lordship. And your work with the Saskatchewan regiment paid dividends. They fared better than the other regiments. Green Beach was the one where the Canadians had the most success."

"Did Colonel Merritt and the others get off?"

"Not Colonel Merritt and Captain Friedmann. They were the last ones on the beach and they surrendered. They are in the bag I am afraid."

"Then it is little consolation to me, sir. They are good men. They deserved better."

"This is a setback only. Some good ideas have come from this. You told the powers that be about the shingle and the concrete emplacements. They just thought that the Churchills could overcome them. If nothing else they will be more likely to listen to the likes of us again. They are training Commandos to become Frogmen too. It is not all doom and gloom."

I finished my whisky, "If you say so, sir."

"Tom, you can't win every time."

"But that shouldn't stop you trying, sir."

The Brigade licked its wounds and assimilated new recruits. On September the fifth I was summoned to the office where a staff officer waited for me in Major Foster's office.

"Sit down, Tom. This is Major Fleming from Intelligence."

Major Fleming was a thin nervous looking chap who chain smoked but, as I came to learn, he had as sharp a mind as any. He had, I later discovered, been taking an interest in me and my team. "Lieutenant Harsker, I have heard a great deal about you. You are the chap that Lord Lovat goes to when he wants a job doing. Lord Mountbatten even mentions your name."

I nodded, "Sir." There was little else to say. Any more would have sounded boastful.

"We have a tricky problem." He handed me a photograph of a tank. It looked nothing like the Churchill or any other British tank. "This is a new tank; the M4. It is made in America. The Americans have given us three hundred of them. It is the equal of any Panzer. They were delivered last week to the Eighth Army in North Africa." I nodded and looked at the photograph. Its front sloped and it looked to be more compact than our tanks. "Two days ago there was a tank battle and one of them was captured intact; it had no damage whatsoever. The Germans put it on a tank transporter and sent it back to Tunis. We sent the Long Range Desert Group after it but they were intercepted and all killed or captured. We think there is a spy in Cairo. We want you and your section to go in and destroy it. If the Germans take it apart they will know how to beat it. They will be taking it to Tunis. When they have had their people look at it there will be no secrets. Besides our American cousins are less than pleased that we have lost one of their new toys."

"But surely there must be someone closer."

"I am afraid not. Dieppe cost us some good men. You are the best we have that can be flown out quickly. You can be taken by Sunderland and be there by tomorrow morning. You will be as fast as any troops we have in North Africa. Most are penned close to Cairo."

"Where is 'there' sir?"

"Tunis. We are not exactly certain where. We think they will take it to their headquarters. We would send the RAF in but it is too close to civilian targets and... well there are certain issues which need not concern you but suffice it to say we do not wish to upset the local populace." He gave me a look which told me he knew more than he was telling me. "We may well need their help in the near future. Bombing is out. You need to be careful not to injure locals."

He handed me an aerial photograph. "You can see that they have a large compound. We do not know for certain but this building, marked with an X, seems the most likely place they would take it. Anyway that is the first place you will search"

My mouth dropped open, "German Headquarters is the first place to search?"

He shrugged, "It is as good a place as any. You showed in Dieppe that you can move like ghosts. We believe it is still on the road and has not yet reached there. It is a long way by road from Egypt. And before you ask, we have sent the RAF in but so far we have lost four valuable aeroplanes. You, as they say, are it. If you can't do it then we have lost an advantage."

I knew when I was beaten. Orders were orders. "The Sunderland drops us off. How do we get out?"

Major Fleming smiled as he lit another cigarette, "You are confident that you can get the job done and get out?"

"My men and I are not nut cases sir. We do not have a death wish. I believe we will get the job done but I want to know how to get out in case it all goes wrong." I paused, "Like Dieppe."

"Point taken. The Sunderland will wait at Gibraltar. You have two days to complete your mission and the Sunderland will return at a designated time to pick you up. The pilot will give you the coordinates."

I shook my head, "No, sir, we will give the pilot the coordinates. When I have studied the maps I will work out where we can go that is safe." He nodded. "I am guessing that we will not be taking a radio?"

"Correct. You will be out of range of any allied operator. Well the machines you boys have anyway."

"And we haven't got time to get a better one."

"Precisely. You are on the clock Lieutenant Harsker. The Sunderland awaits."

Major Foster said, "But this is unplanned! I have never seen such a vague plan."

"Lord Mountbatten himself said that Lieutenant Harsker was the perfect man for the job. He thinks on his feet was what he said." He smiled, "Have more faith in your men, Major. I can see the Lieutenant's mind working on the plan already."

"I have some ideas, yes. I will need to get my men. Could you have transport ready in say an hour?"

Major Foster gasped, "An hour, Tom, are you sure?"

"The Major of Intelligence is quite right sir, time is of the essence. The last thing they will expect is an attack so soon. If Major Fleming is right and there is a spy in Cairo then the longer we delay the more chance they have of getting the information from London. I am not certain we can pull this off sir but delay decreases those chances of success."

He nodded, "Sergeant Major Dean will go with you to ensure you have all that you need."

Reg was waiting outside. His office was the insulation between the rest of the world and Major Foster. He had heard every word. "This is a tough one, sir."

"I know Reg. Tell Mrs B we won't be home for dinner. I would hate her to waste food."

He shook his head, "I don't believe you sometimes sir. You can think of Mrs Bailey at a time like this!"

I smiled, "What can I say? Mum hated waste." I spied Alan Crowe. "Alan get the section. Meet us at the QM with full gear."

"Right sir!"

His calmness made me smile. I had a good section. When Daddy Grant saw Reg's face his fell too. "Don't tell me, you want everything we have and you want it yesterday."

"Pretty much. Extra canteens, rations for a week, desert camouflage nets and two spare Bergens with Mills bombs."

He nodded and shouted orders to his clerks. Sergeant Poulson was the first to arrive. "Sergeant we leave in forty minutes. Go and get as much ammo as you can and twenty pounds of explosives and timers."

The others arrived. I pointed to the gear which appeared on the counter. "Get the gear and take it with your own to the lorry."

Reg Dean said, "Right my lovely lads, follow me."

Daddy came over to me and, handing me my desert camouflage net said, "Africa again?"

"It looks like it."

"Take care sir, you left some good lads there last time. Try not to join them."

"I'll do my best." The section was waiting by the lorry. They did not need me to organise them. "Just put the gear in the lorry. We'll sort it out as we drive. We are on the clock here."

The two majors headed for the staff car. "We will meet you in the harbour. There is a tender waiting for us."

Reg handed me a haversack, "Your maps sir and the aerial photographs. The Major said to leave them on the Sunderland, sir." He shook his head, "He must think we are wet behind the ears. You look after yourself Lieutenant Harsker. Mrs Bailey would make my life a misery if anything happened to you."

Everyone was so concerned for me. "We will try to pick you up a fez eh?" I climbed into the cab. "Step on it Jones."

"Right sir."

I would have time to go through the material once I was on the Sunderland. As I recalled it would be a ten hour flight to Gibraltar. That would be more than enough time for me to assimilate the data. Tunisians spoke French. That was handy. However we would stand out like sore thumbs. When we had returned the last time we had had the sort of cloaks worn by the locals, they were called a bisht. Mine was in the boarding house. We would need to acquire them. The only advantage I could see was that we were so far behind the front line that their vigilance would not be as great. They would be trying to deter local criminals rather than Commandos. However once we had blown the tank up then all hell would break loose. We needed an escape plan.

The Sunderland was about four hundred yards from the shore. The two majors awaited us and I saw a Royal Navy tender. Major Fleming was still smoking!

"Right Sergeant, get the men and the gear on the tender. Make sure my stuff is there too." As they boarded the tender I asked, "Anything else I need to know sir?"

"The Sunderland won't be able to get you really close to the city. Too many anti aircraft defences. You will have to find somewhere to lay up for the first day."

I looked at Major Foster who shook his head. That was obvious. "How much discretion do we have with the Sunderland sir?"

"It is yours for seven days. We assume if you haven't escaped by then you are either dead or in the bag."

"Quite. Well if that is all sir, we will push off. This is going to be tight enough as it is."

"Good luck, Tom."

"Thank you sir."

The water was remarkably calm as he we headed towards the huge seaplane. That was good. We needed calm water to take off. The crew were eager for us to be aboard. Half of my section had done this before and they showed the others where to stow their gear. The pilot peered from the cockpit. "We'll get in the air and then we will chat. We only heard about this late last night."

I nodded, "An hour ago we knew nothing."

He laughed, "Whoever called them Intelligence was off the mark, eh? Hold on."

The take off was noisy but as we climbed it became quieter. We were in the crew area and I explained our mission. The newer members of the section sat open mouthed as I outlined it. Sergeant Poulson said, "The difference this time, sir, will be getting out. That will be a bit trickier. It looks like the nearest British forces are thousands of miles away."

"More like hundreds but you are right." I handed the aerial photographs out so that they could see them. "Finding this place will be easy. Getting in might not be so hard. Look for a way out and back to the coast."

I needed to talk to the pilot. Where would he be dropping us? If it was on the north coast then we would have a twenty six mile journey. That would mean stealing a vehicle and that would draw attention to us. The best place would be in the bay of Tunis. There looked to be an Arab shanty town. It would mean just a short six mile hike from wherever we camped. I had already decided that would be my suggestion to the pilot. If he couldn't manage that then we had a problem.

George Lowe said, "Sir, it looks like there is a lorry park close to where they are going to be keeping this tank. We could steal a vehicle."

Harry said, "Make it two Kubelwagens. Those Jerry lorries are slow as and the Kubelwagens normally have guns."

"Good, then that is your job. You and your section get the vehicles. We will blow up the tank."

The pilot wandered over. "We should be all right for a few hours. There isn't much traffic this far out. I will get a little shut eye soon. We will have a thirty minute turn around at Gib. Then it is six or seven hours to Tunis. I might push it and use more fuel. I would like to get there, drop you off and be out of there while it is still dark. We are a big target."

I held the map out. "In a perfect world we would like you to land there."

He shook his head. "That is too close for comfort."

"Well if you could drop us say a mile or so offshore. If we had two dinghies then we could paddle in and lose the dinghies."

"I could do that. I'll get on the radio to Gib and have two prepared for you. Now the tricky part is picking you up. Whichever genius came up with this plan did not give much thought to that."

"I know; we met him. He said we had you for seven days."

"There or thereabouts."

"Then pick us up three days after you drop us. At one a.m. here. There is a little bay half way between Cap Serrat and Cap Negro. There looks to be a beach here and no houses. If you land in the bay then you should be hidden."

"It is perfect for me but a bit remote and a long way from Tunis."

"Leave that with us."

"Call signs? We don't want Jerry to be waiting for us."

"We will transmit, '*Scouser*' by torch."

"What will our response be?"

I laughed, "Unless the Germans have captured a Sunderland then it will be you. Just send back the same call sign. You will have to send dinghies over."

"Right. And how long would you want us to wait?" I could tell that he was not happy about stooging around the North African coast.

"If we are not there by two then leave and we will make our own way out."

"Of Africa?"

I shrugged, "There are always ways and means. We are Commandos."

"You are crazy that is what you are. You are the boss. When I drop you off I will fly to Malta. It is a shorter journey. I will be able to get to you quicker. I am off to get some shut eye. There are plenty of bunks if you need to sleep."

"We have flown in a Sunderland before. We know our way around."

When he had gone Sergeant Poulson asked. "How far is it then sir?"

"About seventy five miles as the crow flies. Nearer ninety on the roads and tracks that we will be using." I nodded towards Harry. "When you lads steal the vehicles make sure you get water and fuel." I looked at Ken, "You and George need to work out the best way to use the explosive. George will be stealing Kubelwagens. You get promoted; you become explosive expert!"

"I think we set off something near the fuel and the ammunition. If the hatches are closed then the explosion will be greater."

George nodded appreciatively, "You have done your homework. I will talk through some ideas I have. You should be all right."

"I want you all to get some rest and eat and drink as much as you can. This is going to be a long three days." As they wandered off I said to Sergeant Poulson, "It is a shame we haven't got those thobes and bisht we used last time."

"We could always steal them again."

I had a thought, "Or perhaps buy them. I'll find out what currency will work best. That would be safer." I should have thought of that when I had been briefed but the Major had hurried us so much I had not had time to think properly. I began to get a bad feeling about this operation. Such haste could lead to mistakes and mistakes cost me their lives.

I didn't sleep, as the rest did. Worries about the operation filled my head. The last time we had done this we had only had to travel fifty or so miles to friends. Here we would have more than that and we relied upon a Sunderland aeroplane being able to land, at night and for us to find it. The odds were rapidly stacking up against us.

I pored over the maps and the photographs. I had to learn what the ground looked like. I might not have either the time or the luxury to read maps when we were in action. We needed everything in our heads. This would be our most dangerous operation to date. We were not a Channel away from home; we were a continent. This could well be our last operation.

Chapter 9

Someone in England had wanted us to succeed. Major Fleming was in charge and he got what he wanted. We were furnished with silver coins. To me they did not seem much but I was assured that they would purchase our needs. The two dinghies were taken on board and they were already inflated. Finally we received an update on the tank. It had been seen on the tank transporter and was still some miles from Tunis. The coast road was not the best and they had to move at the speed of the tank transporter. Scouse Fletcher asked, "If the spotter plane can see it why can't the RAF destroy it, sir?"

The air attaché shook his head, "The Spitfire which saw it was well out to sea. If it had closed with it then the Luftwaffe would have descended like hawks. Believe me it was tried."

We boarded the Sunderland for the last leg. The pilot had assured me he would use full speed. It was in all our interests to do so. "Besides, it is just a short hop to Malta. I could get there with the petrol in my lighter."

We left Gibraltar just as the sun was beginning to set in the west. The gun crews were closed up and looked more apprehensive. Flying out at sea we had been safe. Now we flew through enemy air space. The aircraft was in complete darkness. We needed to be invisible. We had checked the weather forecast and the seas would be calm when we landed. That was useful, not only for us but for the Sunderland which had to land. I had managed a short nap and now, as we set off I lay down again. We had over six hours of flying ahead of us; even a few hours of sleep would help.

Sergeant Poulson shook me awake. "We are an hour from Tunis sir."

"Right, Sergeant."

He grinned, "Al Jolson time eh sir."

I nodded, "Let's get ready, Sergeant."

The co-pilot came out not long after we had all blacked up. "Touch down in thirty minutes. Are you ready?" We nodded. "You are in luck tonight. There is no moon and the skies are cloudy. The weather might change in the morning. I am not certain if that helps or hinders."

"Rain and a sand storm would help."

"Then we will pray for that."

I realised that if the weather was too bad we would not be able to be picked up. Then my ingenuity would be tested if I was to get my section back home safely! We made our way to the hatch at the side of the aeroplane. The two dinghies were already there. We would be crowded on the two rubber boats but three would have been too difficult to manage. I glanced out of the dorsal bubble. In the distance I could see twinkling lights. There was no blackout in Tunis. The reflection showed that we were descending towards the sea.

The Flight Sergeant said, "Here we go gents. Be ready to bail out as quickly as you can. The pilot will turn away from you as he takes off. The back draft from the propellers will act like a wind and give you a head start." He shrugged, "It is the best we can do I am afraid. It is just too dangerous to go any closer. These are big noisy buggers!"

"It will be fine, Flight. Thanks for the lift!"

As we came down lower I saw spray being blown behind us from the huge Pegasus engines and then the slight jolt as we touched the water. Landings were always smoother on sea planes.

"Get the hatch open!" We were covered in spray but we needed to get out as soon as possible. Our Bergens were stacked next to the hatch with Tommy guns already attached. As we slowed we threw out the two dinghies. They were attached by ropes. As soon as we had slowed enough we leapt into the two dinghies. The crew handed us our bags.

"Good luck lads, and see you in a couple of days."

The hatch slammed ominously as the pilot began to turn but we had no time to ponder our fate. "Paddle!" Sergeant Poulson was at the stern of one dinghy and I at the other. We would be the rudders and the steering paddles. The other four in each boat just had to keep paddling in unison. It was a race against time. We needed to be ashore as soon as possible and then find somewhere to lie up. Even though it was a cloudy sky I could see Tunis. Its irregular shadow rose in the west. Suddenly it was as though we were pushed in the back. The Sunderland's mighty engines, just forty feet from us increased power and we hurtled through the water. It was just the start we needed. We had got over the initial inertia quickly and it spurred on the men. They were competitive and the two crews would keep going until the muscle burn kicked in and they could paddle no more.

We were within two hundred yards of the beach when we saw the searchlight of the harbour guard boat. It would go from La Marsa east and then back. We knew about it but had no idea of the timing. We saw it as it began its turn east. The beam from its light illuminated the spot we have vacated ten minutes earlier. We had been lucky. The sound of the surf and the waves had hidden its engine from us.

I hissed, "Slow down a little. Let's make sure the beach is clear." The last thing we wanted was for a Tunisian fisherman on the beach to see us. There was no-one and we rolled in on the tiny, inconsequential waves.

Crowe and Hewitt leapt out and pulled the painter to drag us on the shingle beach. We gabbed our Bergens and jumped into the water. We pulled the dinghies out of the water and ran with them towards the low dunes and scrubby sand ahead. When we reached them we dropped the dinghy. "Shepherd, Fletcher, go and get rid of our tracks." They dropped their Bergens and ran off. "Get these dinghies punctured and bury them in the soft sand." There was the sound of hissing as the daggers punctured the boats.

I knew that they would be found but I hoped it would not be a for a day or two. It was too dark to see my map and I could not risk a light. We had to find shelter and find it soon. I knew from the maps and photographs that there were two rivers. One was wider than the other. When we found one I would know where we were. If there was a road ahead of us then we had landed at the wrong place and we might be in trouble.

"Take charge, Sergeant."

I headed inland and ran for two hundred yards. I did not cross a road of any description. It meant we were in the right spot. I turn right and headed north. I was guessing we would find the river. Two hundred yards later and I found it. To be honest I could have found it with my eyes closed. It stank! I guessed it was the main drain for the myriad settlements further inland. I ran back down the sand and scrub until I found the section. The dinghies had been covered and Shepherd and Fletcher were back.

"Shepherd, take the point. Let's find some shelter."

We moved in an arrow formation. Our eyes flicked from the ground to the land around us and back. There was danger everywhere. We had travelled about a mile when Shepherd stopped. He pointed to his nose then to the right. There were people in that direction. I pointed left. He began to move closer to Tunis. I glanced behind. Dawn was an hour away. In this part of the world it was a lot more sudden than in France. We needed somewhere to hide and soon.

It was when I turned back from looking east that I spied it. There was something ahead and to the left. I overtook Shepherd and ran towards it. It was an old mud hut. The roof and the upper walls had collapsed leaving just three walls that rose five feet high and a fourth that was just two feet high. Wind and water had eroded the side facing the Gulf of Tunis. This would have to do. I circled my arm and my section quickly occupied it.

Some of us had done this before and the others merely copied our actions. We rigged the camouflage nets over the top of the walls. The fact that they were uneven actually helped with the disguise. We each put our Bergen in our own space. Soon we were invisible. Before we had left Gibraltar we had arranged the guard rota. Lance Sergeant Gowland and his team had first watch. I drank some water and forced myself to eat something. It was an orange we had each been given in Gibraltar. As rare as hen's teeth in England it was a luxury we savoured. I even ate the peel. I curled up in a ball and fell asleep. It would not be a deep sleep. It never was when I was in action but I would rest and, when I awoke, I would be refreshed.

It was just daylight when Harry woke me. We had left a tunnel to the entrance, which faced the sea. I slipped my binoculars out of my Bergen and crawled to the entrance. I could see a small fishing fleet of lateen rigged ships heading out to the sea. I crawled along the wall and looked towards the harbour of Tunis. I saw the masts and antennae of warships. They would only be destroyers and E-Boats but they would be German and they would be dangerous. I moved around to view Tunis.

My map was in a case around my neck and I held it on the ground before me. The building we sought was two miles away due west. It was close to a major crossroads. It was not in the town proper but on the outskirts. From the photographs it looked to have been erected recently. With typical Teutonic efficiency it was all straight lines. That would help us. I used the glasses and saw the Swastika flying. I could not see the building; huts interfered with my view. I knew where we had to get to. The problem was all the people between it and us. We would have to hit it quickly. We could not afford to spend two days in this dilapidated hovel.

I completed a full circuit and saw some inhabited mud huts a mile to the north of us. There was nothing else close. There was a large patch of water to the south. I saw birds rising from it. That would be a place where the locals would go. There would be eggs, fish and fowl. We had been lucky again. Once back in the camp I drank sparingly from my canteen. The last time we had been here it had been almost winter. This was late summer. It would be hot and dehydration would be a problem. I waved over Fletcher and Shepherd and spoke quietly. "Shepherd watch the north. There is a village a mile away. Keep your eye on it. Fletcher do the same to the south. I didn't see anything but you never know."

An hour into our watch a squall swept in from the Bay of Tunis. It was not heavy rain but it was driving and relentless rain. I took my oilskin from my Bergen and huddled beneath it. I was thankful I had not left it in Blighty. Although it stopped an hour later it set the pattern for the day. Sergeant Poulson relieved us and when we rose at three another shower had swept in. The ground on which we sat was sodden and our clothes covered by a patina of mud. It helped to camouflage us. We needed no makeup. Our hands and faces were also speckled with splashed soil. We were all rested and, as we ate our main meal of the day I sat with Sergeant Poulson and Lance Sergeant Gowland and ran through the plan again.

"We move out as soon as it is dark. I know there will be locals about but we try to avoid them. I want to be as close to the compound as we can before midnight. We will need as much of the darkness as we can to get into the mountains where we can hide. Jerry will have every aeroplane he can looking for us." I pointed to the map. "The road from the compound is a good one to here. It is the last twenty miles that will be tortuous."

Polly nodded, "To be honest sir it is getting in the compound that worries me."

I took out the aerial photograph, "There are two entrances in and out. This is the main one; the one facing Tunis. The one on the far side looks to be a small access road to this huddle of buildings. I am guessing that this is the one the German soldiers use. There will be the Tunisian version of a pub there. Locals will know how to milk soldiers; they always do. They will be used to men going in and out. That is how we get in. Once we are in there will be little security within the compound. We take the field caps of the Germans and, in the dark, we might pass for German. There are four of you who have a little German; it is enough to speak with me and that might lull any Jerry we meet and give us the edge."

Lance Sergeant Gowland nodded, "Do you want us to disable the other vehicles, sir?"

"If you have the opportunity but the priority is stealing two. Then you can disable and booby trap until we get there. We will leave the same way we came in, through the small gate and then to the main road. If you have a choice of Kubelwagen, take the ones with the machine guns."

The rain stopped and we all watched to see if any locals investigated the mud ruins. Our camouflage must have been good for no one came. I had the men put their oil skins on. They would cover our Bergens and they came down to our waist. With the hoods on them they might be taken, in the dark, for the Arab cloak, the bisht. When we left, at dusk, we saw why no one had approached the ruin. The ground all around had become a slippery morass. The sand and shale like soil had mixed into a grey mud which made walking harder. I was grateful for the rubber soled shoes which gave us more grip. I led. My French and the map in my head were our best weapons until we reached the German compound.

We had just a mile to cover before we came to the first road. I used the word road but what passed for a highway was in a poor state of repair. That suggested they were little used by the Germans. The huts we had seen were a mile to the north of us and, with nothing else in sight, we slipped across the road and then waited. The sand and soil had given way to soil but the rain had made it muddy. I looked down and saw our prints. They would be able to follow us. I took out my binoculars. The German flag was flying a mile and a half away. I could not see the actual compound for there were huts in the way. I decided to head north and west to go around the huts and the compound. That way we would approach our gate from what would be, I hoped, the quiet side.

The rain returned. This time it was heavier rain. I took advantage of the rain storm and led the men as quickly as the ground allowed. As we approached the first of the houses, to our left, I held my hand up and we dropped to the ground. A mother and two children ran, just eighty yards from us, across the track and into a hut. Then there was no one. I took a chance and led the section through the huts. Anyone with any sense was sheltering. The rain was pounding now. It suggested it would not last long. Our luck held and we emerged from the huts having saved ourselves a muddy detour.

Once we had cleared the huts I saw the German compound to our left. There was wire all around it. I saw, close to the wire, wooden warning signs. I could not read them but I guessed that they marked a minefield. We now had to negotiate the many small huddles of huts which surrounded the wire. The rain helped. No one but a fool would venture forth on a night such as this. What had Noel Coward written? *'Mad dogs and Englishmen'*! That was us.

As we approached the western end of the compound and the road we slowed. There was vehicular traffic on the highway. It was not a great deal but enough for us to have to time crossing it well.

We huddled behind a hut adjacent to the road and watched the road from the north west. I heard a convoy approach. The lead vehicle had slits of lights and they were driving cautiously. I saw that the convoy was led by a Kubelwagen. There was a truck which passed us, slowly, and then five petrol tankers. A small armoured car brought up the rear. When they had passed the road appeared to be clear and I led the section across the road. We ducked behind a deserted workshop of some kind and I looked at my watch. It was a quarter past ten. We had made good time. I took out my binoculars and risked a look down the road. I saw the convoy at the entrance to the compound, about half a mile away. We were almost there.

I waved my hand and we moved parallel to the road down the back alleys of this shanty town. We heard voices within the huts as we passed but no one emerged. The rain had lightened somewhat but it still fell. Then, as we neared the entrance to the compound, three hundred yards to our left, I saw lights and heard noises and voices. It was the clinking of glasses and the voices were German. I pointed to the right. It was away from the light and towards the shadows of what looked like a shop during the day. It was shuttered.

I took out my silenced Colt. The others did too. We waited, hidden by the boxes upon which goods would be stacked during the day. Light burst from the building thirty paces away. Five Germans staggered out. One of them shouted, "Come Heine. It is pouring down out here! You will have to peel potatoes for a month if you are late again." I heard an indistinct response. The German waved a hand and said, "You and Kurt are on your own. I will tell Stephan at the gate that you are on your way. You do not have long!"

The five headed across the road. I waved for the men to stay where they were and I crossed to the building which I now knew was a bar of some description. I could hear voices from inside. An Arab voice speaking halting German said, "Effendi, it is late. There is a curfew. I will be in trouble. Your friends have gone."

"Mustapha you are the son of a whore. Piss off!"

"I must go now! I cannot risk breaking the curfew. I will clean your mess in the morning."

I pressed myself against the wall. The Arab came out. He was clutching a leather bag. That would be the takings; I had no doubt. He looked at the sky and pulled the hood of his bisht up. He ran around the corner and I heard a moped start up. He rode back up the road the German convoy had used. I waved my men forward. This was a chance not to be missed. I listened at the door.

The German who had told the Arab to go was speaking, "The thing is, Kurt, I don't really like Arab women. I mean they are pretty enough but the young ones have not enough meat on them. I like something I can get hold of. You know what I mean? And this Arab beer is like piss. Heinrich is right about that. But we stay here for a bit. I am not getting wet." He giggled drunkenly, "At least not outside!" I heard the sound of loud slurping.

From the noises I had heard the two Germans were the only ones within and one of them was so drunk that he could barely speak. I pointed to Sergeant Poulson and Lance Sergeant Gowland. I mimed knocking someone out. They nodded. I stepped into the bar. It was lit by candles. One soldier was face down on the table, his beer dripping on the floor. The other was in the act of drinking when I pointed my gun at him and he froze mid drink. Polly was behind him and had tapped him with the sap before he knew it.

"Harry, check the back." The others came in. "Tie them up." I took Heine's hat and replaced the comforter I wore. I searched them but they had nothing on them that would help us.

Harry returned, "Nothing out there and no beer left either." He sounded rueful. It explained why the barman had gone. There was nothing left for the Germans to steal. I looked at my watch. The barman had left before ten thirty. I guessed that was curfew and, from what the German had said, the time they had to be back inside the compound. If the German army was anything like ours then the sentries would try to help out any comrades stuck outside.

"Harry, you are the same size as the other one, put his hat on. Sergeant Poulson we will pretend to be the Germans. Slip over the road as soon as we have their attention."

"Sir."

"Harry, just sing in German and sound drunk. *'Lilli Marlene'* will do. Leave the talking to me. Lean into me as though I am supporting you. Have your sap ready. Sergeant you keep your Colts trained on the two sentries. If we don't subdue them you will have to shoot them." He nodded. I said, loudly and in German, "Right, Kurt, let us go!"

I sang with Harry and we were deliberately slow as we staggered and did the drunk's tango across the road. Three steps forward, two steps back. An occasional pirouette. We kept our heads down. With the rain it was understandable. As we began to cross the road I glanced up and saw the two guards approaching, "Hurry you idiots. Heinrich told us you would be late. The Feldwebel will be here soon with the relief. Get a move on."

"Come and give me a hand, Kurt is a dead weight." I giggled as though drunk, "I think he has pissed himself."

The two Germans obligingly put their rifles down to help me as we approached them. I deliberately staggered a little and the two of them ran to catch what they thought was a falling Kurt. Harry was a big man and he brought his fist up in an uppercut. I swung my sap and it smacked into the side of the German's head. Harry gave his man another tap with the sap and we dragged them into the guard hut.

Sergeant Poulson and the others joined us, "Quick tie them up. We only have minutes. Scouse, you and Ken get their rifles and caps. The relief will be here very soon. Go and patrol outside."

This complicated matters. The relief would be missed, eventually. It shortened the time we had to do what we needed to do. We had barely tied them up when I saw the three Germans approaching us. I took out my Colt and we waited in the shadows of the guard hut. Shepherd and Fletcher were on the road. The Feldwebel stood less than ten feet from me under the shelter of the guard house lean to.

"You pair, what the hell are you doing?" One of them must have made the mistake of turning for the Feldwebel said, "You are not..." As he raised his rifle I shot him in the head. The other two swung their rifles but four silenced bullets ended their lives.

"Get them in here. Hewitt, take Groves, Shepherd and Fletcher. Put these two Germans in the bar with the others." They picked up the unconscious Germans and headed back across the road. I grabbed the grenades and ammunition from the three dead Germans whose bodies were stacked up inside the guard hut. "Sit them around the table and turn up the oil lamp. George I want this place booby trapped. When they come to see where the last watch is they will look through the window and when they open it we will have warning that they are on to us." The last thing I did was to take any papers they might have from their jackets. They might prove useful.

"Sir."

I stepped outside while they set the scene. My four men raced back from the bar. The rain had eased. I looked towards the main buildings. The vehicle park was to the left of us and opposite was the building which had been marked with an X. I hoped it was not guarded. The barracks were on the other side of the compound behind the headquarters. I guessed that there would be no one there during the night.

My men came out of the guard hut. George was the last one out and he carefully set the booby trap on the door. I pointed to the vehicle park and Harry led his men away. I began to trot down to the mysterious building. The place was eerily quiet. As we approached I saw that it was not guarded but there was a padlock. We had no bolt cutters. We stood next to the door. The lock was a good sign. I nodded to Scouse. He took out some wires and within two minutes had the lock opened. He slid back the bolt and we pulled open the doors. There was little light but we saw, ahead of us a tank. It was the M4 and it was still on the back of the low loader!

I whispered, "Right Ken, take Fletcher and Crowe, do your stuff."

"Sir."

"Sergeant Poulson, there should be a tool kit on the M4. Find a spanner and open the drain plug on the petrol tank." It was only the Germans who used diesel. As the Americans found out when they used the M4 they burned so easily their crews called them Ronsons.

"Sir."

I went to the low loader. There was little of value in the cab. "Hewitt, see if you can find anything which will explode or burn. Stack it under the low loader." There was an office and I went in. There were boxes of files and paper work. I carried them out and laid a trail to the office from the tank. The office was made of wood and it would burn. I saw they had a duplicator machine, Gestetner, it used an alcohol based fluid. I found a large bottle and I soaked my trail of files.

When I returned to the M4 I could smell the petrol which was a viscous, shimmering snake spreading across the floor. Hewitt was stacking blocks of wood beneath the low loader. I went to the door and checked outside. All was silent. Ten minutes later Groves and Fletcher climbed out of the tank.

Peter Groves nodded to the turret, "Shepherd is just finishing off, sir." He took a German grenade and, breaking the top he jammed it beneath the track close to the pooling petrol. He looked up at me. "I found it in the bar. Seems a shame to waste it."

"Well done, Groves."

He patted his battledress, "I have another one sir. Oh and Shepherd said he is setting the timers for fifteen minutes."

"That should be enough time to give us a head start. Sergeant take the section to the vehicle park. I will come with Shepherd when he has finished." I took the opportunity to unsling my Thompson. If we had to leave in a hurry then we would need all the firepower we could muster.

Ken climbed out of the hatch, "We have sabotaged the engine, the tracks, the barrel and the last one is with the ammunition which they obligingly left."

"Any charges left?"

He held up one two pound charge."But I have no detonators left."

"We will use a Mills bomb as a detonator. We rig it across the door as a booby trap in case someone comes before the bombs have gone off."

We used the thin parachute cord we favoured and made it so that anyone opening the doors would set off the grenade and then the charge. Hopefully that would ignite the petrol which had now reached the door. We hurried towards the vehicle park. Forty five minutes had elapsed since we had entered the compound. I wondered why they had not investigated the dead Feldwebel. We almost tripped over the three dead Germans by the side of the road. We hurried on and found two dead German sentries. They each had a bullet hole in the head. I took their field caps and sand goggles and added them to the ones we already had.

Polly was waiting, "Sorry about the three Germans, sir. We saw them heading towards the gate. We used the silencers."

"You did right and I didn't hear a thing. Where is Harry?"

"I haven't seen him yet. Probably still disabling vehicles."

"Spread out. The Kubelwagens were at the far side of the compound. Slash any tyres you see on the way through."

Our daggers were sharp and I heard the hiss as air came from punctured tyres. I heard a, "Hist!"

I saw Peter Groves waving at me. "Follow me."

I reached him, "This way sir. We have three Kubelwagens. They all have a machine gun. We have immobilised the rest." He laughed, "We peed in some of the tanks."

That was even better. The vehicles would start but stop within a few miles.

I reached the Kubelwagens. Handing the field caps and goggles out to those who did not have them I said, "Will they start first time?" The men donned them and put their comforters away. As a disguise it was thin but better than nothing.

Harry shrugged, "Sorry, sir, there is no way to find out. We have cans of water and fuel in the back. One of them had a warm engine. That will certainly start. They all have full tanks. They should get us where we are going."

"Right, get aboard. You all follow me." I took off my Bergen and stuck it in the back seat. "Scouse, get on the machine gun. Shepherd take Fletcher's Tommy gun. Your job is to watch the other two cars. If they get in trouble then let me know. Have your silenced Colt close to hand. Remember do not fire unless I give you the order. We will try to use as much bluff as we can eh?"

"Sir."

I placed my Thompson next to me and close to the gear stick. I turned the engine over. It sounded inordinately loud but after a couple of splutters it started. The other two did the same. Ironically Harry's took the longest to start. I saw lights coming on in the Headquarters building. The charges were due off in five minutes. It was time to make a hasty exit. I put it into gear and put my foot down. It leapt away towards the gate filled with dead Germans. We were on our way home! We just had almost eighty miles of enemy occupied and rough terrain to negotiate.

Chapter 10

As we raced through the gate I heard a klaxon sound. They were awake and men were spilling from buildings. I spun the wheel right as we left the compound. It was pitch black but we could not risk lights. I had to pray that I had the roads in my head. We had travelled just half a mile when there was a crump behind me. Shepherd said, "The guard hut just blew up sir! They must have triggered the booby trap."

I could hear the worry in his voice. Would his explosives detonate on time? "Don't worry Ken, your bombs will go off."

Half a mile later there was an enormous bang and then a series of smaller ones. Suddenly the night was lit up as the whole of the building erupted in flame. "My God, sir! You should see this!"

"I'll take your word for it, Shepherd. It is a bit too dark to risk turning around."

"The Germans are running around like lunatics, sir. The whole of the building is on fire and it is spreading!"

I kept my foot down as we drove on the relatively straight road which led to the coast. We had two towns to navigate our way through, Mateur and Zana. Zana was just a few miles away. I had decided to try to bluff my way through the small hamlet. We reached it ten minutes after leaving the compound. There was a glow behind us in the dark and I worried that might initiate questions. I slowed down as we approached it. I suspected there would be troops of some sort and the explosion was so loud that they would have heard it. I was right. As we approached the outskirts of the village four Germans stepped out and shone a light into my eyes.

"Are you trying to blind me fool!" I lowered my voice, "Have your Colts ready and wait for the signal."

A Feldwebel held out his hand, "Papers!"

I saw that the other three were suspicious and their rifles were levelled at us. Scouse just grinned at them. It must have disconcerted them for they could not hold his gaze.

The Feldwebel looked at the papers I had taken from the German NCO. He handed them back to me, "What are you doing out here? We heard an explosion and saw a fire. What is going on?"

I nodded, "Saboteurs. We are hunting them. Did anyone come through here?"

The four of them relaxed and their guns lowered slightly. "No, you are the first. Who was it? Arabs? The Tommies?"

"We have no idea. We were just ordered to get to Mateur and set up a road block. Of course now that you have held us up they might escape."

"We are just following orders."

Just then, the fifth German, who was hidden by their Kubelwagen stood, "It is headquarters, we are to look out for three..."

He got no further. Our three Colts came up and four fell quickly. The radio operator managed to dive into cover. Peter Groves leapt up and ran after him. I heard two soft phuts and Groves returned with his gun still smoking, "Well done Peter that was quick thinking."

I got out and waved the others forward. "Quick we need to get rid of the Kubelwagen and the men, silently. George drive it to the west end of the town, Make it look as though we ambushed them there. Scouse take the radio. It might come in handy. Take anything you can from the Kubelwagen," I pointed to the jerricans, "those especially. George, disable the Kubelwagen when you have ditched it. Peter take the machinegun from it. We can always use an extra weapon."

I waved Sergeant Poulson to join me.

117

"Change of plan. I have no doubt that the Germans will investigate when the radio operator doesn't get back to them. Instead of going to Mateur we will head north and then cut west. There is a road we can take which misses Mateur; it goes between two lakes. It is a longer road; about twenty miles further but we have enough fuel and, besides, we have little choice."

"Right sir."

"We might as well top up the tanks while we wait for George."

Peter Groves said, "I will set this machine gun up at the rear of the Kubelwagen sir. It will give us a sting in the tail."

"Good idea." Groves was becoming more confident. This operation had been good for him. I would be able to promote him soon.

Once the others returned we remounted and I lead us to the north. Our road cut west four miles along the highway. It would still be dark by then but soon after we would have to contend with daylight and the Luftwaffe. I counted on the fact that they would not be looking for three vehicles which were going due west. With the field caps and goggles we would pass a superficial examination but it would not take them long to find their dead men and then suspicion would be on every vehicle.

We made good time on the road. It was well used. We passed huts and small villages but the locals kept themselves hidden. As the dawn broke from the east my heart began to sink. My original plan had been to disappear in the mountains before dawn. That idea was now out of the window. We reached the crossroads close to El Alia. We turned west. Already we could see Lac de Bizerte. There would be a garrison at Bizerte. We could run into their patrols. That was a town we would avoid at all costs.

Thin grey dawn did not brighten the day over much but, at least, there was no rain. We pushed on. The Kubelwagen was not a comfortable vehicle but it was speedy and we ate up the miles. We had one more obstacle before we passed the lakes, Menzel Bourguiba. I suspected there might be a garrison there but it was a much smaller town than Mateur. Scouse pointed to the left, many miles away, "Sir!"

It was a scout aeroplane and it was over Mateur. They were looking in the wrong direction. I slowed down and stopped in a defile where we would be hidden from view. The others gathered around me. "Take on water, and refill your vehicles with fuel and water. The spotter plane is well to the south west. We hit Menzel Bourguiba soon. I will try to bluff our way through again but I think they might be on to us. Stay close and if we have to hit them then hit them hard. The reason I didn't pick this route in the first place is because there is one bridge across the river which joins the two lakes. It is a bottle neck. Have grenades ready in case they try to stop us."

I saw my more experienced Commandos exchange looks. This would be more than a little tricky.

"Ready?"

"Yes sir."

We started the cars. Dawn had now finally broken and I saw the small town, a sprawl of huts and humanity, spreading out below us. We moved sedately towards the town. It was morning and there was a market on. The throng of people slowed us down. I saw uniforms of the Afrika Corps but they looked to be off duty. Where was the road block? Some of the soldiers waved at us and we waved back. The locals got out of the way of the three Kubelwagens which were the only motorised vehicles in the village. Once we had passed through the village we saw the bridge and, to my dismay, there was a German presence. There was a half track. It had six men lounging around it and there were two men on the heavy machine mounted at the front. Although it was not totally blocking the bridge it would be a tight fit to get across it. I also saw the antennae of a radio. They would seek confirmation of our identity.

"Have grenades ready. This could be tricky."

"Right sir!"

A lieutenant stepped forward with his hand up, "Halt! Papers. Where are you going?"

"We are heading for Mateur."

He looked at me suspiciously. "Then you are going the wrong way."

"Am I? It is these signs they are either in Arabic of French. Should we turn around?"

"Wait, let me check these papers."

"Of course and thank you for keeping us straight!"

I saw the Germans relax. I had a grenade between my legs. I took out the pin and held it loosely. I nodded to Scouse. We both threw our Mills bombs at the same time and I grabbed my Thompson and sprayed the men on the bridge. "Duck!" The two grenades had fallen inside the half track but we were so close that, when they exploded, our vehicle rocked.

I dropped my gun and floored the accelerator. We leapt through the gap, scraping along the side of the half track and the bridge. Behind us I heard the machine guns from the others as they ensured that no one was left alive. As we reached the other side and turned slightly left I saw the grenades the others had thrown under the half track. It lifted up and fell into the river. More importantly it took half the bridge and one parapet with it. They would struggle to get heavy vehicles across the bridge. We had bought a little time but we had shouted where we were. The Luftwaffe would soon be hunting us.

"Are either of you hurt?"

"No sir."

"Sorry I didn't get a grenade off."

"Don't worry Shepherd, we didn't need it."

We had less than fifty miles to go and I could see the mountains ahead. We had to move quickly and work out how to deal with aeroplanes. I saw that there were trees covering the mountain sides. If we could reach them then we had a chance. The road, however, was not a good surface and it twisted and turned. We were no longer able to maintain our speed. However it took the Germans more than an hour to send an aeroplane to the right place. We saw their Fieseler Fi 156 Storch aeroplanes, all three of them, buzzing like flies in the distance but it was not until we began to ascend the twisting road towards the mountain that one headed closer to us.

"Sir, Jerry!"

"Wave at him. They might think we are friendly. Tell the others not to shoot!

Shepherd shouted, "Don't shoot, wave!"

He circled over us and then flew lower. It was really tempting to let him have it but he would radioed that he had seen us and was investigating. We had to carry on with the bluff. He circled away and headed due east. He was going back to the airfield. We had been seen. If they sent fighters we were in trouble. I saw a road to the left approaching and it led into the trees. I threw the wheel around so sharply that poor Scouse nearly fell out. I gunned the motor down the track until a canopy of trees covered us. I stopped.

"Jerry has seen us." I took out a map and an aerial photograph. "This road runs through the forest for a few miles. It is parallel to the road we need. We drive along it, relatively slowly. If we move fast it will make it easier for Jerry to spot us from the air. If they think we have lost them then they will widen the search."

"What if they get ahead of us, sir?"

"Then, Peter, we will have to think of something else. We have another seven or eight hours of daylight. This cover helps us. Let's use it. George check that Groves is all right with the MG in the rear Kubelwagen. We may need a sting in our tail! When we are close to the main road again we will scout it out and choose our best moment to leave the cover of the trees."

We listened to the German radio. They knew we were to the north and they had patrols out looking for us. Ominously I heard the word Luftwaffe.

"I think we sit tight until we know where the aeroplanes are."

We were about to move off when we heard the sound of aeroplane engines. We could not see them but the roar of their engines as they approached told me that there were three of them. They sounded like 109s. The flight was using the road as a marker and they zoomed to the north of us. The engines faded and then returned in the opposite direction. They faded again and this time, when they approached, came at us on a north west to south east alignment. They flew in the vicinity for forty minutes. Then they left.

"Time to head to the road."

The odds were that there would be vehicles on the road. Had we left when the aeroplanes were above us we would have been spotted and, more importantly, attacked. We moved cautiously. When we were, according to my reckoning, two hundred yards from the road, I sent Ken to scout it out. I heard vehicles using the road but I could not see them. He was away twenty minutes.

"Sir, there are Germans on the road. They have no road blocks and the vehicles are mainly motor cycles and Kubelwagen. There were plenty going up and down the road."

I got out and joined the other two cars. "There are about five hours of daylight. We have to be across this road and close to the beach by dark." I pointed to the map. "There is another track across the road. It parallels the main road too. We will go to the road and nip over one by one. Polly you go first and then you Harry. I will be tail end Charlie." I pointed out their route. "You wait at the main road. It should take us no more than twenty minutes to reach it. If you hear firing then you are on your own and you take your own decisions."

"We can't leave you behind sir."

"Sergeant, they are looking for three Kubelwagens. If any of us are attacked it gives the other two more chance to reach the rendezvous. It isn't open for debate. It is an order."

We stopped ten yards from the entrance and I went to the edge. A pair of motorcycles came from the west and I ducked behind a tree. Their engines faded, I waved across Polly. There was no one else and I waved across Gowland. I ran back to the Kubelwagen. "Ken. Go and see when the coast is clear."

"Sir."

I edged the Kubelwagen closer to the edge. He waved me forward and I drove next to him. We had just emerged when the two motorcycles he had seen heading east came back. I acted instinctively I turned and headed towards them. They could not fire at us and it took them by surprise. "Use your Colts as they come close."

The Germans tried to turn; that should have warned me but it did not. One slid and spun into a tree. "Use the machine gun. We have to stop him." The second motorcyclist's turn had allowed me to close with him. Scouse stitched a line of bullets across his back and he was down. I had just managed a three point turn in the road when Ken shouted, "Sir, a German lorry! It is right behind us."

I saw, just ahead of us, the track we had first taken into the woods. It might be too narrow for the German lorry. Ken's Tommy gun barked and I heard a heavy machine gun fire in reply. "Save your bullets and hang on!"

I spun the Kubelwagen through the gap and on to the track. I turned so quickly that I almost turned the car over. This time I did not drive sedately through the woods, I gunned the motor and drove as quickly as I could. Ken shouted, "They are following!"

"Good!"

My mind, like my engine, was racing. The other two would have heard the firing and obeyed my orders. My disaster might just help to save them. I would then be free to make my own way to the rendezvous. Perhaps this accident might be a happy one. I did not use my brakes when I turned, I used the gears. It was more efficient although definitely more hazardous. We established a lead. When we were on the last part close to the road I said, "Ken, get a German grenade ready." When I saw the track lighten as we approached the road I stopped and jumped out. I grabbed the grenade from Ken. In the distance I could hear the German lorry as it laboured through the woods. I had minutes only. I improvised a booby trap jamming the grenade beneath a broken branch.

I jumped back in and drove straight across the road to the track on the other side. Luck was on our side and the road was clear. We plunged into the woods. The track went right and then, after forty yards turned sharp left. I had to stop this time to negotiate the tight turn. We had just turned when I heard the crump as the grenade went off. I hoped I had disabled the lorry. In all events I now had the distance between us. We were at least eighty yards or more ahead and they would not know which way we had gone. We hurtled through the woods. Scouse and Ken had to cling on for dear life.

I did not pause at the main road. The trees ended some seventy yards before the road. I could see it was clear. I just hurtled out. It was much easier travelling on the main road and it was, amazingly clear. I could see that the road was heading up into the mountains. It was exposed and bare. If anyone was on the road behind us or ahead they would see us. I slowed down.

Scouse turned, "Sir?"

"We have to pretend to be Germans. There was no radio on the motorcycles. The lorry would just have seen our back. He might assume that the three of us are still together. Until we are rumbled we pretend to be Germans."

We managed another three miles before we met a vehicle coming the other way. It was another lorry with a dozen men on board. They pulled next to us.

"Have you seen the Tommies?" I asked the question before they did.

The driver said, "No. We heard on the radio that there was shooting in the woods ahead."

I pointed to the north east. "We were in the woods. I heard something but I thought it was in this direction. I have to get some more fuel. We are running out."

The driver nodded, "There is a fuel dump twenty miles up the road at the road block. Can you make it there?"

I tapped the jerry can which was attached to the front. It had a little in. "I can refill for a few more miles if I have to."

He waved and carried on. We drove on west. The place he mentioned had to be Tamra. We would need to turn off before then but it was handy to know where the Germans were in strength. The Messerschmitt 109s returned half an hour later. This time they did not fly as a flight but as three individuals. They appeared to be flying a box pattern. They were still searching for three vehicles.

"When they come over look up and wave."

One flew really low. I looked up and waved. Ken did the same. He waggled his wings and flew on. We had fooled them but it would not last long. We had to watch them flying overhead for another thirty minutes as we headed down the road. Worryingly we saw nothing else coming the other way. We were five miles from the turn off when I heard firing from up ahead. One of the fighters dived and strafed something I could not see beyond the brow of the hill we were climbing. They must have been on the edge of their endurance for it peeled off and headed south. I heard more firing and this time I recognised the sound of Thompsons. It was my men. Then there was the sound of rifle fire.

Scouse turned and looked at me. "Yeah, Scouse, it is our lads. Let us approach, slowly, slowly."

I saw a thin spiral of smoke beyond the hill. There were woods close by and, when I drew close to the brow of the hill I turned off into the woods and drove the Kubelwagen through the thin trees. I grabbed my Thompson and led the other two through the woods. We reached the brow and saw, in the hollow a burning Kubelwagen. The other was stopped and I saw twenty Germans. There was a gunner on their lorry with a machine gun trained on them. The other vehicle was a Kubelwagen. Four of my men had their hands above their heads and two lay on the ground. One was moving but one was still. We did not have long and I led my last two men through the woods. The attention of the Germans was on the prisoners and I saw the officer shouting at Poulson and then slap him hard.

I stopped, "Ken, you shoot the gunner. Scouse, the NCO! We use our silenced Colts until we run out of ammo. By then our lads will have taken cover and we will be able to use our Tommy guns."

"Sir!"

We moved on and I could hear the German now; he was speaking English. "Where is the other car you stole?"

I saw that Sergeant Poulson had been struck a number of times.

"Unless you tell me where your comrades are I will put your wounded fellow here out of his misery!" He swung his gun around to aim it at Alan Crowe . I could see his chest rising and falling. He was alive.

I nodded to Ken as I took aim at the German. The three of us fired together. The officer sprouted a third eye as the gunner fell dead and the NCO was thrown to the ground. I switched target and fired. I kept firing as I moved around. Sergeant Poulson and the rest of my men had also reacted and they grabbed the fallen guns and began to fire. The air was filled with smoke and the sound of German rifles. It was over really quickly. Our twenty .45 bullets did a great deal of damage in a small area and at such close range. The German rifles just mopped up.

"Scouse, fetch the Kubelwagen." I ran to Crowe who was now being tended to by Hewitt. "I am afraid that gunfire will bring the wrath of the Afrika Korps upon us. Get a medical kit for the two lads and put them in the Germans vehicle."

Sergeant Poulson shook his head, "Groves is dead sir. There isn't much left of his head and chest. That 109 gave him a full burst. That is how they caught us."

"Post mortem later." I grabbed Groves' dog tags and his Colt. "Sorry son, I let you down. God bless." The dog tags were bloody. I jammed them in my battledress. "Follow me." I went to my Kubelwagen, "Shove over Scouse."

I made sure the other two vehicles were both loaded and then I floored the accelerator. We only had to drive two hundred and fifty yards before we reached our turn off. I took it slower this time. I did not want a trail of gravel showing where we had turned. "Ken, nip out and sweep up when the last Kubelwagen has passed." He jumped out even as we were moving and I drove slowly along the rocky track until I reached some bushes. Ken rejoined us and I set off.

There were trees but it was no constant cover. The track was wide enough for our Kubelwagen and the surface was poor. We would be able to travel at no more than fifteen or twenty miles an hour. The only saving grace was that the Germans could travel no faster. Our danger was aeroplanes. That hazard would only cease when darkness fell and that was still three or four hours away. I did not go the direct route. It was too steep. One of the tracks followed the contours of the hill and provided the best cover. Forty minutes along the track we heard an aeroplane engine and I stopped. We were invisible. I could not see the 109 but I knew it was there.

I dismounted and went back along the track. I had noticed, just before we stopped that some of the rocks over which we had driven were a little unstable. The recent rain must have washed out the ballast. "Quick get the sand shovels and lever these stones down the hill. It will slow down pursuit if they do find out where we have gone."

It did not take long to loosen and send crashing down the hill side ten large rocks. Anything but a half track would struggle to pass.

I listened and heard the 109's engine receding in the distance. "Right, let's push on. Take on water too. Food can wait."

It was tortuous going. The track twisted and turned along the hillside but always it climbed. Hewitt and Crowe were in Sergeant Poulson's Kubelwagen. It was now in the middle of our small convoy. George and Harry, old friends both, brought up the rear. They would cover our backs if danger threatened. It was two hours to sunset when we reached the top. We could see the sea! When I looked at the track I saw we would be following then my heart sank. It was an even more daunting route down than the one we had taken to the top. There were sheer drops at the side of the pitifully thin track and we still had four miles to go. I could, at least, see the beach which I had identified back in Gibraltar. Now we had a chance. A slim one but we would take that in a heartbeat.

Chapter 11

We drove down the steep hill very slowly. I suppose we could have walked down the hill side and that would have been safer but we had our Bergens and we had a wounded man. Crowe had a concussion and a bullet hole in his shoulder. He was lucky the bullet had gone right through but we could not carry him too. It meant that we went down the hill at walking speed. We were fighting the terrain and fighting nightfall. The sun sets far quicker around the Mediterranean than back at home and we watched the sun as it set before our eyes. We were still a mile and a half from the beach when the lights went out, quite literally. A perfect night for a raid, there was no moon, it was the worst of nights for such a descent. We tried to continue, in the dark, but when one of my wheels went over the side and we lurched alarmingly I decided we had best walk. Had Ken not thrown himself to the opposite side of the Kubelwagen then we would have fallen to a rocky death.

"Everybody out. We walk from here on down. Ditch the field caps. We fool no one now."

Our Bergens were now almost empty. Sergeant Poulson, use four of the Bergens to make a litter. Spread the rest out between the other bags."

"Sir."

"Harry and George, find two strong branches."

"Sir."

"You two disable the three Kubelwagens. We might as well make it hard for Jerry eh?"

"With pleasure, sir."

I took out a torch and the maps. Using my cape to hide the light I studied the map. The path looked straightforward. If we could reach the beach by twelve then I would be happy. I turned the torch out and repacked the cape and torch in my Bergen. The extras from the other Bergens did not make it too heavy. Now that we did not have the sound of the Kubelwagens' engines I could hear noises further away. There were vehicles and they were struggling. I guessed our trail had been found.

"Scouse, you and Ken had better booby trap the Kubelwagens with the last of the grenades. I think Jerry is on the way. At least this way we will have an idea of when they are close."

The litter was ready by the time the booby traps were prepared and in place.

"Take it in turns to carry Crowe. Half an hour each eh? Ken you are tail end Charlie. Keep those ears open."

"Sir."

We began to descend. At first I tried to follow the path using what little light remained. It was no use. I fell twice. We were stumbling in the dark. I risked a torch and we made much better time. After half a mile it was much easier going and we made quicker time but the sound of the Germans grinding up the other side of the hill in their vehicles drew closer. We halted twice to change stretcher bearers and soon I found more sand under foot than rocks. My other senses kicked in and then I smelled cigarettes and wood smoke. There were people ahead. I turned out the torch and hissed, "Scouse, Sergeant, Come with me. Harry take charge."

I drew my Luger and headed towards the beach. I saw that what I had taken to be rocks were in fact two mud huts and there were three small fishing boats drawn up on the beach. When the aerial photograph had been taken they must have been out at sea. I waved my hand for the other two to flank me. The smell of smoke grew stronger and I realised that it was not tobacco it was marijuana. I had smelled it before. Then I heard voices. There were four of them and they were speaking French. They had thick accents but they were talking about what a good catch they had made and how they would sail to Bizerte in the morning to sell it. We could not board the Sunderland with these here. I waved Sergeant Poulson around the back of the huts and I stepped out into the light of the fire which had been hidden by the huts.

There were four men there. Their eyes opened wide when they saw us. I lowered the gun and smiled. One of them took it as a sign of weakness and ran from the fire. He ran straight into Sergeant Poulson's fist and he was dragged, dazed back into the firelight.

I spoke in French, "We mean you no harm. I promise you that you will be safe. We will not be here for long."

One of them grinned. He was the oldest of the men and had a white beard and moustache, "English?" I nodded, " My name is Mustapha al-Berkite. This is my home and these are my sons. Even the stupid one who runs into your soldier's fist." He shook his head. "I like Tommies. You are welcome to our fire, effendi. Sit and have some stew. It is good."

His English was reasonable and I saw my men relax. "Thank you for your hospitality." I turned and shouted, "The rest of you come and join us."

The others came, with the stretcher. Hewitt said, "Sir, Crowe is starting to come to."

"Good. These chaps have offered us some food. I suspect they don't have spare bowls. Break out your mess kit. Scouse you had better eat first and then keep watch for the Sunderland."

"Yes sir."

I went to Crowe who had his eyes open. He looked up at me, "Sorry about this, sir."

"You can't help getting wounded."

"How is Peter?"

I shook my head. He didn't make it."

"He always said he didn't have much luck."

Sergeant Poulson brought me my stew as Hewitt brought Crowe's. "He was right there, sir. He was a brave lad but he made a mistake." I started to eat and waved my spoon so that he would go on with the story. "After we lost you we pushed on as ordered.

It was all going well and then the fighters arrived." He shook his head, "I don't know what he was thinking. We were waving at the fighter pretending we were Jerry and suddenly he opened fire with the machine gun. The fighter fired instantly and that was when he bought it. The bullets shredded the tyres and it flipped over. We stopped to see to Harry and George. The 109 dived again and I thought we had had it but they had sent for help. Hewitt and I were helping Harry and George when the Germans arrived. Young Alan here opened fire with his gun and he was shot. He fell awkwardly and bashed his head against a rock. The rest, you know, sir."

"It was just bad luck, Sergeant."

"No, I should have secured the perimeter first. Harry and George weren't badly injured."

"But you didn't know that, did you?"

"No sir."

"And I would have done the same. It is not a disaster. We are here and now we have three hours to wait for the Sunderland."

Just then I saw a flash on the hillside above us and there was an explosion. The Germans had triggered our booby traps.

"That's torn it sir. They will be down here before the Sunderland arrives. It took us about two hours to get down."

"I know." We had used all of our explosives up and there would be no more booby traps. We had plenty of ammunition but, even if we held them off there was no way we could safely escape in rubber dinghies. We would just get the air crew killed and the four Tunisians. That triggered a thought.

I pointed up the hill, "Mustapha, they are Germans and they will be here soon. If they find us they will shoot. You and your sons might be injured."

"If it is God's will...."

"However if we left the beach on your fishing boats then they wouldn't find us would they? You could say that we stole them."

"We could not do that, effendi. They are our livelihood and besides we have given you hospitality. Custom dictates that we defend you from enemies."

They were old fashioned and well meaning values in a world which no longer cared about such things. "I have a compromise."

"Yes?"

I took out the coins I had been given, "We would like to hire you to take us out to sea."

"Back to England?"

"No Mustapha, just a mile or so out to sea. Where we will not be seen by the Germans. We have an aeroplane coming to take us off." I saw him debating. "You could carry on to Bizerte and be there when the market opens to sell your fine catch."

That decided him, "We will do it. You need to spread your men out in the four boats. The stretcher will be too big to take."

Crowe said, "Don't worry sir. I can walk. I have been enough trouble."

"Then you have a deal." I handed him the coins which would have been the equivalent of a month's wages for all four of them. "Get to the beach lads, we are going fishing!"

Mustapha shouted to his sons.

"Hewitt you and Sergeant Poulson go with Crowe. The rest of you choose your own boat. Scouse, you are with me. You have the signal to make."

It took longer to load the boats and to launch them than I had expected. It was eleven thirty by the time we managed it. They hoisted their sails and we laboured our way out into the inky blackness of the small bay. Scouse and I were with Mustapha. The others were following. When the fire became a distant glow I said, "Here is far enough."

He lowered the sail and threw a rock attached to a rope over the side. It was a crude but effective anchor. We still drifted but much more slowly. We would not move far.

"Effendi, how will the aeroplane pick you up?"

"It is a seaplane. It can land on water."

"Ah." We bobbed on the water in silence until he said. "We do not like these Germans. They are cruel and have no sense of humour. We want the French and the English to come back."

I nodded, "Your English is very good. Where did you learn it?"

"I worked on ships before the war. They carried passengers from Gibraltar to Malta. They were rich English people. They were kind and they tipped well. I liked them. Even then the German passengers were, how you say, unpleasant. I like Americans too. There were never many of them. They gave even better tips." He patted the boat. "When the war in Spain stopped the ships I used my tips and bought two boats. We now have three."

"Do the Germans bother you?"

"Not here. They never come to this bay but when we are in Bizerte they watch us and they have rules for everything. Soon you will drive them out eh, effendi?"

"One day, Mustapha, one day."

Just then a searchlight played out across the bay. Its beam did not reach us but it told us the Germans were there. We stopped talking and watched as the light played across the black water.

I looked at my watch. It was twelve forty five. The Germans had settled down for the night. They were waiting, no doubt, for us to return. They knew we had come down the hill and could not see us. I saw torches flashing on the hill side as they searched for us. Soon they would know where we were. I looked at my watch again and Ken, in the next boat along, said, "I heard engines, sir. It sounds like the Sunderland."

"Start sending the call sign, Scouser. We don't want him landing on top of us." Scouser kept his back to the shore to hide the flash of his light and he aimed it east. That was where the sound of the engine was coming from. The noise grew but there was no response as yet. Perhaps it was not the Sunderland. Had the Germans called in one of their Focke-Wolf Kondors? Then there was a flash in the night. I heard the relief in Scouse's voice as he acknowledged. "It's them sir. They are going to land west to east."

I guessed that would be to aid their take off. Suddenly the huge Sunderland appeared almost above us. I saw Mustapha's sons cowering in the well of their boats. He snorted, "They get that from their mother! She was afraid of her own shadow too!"

133

There was a burst of hopeful firing from the beach. They had no chance of hitting at that range. The Sunderland turned and I saw it heading almost directly for us. I hoped the lieutenant knew what he was doing. He did. The Sunderland stopped less than twenty feet from us. The swell from its floats made us bob up and down alarmingly but we were not swamped. The flying boat edged its way to us. The hatch was open. The Flight Sergeant said, "Best get a move on gents. I think we will have company soon."

"Bye Mustapha. Thank you again."

"Don't forget effendi, come back and drive these Germans from my land."

"We will."

I scrambled aboard, followed by Scouse. "Right sir."

We moved forward and picked up the others boat by boat. As soon as Sergeant Poulson was on board the Flight Sergeant said, "That is it sir! We can take off." The motors began to roar as the pilot opened the throttles. "I reckon the Germans know we are here. They will send night fighters up. I am off to the nose." He pointed to the hatch. "If things get dicey you can open this and have a pop yourselves."

"Right."

"Hewitt, get Crowe stowed safely. The rest of you get your Tommy guns. If we are attacked then we will open the upper half of the hatch and make ourselves useful."

We began to climb and bank as the pilot resumed his flight west. I had no doubt that the Flight Sergeant was correct. The Germans on the beach had to have a radio and a Sunderland was a tempting target. The Germans called them a Flying Porcupine but at night the Germans would have the advantage. We were thirty minutes from the pickup point when we heard a shout from the gunners above. "You lads watch out. There are two 110 night fighters coming in. They will try to get below us."

"Get the hatch open. Poulson and Lowe, come with me. The rest be ready to change positions when we empty our guns."

The air was rushing in at us and I was glad I still had my sand goggles. I put them over my eyes and it became much easier. I saw nothing and then I saw the tracer as it came from the four nose machine guns of the German night fighter. It was below us. "Fire! Give him the lot." I ignored my own rule and emptied the magazine. I made a space and went to reload. Ken took my place. By the time he had emptied his the 110 had soared over us.

The gunner above us shouted, "Well done Army! That gave the bugger a shock." They tried two more attacks but none were on our side and they eventually gave up.

The Flight Sergeant returned with a big grin on his face. "Well this is a novelty, sir. Passengers who actually do something useful. You didn't hit him but you put him off enough so that he just gave us a couple of bullet holes in the wings. I think this calls for some cocoa!"

Hewitt had used the medical kit in the galley and made a better job of patching up Crowe. He would still need to be seen in Gibraltar by a doctor but my medic's professional pride was intact.

After the cocoa I fell asleep and had to be woken as we taxied to a buoy at the flying boat dock. The pilot shook my hand. "Well done Lieutenant. We heard in Malta that you had pulled it off. They sent a Spit over to take photographs. You did a damned fine job of demolition."

I nodded, "We lost a man."

"Small price to pay but I understand what you are saying." We walked along the wooden jetty to the small barracks we would be using. The flying boat needed repairs and refuelling. There was no rush to get back. "And now what? Will you get some leave?"

"I hope so but you know what it is like."

He shook his head, "Aye, mate. I certainly do."

Part 3

English interlude

Chapter 12

I borrowed notepaper from the flight office in Gibraltar. I was tired; the four hour wait in Gibraltar had been filled with reports and debriefs from Intelligence. They were taking no chances. If the Sunderland went down on the way back to England they would have their pound of flesh. I was tired and needed a bed but I would not be able to sleep until I had written to the family of Peter Groves. I had had to write such letters before. Thankfully those occasions had been few but it was still the hardest part of my job. Technically Major Foster should have done it but he didn't know the men as I did. We had all been in harm's way together and suffered the same dangers and privations. Dad had always hated that part of the job too but he had once said to me, "We owe it not only to the families but the dead themselves. It shows that we value the sacrifice that they made and that we will remember them."

I spent well over an hour remembering and writing. Peter had been quiet and thoughtful. When they had gone out for a beer he was always the one who helped those who could not handle their ale back to the digs. When someone had had difficulty with a new skill which Peter had he had been patient and showed them how to do it. As I was writing it John Hewitt had come by. He saw what I was doing and sat next to me. "He had met a girl you know, sir, Margaret. Her mum has a boarding house just four doors from Mrs Bailey. It was early days but he was keen."

"I didn't know."

"No one else did, sir. Peter didn't want the mickey taking out of him." He shook his head. "I think the lads think because I am the medic I am the priest too. They confide in me."

"I am sorry."

"No sir, I take it as a compliment. They know I will keep my mouth shut." He stood and yawned. "Anyway sir, I just thought you ought to know."

I was learning more about my men all the time. Once written and sealed in the envelope I rested my head against the fuselage and fell asleep. It was not a restful sleep. Writing the letter had triggered memories of all the others I had had to write and the soldiers who had died and would never be coming back.

The flying boat landed in the early afternoon. The radio operator had warned the camp that we were returning. There was a reception committee. A staff car was there with Major Foster and the smoky Major Fleming. Sergeant Major Dean also waited with a lorry. The tender was large enough to take us all and I was the first to step ashore. Major Fleming leapt upon me as though I was prey. "Good job Harsker! Now tell me..."

Major Foster held his hand up, "Major Fleming, not here. Wait until we get back to camp." He shook my hand. "Damned fine job. I was happy to let you have the day to recover but our colleague here was keen to debrief you."

"That is fine sir." I hesitated, "We lost Peter Groves."

"Sorry about that. He was a good lad."

I had the envelope in my hand. "I don't know his address."

Reg Dean stepped forward, "I'll take that, sir. Leave it with me. I'll look after the lads and congratulations from me, sir. You can tell me all about it over a pint, tonight. It can wait until then." He shot a look at the Major. A recruit would have quailed before it but the Major seemed oblivious to his own insensitivity.

I sat in the front with the driver. Sergeant Poulson had taken my Bergen and Tommy gun. We drove in silence to the camp. Clouds of smoke wafted from the back. You always knew where Major Fleming would be. As we entered the office Major Foster said to the duty sergeant, "Get some tea sent from the mess eh? You hungry, Tom?"

"No thanks, sir. They fed us on the Sunderland."

The major from Intelligence took out a notebook. He did not wait for the tea, "Now we just saw the photographs the Spitfire took. What was the damage, exactly?"

I looked at Major Foster who rolled his eyes and then looked heavenward. "Sir, we did not hang around. We saw and heard the explosion. The whole building went up. Everything in it was burned."

"Yes we saw that. I meant how did you sabotage the tank?"

"You didn't ask that, sir." I was beginning to become irritated. Too many of these staff officers never got their hands dirty. They had no concept of what the soldiers on the ground actually did. "You need to be more precise in your questions, sir!"

He was not in the least put out by my comments, "I thought I had. Well go on then. How did you blow it up?"

"My men put demolition charges in the engine, the ammunition, the barrel, the low loader and we opened the petrol tank."

He looked up, "Your men? You mean you did not supervise it yourself? It was an important job. I hope your sergeant knew what he was about."

I smiled, "It was not my sergeant. It was my new private, Shepherd."

"A private!"

The tea arrived and as the cups were placed before us Major Foster said, "In the Commandos we trust our men, all of them. Tell me, Tom, have you any doubts that the tank was destroyed?"

"I guarantee it."

Mollified Major Fleming lit another cigarette. I sipped the hot sweet tea. "So Lieutenant Harsker how did you get out?"

I told him how we had stolen the Kubelwagens and made our way north. He scribbled away furiously. He asked for clarification a number of times but seemed satisfied. When I had finished he looked at his notes. "Very resourceful. I can see why his lordship rates you so highly. Tell me do you think the fishermen were typical of those in the area?"

I shrugged, "Possibly. It is hard to judge. Mustapha liked the English."

The Major scribbled some more. Major Foster said, "One thing, Tom. You tied up a great number of Germans. That would have helped General Montgomery in the desert. Those 109s and 110s couldn't shoot down any of our aeroplanes while they were hunting you. You did more than we could possibly have hoped."

"I suppose." At the time I had not thought of that but the Major was quite right. There had to have been more than a hundred men hunting us.

"Hmn." Major Fleming put down his pen and smiled, "So, I bet you are keen for your next mission eh Lieutenant? I can see you are the type who likes excitement!"

Major Foster snapped, "Lieutenant Harsker is not a glory hunter. He does every job as professionally as he can."

Major Fleming looked nonplussed, "But when I read of the medals he had I thought he sought the accolades!"

"The medals were earned. They came as a result of being put in a difficult position and the Lieutenant extracting himself and his men from that position."

I stood, "Sir if I could go and write my report. I would quite like to get back to my digs for a bath."

"Of course. Use the Sergeant Major's office and I will finish up here."

I had almost finished when Sergeant Major Dean returned. I looked up, "Almost finished, Sarn't Major."

"No rush sir. Mrs B was right upset about poor Peter Groves. She thinks of them all as her bairns."

"I know. We are lucky we haven't lost more."

139

He went to his desk and took out a sheaf of papers. "The Major has given you all a week's leave. I have your travel warrants."

"Thanks, Sarn't Major."

"We have a new draft of Commandos in next week. They are the replacements for those killed and lost at Dieppe. The Brigade is coming back here for a while. The Major said it was something to do with lessons learned at Dieppe."

I signed the report and sat back, "The trouble with lessons in this school is that they come at the cost of someone dying and not just a caning."

Sergeant Major Dean nodded and lit a cigarette, "Major Foster said that Lieutenant Colonel Merritt has been put up for the VC for what he did at Dieppe. He did all right." He nodded to me, "You trained him and his lads well, sir. You should be proud. He is alive, although a prisoner now; him and the hundred men he had left with him, but that is down to you and your lads."

"That's what I mean Reg. Those lads from Saskatchewan weren't ready to face the Germans. They needed more training. They were thrown in at the deep end and their loss was a waste."

"The trouble is, sir, that the ones with experience, like you and your lads, you can't do it all on your own. You had to go through what those Canadians did. The ones who come through will be stronger."

"But what good is that behind a POW wire?"

He had no answer to that, "The Major's driver is outside sir. He is waiting to take you to your digs. Mrs B said she would have water ready for your bath." He handed me the travel warrants and leave chits. "You'll be more yourself after a leave, sir."

"More myself?"

"Yes sir, positive. You are the half full bloke. It's one of the reasons the lads will follow you anywhere. You never give up. Don't give up on yourself, sir. You lost a man. Most would have lost half of the section at least. Think about the ones you brought back."

Perhaps Reg was right. I was tired and a tired man never thinks straight. The trouble was every time I met someone whose war was behind a desk I became irritated. They moved flags around on a board and never thought for one moment about what the flag represented. Peter Groves had hopes and ambitions. They ended on that North African road. He had made one mistake and it had cost him his life. If Major Fleming made a mistake the worst that he would suffer would be a reprimand.

The slamming of the car door brought Mrs Bailey to her front door. I could see that her eyes were red and puffy. As I entered she said, "Poor Peter and poor Margaret Little! They were walking out you know, Lieutenant."

"I know, Mrs Bailey." I put my hand on her shoulder to comfort her and it seemed to open the floodgates.

She threw herself into my chest and sobbed, "I know what she will go through. She will end up like me, Lieutenant." She spoke between sobs."She'll never have bairns and she has lost the love of her life!" She was crying not only for Peter and Margaret but for herself. It was hard for her. Each death reminded her of her own lost love.

"She is young enough. She can find another young man."

Mrs Bailey stepped away and looked at me, "But until this war is over every young man could end up like Peter Groves couldn't he? It has to end, Lieutenant, it has to!"

Her words were still with me as my train took me north. The newspaper I had bought spoke of the Russians being attacked at Stalingrad. The propaganda suggested that they were holding out. I did not believe such reports. The German Blitzkrieg was a frightening phenomenon. I had witnessed it firsthand. I knew that it was not going well in the desert. The new general, Montgomery, was barely holding Rommel. We had seen plenty of Germans around Tunis. They had enough men to end the war in the desert and our troops had to risk the bombers and submarines in the Mediterranean to get there. Even my optimism was failing. We needed a victory and we needed it soon.

As usual I had not warned Mum of my impending arrival. I was always too keen to get to the station and get on a train. I always forgot to ring. Part of me also worried that the train would be delayed and she would worry. That journey was just such a one. We were held up north of London. German bombers must have missed their target or perhaps they had deliberately targeted the junction. Whatever the reason we all had to walk two miles with our cases to the next station where small local trains were used to take us on. I reached the station closest to Mum and Dad's at ten o'clock at night. Taxis in England were unheard of at that time of night and the telephone box was out of order. I shook my head. It would have to be Shank's pony. I began to walk. I wished that I had brought my Bergen. The kitbag was hard to carry!

I stepped out quickly and noticed just how dark England was with a blackout. This, however, was easier than when we travelled at night normally. That was behind enemy lines. There we would have to keep our eyes open for the enemy. At least the worst I could encounter here would be a poacher. It was eleven forty five when I tried the door. Surprisingly it was locked. I knocked and felt foolish for doing so. I had a key somewhere. I just couldn't remember where. In peacetime we would have had an external light but there was a blackout. I heard Mum's querulous voice. "Who is there?"

"It's me, Mum. Tom!"

She flung the door open and threw her arms around me. "Why didn't you ring?"

"The telephone was out of order." A white lie never hurt.

"Come on in. I bet you haven't eaten. I am not certain I have anything in. You should have rung!"

I put my arm around her and led her into the sitting room. There was a dying fire and the crossword puzzle next to her chair. "It's fine. I had some food on the train, " I lied. Another white lie would not keep her awake at night feeling guilty for not feeding her son. "Where is Mary?"

"She is training to be a ferry pilot. She has her wings now. She said she didn't want to sit and do nothing while you and Dad were saving the world."

I laughed, "What a goose! Where is Dad?"

"London. He will be back for the weekend. How long is your leave?"

"Just a week."

"Well you can see him then."

"Why the locked door, Mum? Is it because Mary isn't here?"

She shook her head, "No. They have a prisoner of war camp twenty miles away. A couple got out last month and they were caught four miles from here. Your Dad suggested it."

I knew they had to put prisoners somewhere but why near my Mum? "I shall root out my key then."

"Oh we had the locks changed not long ago. I have a spare for you." She suddenly stopped. "Leave? This isn't Christmas. Why have they given you leave?" Mum was clever and she knew enough about the military to work things out for herself. "You have been in action again, haven't you? You have been over there. You were on the Dieppe raid!"

"Yes Mum."

"That was a while ago! You have been away again!" She shook her head. "There are other men in the army apart from you Tom!" She became tearful.

"Mum, I am fine." I put my arm around her until she stopped crying. "Were you like this with Dad in the Great War?"

She managed a smile, "No. But I know better now. I believed all your Dad's white lies. Then I spoke to Ted and the others. Now I know the truth. Besides I carried you for nine months. You are too precious to be thrown away."

"And I won't be." I rubbed my hands, "Now I have had food but I could do with a nice whisky. Has Dad left any?"

"Of course. You sit down and I will get you one." She kissed me on my cheek, "It is good to see you, son."

I managed to cheer her up by talking of inconsequential things; the shortages, the weather, what Auntie Alice had been up to. Soon it was one o'clock and we were both ready for bed. She put her hand to her mouth, "I have not even aired your bed! What kind of mother am I?"

I kissed her on the cheek, "The best. Listen any bed will be fine. I am not picky any more. I could sleep on a clothes line and be happy enough."

She shook her head, "You get more like your Dad every day. I'll make you a hot water bottle, at least."

I had the luxury of a lie in and a cooked breakfast. I have no idea where she got the bacon and the sausages from but they were delicious. The ones we had at camp were mainly gristle and watery bacon. This was home cured bacon and farm sausages. I was home and it felt like there was no war.

"I think I'll take one of Dad's guns and see if I can pop a bunny or two."

As I left she said, "I'll get your uniform clean for you. Goodness only knows what these stains are."

Coniscliffe Woods a mile or two from our house, teemed with rabbits. The owners were happy for locals to keep the rabbit population down. I suspected that with most men my age away at the war there would be more rabbits than the land could support. As I left the lane and headed towards the wood I saw old Joe Carlton, "Now then Joe, what are you up to?"

He knuckled his head, "Eeh, Lieutenant Harsker. Home on leave are you?"

"Just a week. I am off to get a couple of rabbits. What are you up to?"

"Well I patrol this area every day now. Home Guard you see. We had a couple of prisoners escaped not long ago; from the POW camp. The missus and the other women were a bit jumpy so we each take it in turns to patrol. It makes it seem like we are doing our bit."

"I would have thought that any Jerry who escaped would be away on his toes."

"You'd think so wouldn't you? They must have the dozy ones yonder. Any road I'll come with you, if you don't mind. A bit of company would be nice and I'd like to hear what you have been up to. You and your Dad are the local heroes."

I sighed inwardly but outwardly I smiled and let him ramble on about Dad's exploits in the war and how I was his double. Joe did have one skill which was invaluable. He knew exactly where we would find the bunnies. Between us we bagged six. He had a family and I just took the two; I let him have the rest. The two would be more than enough for the three of us. On the way out of the woods he spied some mushrooms. "Here you are sir, these will go nicely with the rabbit stew. That rain we had last week and the warm weather has brought them on a treat. They don't last long. By this time next week they will be past their best." We picked wild mushrooms and I carried them in my cap with my rabbits over my old hunting jacket. It was like being fifteen and out with my Dad again.

We parted at the end of the lane. "See you again, Joe, and if you want some company next time you patrol give me a knock."

"But you are on leave, sir!"

"And believe me walking through an English wood will be a leave for me."

When I entered the cottage I saw that Mum had cleaned it top to bottom. It smelled of wax polish. I had no idea why; it was just me. "I rang your father. He is coming down early. He will be on the last train tonight. Could you pick him up in the shooting brake?"

"Of course." I held up the rabbits and the mushrooms. "I have dinner!"

She shook her head and wagged her finger, "After you have gutted and skinned them we have dinner. And do it out the back! I have just cleaned the kitchen."

I sighed as I went to the outhouse. What was the point of cleaning anywhere if you couldn't actually use it? Still she was right about one thing the smell of wax was nicer than the smell of gutted rabbits. Considering they only ate grass they stank when you cleaned them out. I got rid of the guts and washed the carcasses under the tap in the yard. When they had drained I held them up. "Is it safe for them to enter?"

She laughed, "You are not so big that I can't give you a clip!"

It was my turn to laugh, "In all the years growing up in this cottage I can never remember you giving me a clip of any description."

She took the rabbits, "I was being metaphorical!"

It was a dream driving the shooting brake after the Kubelwagen. The gears were smooth and the accelerator responsive. The best feature, however was the upholstered seats. My back had still not recovered from the race over the mountain!

Dad's train, inevitably, was late. I didn't really mind as everyone came over to talk to me. Being the last train lots of people were being met. As I found when talking to Joe, everyone regarded me as somehow special because I had been decorated and they had read of the exploits of the Commandos. Harry Charlton, the stationmaster, asked, "Why don't you wear your uniform? Everyone would like to see that."

"Mum is washing it."

"Aye well next time you come down, wear it. The wife thinks you look really smart in that. You look like Errol Flynn!"

"I doubt it, Harry, but it is nice of her to say so."

Just then I spied the train heading towards the platform. As it stopped it spewed steam and smoke. The doors clattered open and the train disgorged its passengers. I stood and waited. There were other soldiers home on leave and they were being met by families. Dad and I could wait. I heard his name called as he passed down the platform from the first class. I held up my hand and he strode towards me. He shook it, "Good to see you, Tom, and such an unexpected pleasure."

I nodded non committally, "The car is outside. No luggage?"

He shook his head as we walked to the car park. "I keep a spare set of everything at the flat. It saves packing." As I drove down the lane he said, "I am guessing your last operation was harder than Dieppe."

"You knew about Dieppe?"

"I bumped into Lord Lovat and Lord Louis at the club. They were singing your praises then they both went quiet when I asked what you were up to. I guessed it was cloak and dagger again."

I nodded, "Tunisia. Jerry had captured a brand new tank the Americans had loaned us. We had to blow it up."

"At least you didn't have to nursemaid old fogies this time."

"You weren't the old fogey."

We drove in silence. "Was it rough?"

"I lost a man. One of the young lads, Peter Groves. He was a quiet boy; just started courting."

"And you blame yourself."

I flashed him a look, "How did you know?"

"I was the same. Whenever someone went down in a ball of flames I blamed myself. Silly of course. No one man can protect all those who serve with him. You have to accept some deaths as being... well war."

"I don't think I will ever get used to it."

I drove in silence for a while.

"Mountbatten thinks highly of you, you know. You are the chap he thinks of when he has something difficult to manage."

"Oh great, so I can expect all the hard missions can I?"

He laughed, "I shall tell him you want others to do them shall I?"

"No, don't you dare."

We pulled in the gate. "You like the position you are in but you worry about the men you lead. I know the feeling. I still have that problem. When I send a squadron to escort bombers or to attack an enemy I know it is the right thing and I am honoured to have to make those decisions but I hate it when the lads do not return. Part of me stays with them wherever they fell." He got out of the car but, as he was doing so he said, "Keep schtum about the war eh?"

"Of course."

We had two bottles of wine with the rabbit. Mum had used the last dregs of a bottle of port for the sauce and it was delicious. Mum was as happy as she could be with the two men in her life in the same room. We didn't talk about the war but I told her about Mrs Bailey and her burgeoning relationship with Sergeant Major Dean and I told her about the young men I led. For some reason she found it totally fascinating. I realised why later on. Dad moved in the higher echelons of the military. It was all grand strategy and the bigger picture with him. With me it was the minutiae of war and relationships between small groups of men.

"You know it must have been like your father in the Great War. He would come home and tell me about Ted, John, Randolph. Didn't you Bill?" Dad nodded. "I knew all about their hopes and dreams, whom they were seeing, or not. And you are the same. This Mrs Bailey seems a nice lady."

"She is." I told her about her concern for the girl Margaret and her loss.

I saw Dad frown. I had said too much. "So you lost one of your boys?" I nodded. "That's why you have this leave. You must have barely escaped with your life."

I laughed, "That is a bit dramatic, Mum. Peter was just unlucky."

"And that is no consolation. Every time your father went up in one of those string bags I wondered if he would land safely or come back disfigured by fire."

"Mum, the worst I have had is a bite from a German Shepherd!"

My Dad said hurriedly, "That is the dog, Beattie and not a cross German!"

She scowled at him and I thought they were going to row. Instead she burst out laughing. "I can never win with you two can I?"

He went over, sat on the arm of her chair and put his arm around her, "Some would say you won when you got me, my love!"

In answer she gave him a push and he fell flat on the floor, "I hate to say it, Dad, but you asked for that didn't you?"

"I guess I did!"

Mum was happy, over the next two days, just to have Dad and I ramble around the countryside, enjoying pints in country pubs and watching the end of autumn. She busied herself in the kitchen making bramble crumbles and stews with the cheapest cuts of meat and suet crust lids. She had her two men home and her world would have been perfect if Mary had managed leave.

148

Dad and I even joined Joe for one of his Home Guard patrols. Like me Dad was sceptical about the danger a roaming POW would pose. "I was hunted in the French countryside in the Great War and Tom here has had to hide behind enemy lines. Neither of us were any danger to the locals. The soldiers? Yes. I think the civilians will be safe enough." Dad was a senior officer and I saw the relief on Joe's face. His mind was at rest.

Chapter 13

On Saturday Dad took Mum and me out for a drive and a lunch at a nice country pub, *'The Stanley Arms'*. It was a couple of villages away but a lovely drive. Although the food was not as good as it had been before the war the roaring fire and fine ale more than made up for it. We had a really good time and Mum laughed at every one of Dad's jokes. We all forgot the war. That was a dangerous thing to do. There was no hurry and a leisurely drive saved precious petrol. We took our time.

We were just three miles from home when we were stopped by the Home Guard. Joe was in his sergeant's uniform. "Trouble Joe?"

"Yes sir. Prisoners escaped from the POW camp. Three of them." Dad nodded, "They killed a young chap. Alan Raysworth from Tolesby way."

Dad suddenly became serious. "That is just up the road."

"Yes Group Captain. The regulars are blocking off the roads to London and the coast. They seem to think they will head east. We have been given this area, to the west."

One of the men, Albert, said, "This time we shoot first and ask questions after. Murdering buggers!"

Dad said, "I know what you are thinking, Albert, but we do this properly." Albert nodded. "Now is this it? Have we the complete Home Guard here?"

Joe said, "We are only short of Albert's lad, Walter."

Albert shook his head, "He went to check on his young lady and her mum." He pointed north. "They live Stanhow. It is closer to the camp. I told him the regulars would check it out but he wouldn't listen. Sorry, Group Captain."

"Don't worry Albert. If ten of us can't catch three prisoners of war then one extra youth would not help. Right. Tom and I will go home and get our guns. I reckon they would head for the woods. They could lay up there. If I was Jerry I would wait until nightfall when the hue and cry had died down and then steal a car. The woods would be a good place to wait."

Joe nodded, "We'll meet you there, sir."

Once home we quickly changed into more suitable clothes. I put my Luger in my belt and took my twelve bore. Dad smiled when he saw my Luger. "Just like mine in the Great War."

"It is always handy when we are in France. It confuses the enemy."

As we left Dad said, "Lock the door, Beattie, and don't open it unless you know who it is. Even if they steal the car you stay in here. There is less than a gallon in the tank. Even if they take the car they won't get far."

She nodded and I could see fear on her face, "I will Bill. You two be careful."

"We will be."

As we headed down the lane I said, "A bit of a long shot this isn't it Dad? I mean they could be anywhere."

"They could but ask yourself this. If you were in a country you did not know where would you hide out?" He paused, "Where did you hide out?"

I nodded, "In a wood."

"Right. I did it when we were shot down. You have shelter. There is normally water and if you know what you are doing then you have food. In addition you can hide and most people can't read signs. You can."

I nodded as I thought about the task ahead. "Their footwear will be different. The ground has been muddy. Their prints will look different from ours."

"And they will smell different. You know when you are in France with your eyes closed. This may be a wild goose chase but we will soon find out. The moment we see tracks we will know if they are prisoners or locals."

The eight members of the Home Guard soon caught up with us. They all had shotguns. That was the weapon of choice in the countryside. All of them deferred to Dad. Not only was he a senior officer he was the senior man in the area.

"Right Group Captain how do we do this?"

"It is like beating for animals." I smiled. He used a simile they would all understand. I saw them nodding. "Keep the man next to you in plain sight and move slowly. Look for signs that men have been passing through; broken branches, cigarette stubs, that sort of thing." I saw enlightenment dawn. They were all pipe smokers. Most countrymen here could get a pipe going and it would happily burn until the tobacco was all gone. Cigarettes were too much work. He pointed to me, "Tom here will go along the path. He has hunted men before."

I nodded but I remembered that the last time I had hunted a man, a rogue Commando, that Commando had died and one of my men had been wounded. I would need to ensure that did not happen again. We wanted no deaths.

We moved slowly and meticulously. These eight knew the land and they moved not only through it but with it. We had had to train my Commandos to do that. These were born with that skill. We were lucky that the woods had been copsed and cleared lately. There were not as many places to hide as there would have been in high summer. I found the first sign a mile into the woods. There was a bit of a clearing. I spied the cigarette stub. Stopping, I picked it up and found that the saliva was still wet on the end. Searching the ground I saw something I had last seen close to Dieppe, the print of a German boot. I held up my hand and pointed down. Dad and the others nodded. I heard the clicks as broken shotguns were readied.

Now that I had found one track I found others. I frowned. There was a fourth set of prints amongst the German boots and it was a smooth print. Someone with hob nailed boots was ahead of us and they were with the prisoners of war. I began to move more quickly for the track was clear. As I was on the path I was able to move quicker than the others and I became the tip of an arrow.

Suddenly the silence of the wood was shattered by a shout. We all stopped and listened. There were voices ahead. Dad waved us forward. The voices were directly ahead and suggested that they were on the path. We edged closer but I was aware that those to my right were now level with me. I dared not shout for fear of giving away our presence.

I heard the German accent and knew that these were the men we sought, "Do not play games with me or I will slit your throat. You are leading us in circles. How do we get out of this infernal woods?"

"This is the way sir! Honest to God I am telling you the truth!"

It was young Walter. I recognised his voice. His Dad heard it too and he could not contain himself. "Walter!"

I raced forward for the game was up. They knew we were close. As we blundered towards the voices I spied the four of them. Walter had a bloody nose and a German had a knife to his throat. The other two also had knives and were sheltering behind the hostage as well. As I approached I saw that the knives were kitchen carving knives. They were no less deadly for that. In the countryside the men took pride in carefully sharpened knives. One false move would result in young Walter dying. Dad and I stopped ten yards from them. The Germans were standing close to the largest oak tree in the woods. It even had acorns left on it.

"One more move and I kill the boy!"

Albert shouted, "Get your hands off my boy you murdering Hun!"

"Albert, stop!"

My Dad's voice was authoritative and Albert obeyed. We were a half circle around them. The German, I guessed he was an officer or NCO shouted, "Lay down your weapons and we will let your friend go."

Dad said, "That is not going to happen. You are outnumbered and you are surrounded. We have shotguns. Surrender now!"

The German laughed, "You think I am a fool. You cannot use shotguns for you would kill the boy and I am guessing that is his father. Do as I say!" He raised his voice at the end. Then I heard him say, out of the side of his mouth, in German, "When they drop their weapons, Stephan, grab them!"

I laid down my own shotgun, taking a step forward as I did so and then said, in German, "There you can have my gun." I whipped out my Luger and pointed it at them, "If you think you can reach it before I empty this gun into you."

The German's eyes narrowed. "That does not change things, Englishman. I will kill him unless you drop your weapons."

I nodded, "What is your name?"

"Why?"

"I would like to know before I shoot you."

"Captain Heinrich Boehm."

I smiled, "Good, Heinrich now let me tell you something. I am a Commando. I took this Luger from a German I killed. I have killed many Germans with this, with my Tommy gun, with grenades and with my knife. I know how to kill. You think that because you hide behind Walter here you are safe." I shook my head. "I can see you and I can kill you. You see that acorn, just above your head?" The acorn was just six inches above his field cap. He flicked his eyes up and nodded. I pulled the trigger. In the silent woods the shot sounded like a cannon. To be fair to the German he did not flinch although his companions dropped to the ground. He glanced up and the acorn had gone.

"I do not want to kill you but you are not leaving this wood alive if you harm the boy. I have eight bullets left and you know what a nine millimetre parabellum can do to you don't you, Heinrich? I bet you have a gun just such as this. At this range the bullet would punch a hole in you big enough for my fist." I was not certain that was true but he had doubts in his eyes. He shifted his head a little. I laughed, "Pathetic, Heinrich! I'll tell you what; how about I shoot you in your right elbow? You won't be able to cut his throat and you don't need your right arm do you? Yes, I think that is what I will do. Now hold still..."

154

The knife was dropped. The other two followed suit. The Home Guard ran towards them; their shotguns levelled. Albert grabbed Walter. Heinrich stared at me, hate filled his eyes. Dad patted me on the back. "Remind me never to play poker with you, son. That was a good shot."

I said nothing. Walter had reminded me of young Peter Groves when he had first joined up. I had not wanted him to die but I had been helpless to prevent it. I had saved Walter and it felt good. We marched them out of the wood. Each German had two men behind them with cocked shotguns pressed into their backs. Dad and I flanked the officer. We tried to engage him in conversation but his grim eyes faced forward all the way to the edge of the woods and his mouth was drawn into a tight slit.

"Joe, run ahead to my house and use my telephone. Ask the regulars to meet us in the village eh?" Joe ran off.

Once we reached the lane people came out of their cottages to watch us. Some followed us. We were like the Pied Piper of Hamlin. We could do nothing to dissuade them. They bombarded the Home Guard with questions.

Joe caught up with us a mile from the village, "They are on their way. The Major in charge said, *'well done'.* " He chuckled, "I think he said it through gritted teeth though, Group Captain. The Home Guard did what a bunch of regulars couldn't." I heard the pride in his voice. The incident would do wonders for morale.

By the time we reached the village green there were forty people following us. Inevitably one who had not been on the hunt shouted, "We should string the bastards up. They killed a young lad and almost killed another!"

The crowd began to murmur angrily. I noticed that the Home Guard stood protectively around us. Dad emptied two barrels into the sky. It deafened and silenced at the same time. His voice was remarkably quiet when he spoke but it had enough authority to cow them all. "We are Englishmen! We are not a bunch of mindless savages! We have laws in this country and you will obey them. Now you have had your excitement for the day. Disperse

155

and go home!" No one moved. He raised his voice, just a fraction, "That is an order!"

They moved, slowly at first but eventually, in twos and threes they returned to their homes..

We stood in silence and I said, in German, "You see what happens when you forget you are not on the front line? I do not blame you for escaping but I do blame you for killing a civilian. You are protected by the Geneva Convention. So are civilians." He did not answer me but just glared. I had seen his like before. On the retreat someone just like him had shot some wounded soldiers not far from Dunkirk.

Just then we heard the lorry as it approached. A young Lieutenant jumped out. He had a grin on his face, "I say chaps, well done. We'll take it from here."

We watched the prisoners board the lorry and were then whisked away. Dad and I turned to walk back to the cottage. Albert said, "Where are you two gentlemen going? We have drinks to buy."

"We ought to get home, Mrs Harsker is waiting for us."

Joe shook his head, "No she isn't sir, she said she would drive down and pick you up. I said we would be in the pub."

I looked at Dad and he shrugged. We had little choice, it seemed. We followed them into the '*George*'. Walter brought me my pint over, "Thank you for what you did Lieutenant Harsker. I thought my time had come."

"You are welcome. How did they get you?"

"I was heading for Stanhow and I cut across a field. They stepped out of nowhere and grabbed me. I couldn't do nowt, sir."

"Don't you berate yourself, Walter. They are soldiers and they were desperate."

"They wouldn't have got you though sir, would they?"

"That is the difference, Walter, I have been trained."

"Would you have killed him if he hadn't surrendered? Would you have been able to hit him?"

"Yes, Walter. That is part of being a Commando."

"Then I want to be a Commando. I want to kill Germans." He looked at me, "You know sir, if they hadn't got me they might have got Ann and her mother. We can't have that."

"Well, Walter, when you do join up you will find that you do not have much choice in who you fight or where you fight but one thing is certain it is better to fight than to give up."

"Aye sir."

Albert had just paid for the round and he came over to me. He pumped my hand as though drawing water, "Thank you sir. That was a cracking shot! I owe you more than I can ever repay. If you ever need anything..."

"Just you and the Home Guard to keep doing what you are doing. Watch our home, everyone's home. It is reassuring, when I am fighting in foreign fields to know that this part of England is safe."

"Aye, we'll do that, won't we lads?"

There was a huge cheer.

I was grateful when Mum popped her head through the door. I had had my quota of beer! She was inundated with comments and praise about what a fine husband and son she had.

As we sped down the lane she said, "Joe told me what you did, son. That was quick thinking."

Dad nodded, "It was the right thing to do. I don't think I was ever prouder of you, Tom. I know that you have done braver stuff." He laughed, "I have seen you do braver things but today you weren't in uniform and yet you handled the situation far better than I could have."

"I don't believe that for an instant, Dad."

"No Tom, I knew it when we were in Africa. You are used to these quick decisions. Your brain and your reactions are honed for danger. My decisions are reflective. I have reports, maps, charts and data. I have young officers who offer advice. You think on your feet and today it showed." He nodded to Mum, "We have a son we can be proud of, Beattie."

She shook her head, "I didn't need today to tell me that. I am always proud of him but, after today, I will be even more fearful. This war can't end soon enough for me."

Chapter 14

The week long leave sped by and it did not seem five minutes before I was on a train and heading back to Falmouth. My interlude from the war was ending. The journey home through a windy autumnal England matched my sombre mood.

As usual I was the first one back. I always liked to be there before my section. I dropped my bag off at Mrs Bailey's, along with my ration book. I handed her a hessian sack. "Here you are Mrs Bailey, four bunnies. I shot them yesterday. They are skinned and cleaned. There was no heating on the train so they should be fine."

"Thank you very much Lieutenant Harsker. I will save that little bit of shin I bought for tomorrow. The lads will enjoy this."

I reached into my kit bag and handed her a couple of bottles. "This is last year's elderberry wine. Mum sent them down. They are a bit raw for drinking but they might add a punch to the stew."

She beamed as though it was a chateau bottled Bordeaux. "Oh you thank your mother. It will be a feast fit for a king."

I changed into my uniform and jogged up to the camp. The leisurely walks with Dad were not enough to keep up my fitness levels. I needed to work hard again and rid myself of the wonderful excesses of Mum's cooking and Dad's wine and whisky. As I approached the camp I could hear the buzz. The Brigade was back. As I walked through the barrier, flashing my pass to the sentry, I saw Gordy Barker, my former corporal.

"Now then sir. Good leave?"

"The best, Gordy. How are things here?"

"We are still trying to whip the new lads into shape. You know what they are like, all fingers and thumbs. Still we are getting there." He frowned, "Dieppe was a bugger, sir."

"I know, still at least Number Four achieved their objective."

"That we did sir but for all the good it did I am not sure."

"We have to think of the bigger picture. I am sure that the powers that be know what they are doing." After speaking with my Dad I knew that there were some clever people planning but some of those in the War Office were still stuck in the trenches.

"Sorry to hear about young Groves, sir. He was a good lad." He shook his head, "You seem to draw all the hard missions don't you, sir?"

I laughed, "I'll bet you were glad to get your own section eh Gordy?"

"Oh no sir, I would give up the stripes in a heartbeat if I could serve with you again."

His voice told me that he meant it. "You know you can never go back Gordy. The past always looks better from the present."

"I suppose you are right. Well I had better get back to the lads. They need watching all the time. Not like the old days."

"Gordy!"

He laughed, "You are right, sir. Look ahead, not back."

Once in the office we all used when in camp I checked to see if there was anything new. There was not although I noticed that all leave had been cancelled. I wonder what that meant. Sergeant Major Dean came in. He handed me a sheet of paper. "Your new Commandos sir."

"Commandos?"

"Yes sir, two of them."

"To replace Groves?"

"I think, sir, they are taking Lance Sergeant Gowland off you as well, sir." I stared at him. "I am just saying, sir and if Major Foster asks then you didn't hear it from me. I just thought you ought to know."

I did not like this. We were a team. Harry and George worked well together as Lance Sergeant and Corporal. They were old friends. Ken Shepherd had fitted in well but we had been lucky. "Why do they have to change things, Reg? If it is not broken then why fix it? Why break up a good tram?"

He chuckled as he handed me a mug of tea, "You are a victim of your own success. Harry is sergeant material isn't he, sir?"

"Well of course but..."

"And you wouldn't want to stand in his way."

"Of course not. Has he said he wants promotion?"

"Not to me sir but other sections need someone like him to lead them. Barker is one of the top sergeants we have. You trained him and were unhappy when you lost him. Poulson, well, he is as a good a Commando as you can get. We need NCOs who can lead."

"You mean I will be losing Polly too?"

"Perhaps, sir. It isn't for me to say. You had best ask Major Foster." I nodded, "Only if you could not let him know it was me as set you off sir, I would appreciate it."

"Of course, Reg and thank you. I didn't mean to bite your head off."

"You didn't, sir. Troop Sergeant Major's need thick skins, sir."

I knocked on Major Foster's door, "Ah Tom come in. I wanted to see you. Take a seat." I sat, "Good leave?"

I nodded, "Actually it was most exciting." I told him about the prisoners of war.

He shook his head, "And there was me thinking you were having an easy time of it."

"Sir, how come I have two new recruits? I only lost Groves."

He shifted uncomfortably in his seat, "I know, Tom. The thing is we need good sergeants. I am promoting Gowland. We are going to make Lowe into Lance Sergeant. We have a corporal coming from Number 1 Commando."

I became suspicious, "Number 1 Commando? Why would someone transfer Brigades and if he is so good why not stay in Number 1 and get promoted?"

The Major buried his face in the report. He was covering himself. "It seems he didn't get on with his officer. There was some sort of bust up and, well, in the interests of the service it was decided to move Brigades. His senior officer really rates him. He was sorry to lose him."

"So let me get this straight sir, you are taking away a damned good NCO and replacing him with someone with disciplinary problems?"

Major Foster laughed but it sounded a little false to me. "No, Tom, you have got the wrong end of the stick. We just thought that his skills might be useful in your section and we didn't want to lose a good soldier."

"Someone up top applied pressure, sir?" Major Foster's silence answered my question. "What skills sir? I have a good demolition team. A good radio man and my men are all round good Commandos. What can Corporal William Hay possibly bring to my team?"

"He is a qualified frogman."

He had me there. We had proved how useful that skill was. I sighed, "Right then sir. When do they get here?"

"They are here already. They came last week and have been just waiting for you to return. We put them up in the barracks but Reg has already spoken with your landlady. There are rooms available in your digs."

"All nicely arranged sir eh?"

"Come on, Tom, don't be bitter." He went to the door and shut it. "You have a week to get them up to speed and then you and Jorgenson are off again."

"Where to this time?"

"Back to Tunisia. Your work there was so good that Lord Mountbatten wants to build on it."

"But it is six hours or more from Gibraltar by aeroplane."

"This is top secret, Tom, but the Americans are going to invade Vichy in Africa. The Americans are keen to get into the war and Vichy is seen as a soft target. They are desperate to get a toehold in this theatre. General Montgomery is building up his forces to begin a major attack in the eastern desert. We can get Rommel between two armies. The LRDG is doing their bit in the eastern desert but you are the only one with experience in Tunisia. The

US Rangers will be used soon but until they have some experience it will be up to you. With Jorgenson's E-Boat we have the chance to operate close to the African coast."

I stood, "I just hope the Americans fare better than the poor Canadians. There are two and half thousand of them either dead or prisoners."

"This isn't the same, Tom. They will be attacking French not Germans and we have the word that many of the Vichy French are keen to join with the Americans."

"Not us?"

"No, I am afraid not. We upset them too much in 1940 when we took their ships. You and your team will gather intelligence and cause havoc in Tunisia and Algeria for we believe that the Germans will have to react and invade Vichy France."

"And divide their forces." I nodded, "Very clever sir. Right I'll go and find these two new lads then."

"We put them in Barracks 2A. They are expecting you." He looked up, "You will tell Lowe and Gowland?"

"Of course sir."

It was better that I greeted them before they met the rest of the section. I opened the door and saw the two of them. They were the only ones in the barracks. Corporal Hay was older than I expected while Private Emerson looked even younger than Ken Shepherd. I had never seen anyone as thin before and I wondered how he had passed his physical for the Commandos. They both leapt to their feet when I entered and stood at attention.

"At ease. I am Lieutenant Harsker and you men are in my section I believe?" They both nodded. "Good, well I need to get to know you. The rest of the section will be back this evening and we have some hard training before our next operation."

"We have an operation coming up sir?"

I recognised the north east in Emerson's voice. He was grinning and looked keen. I smiled, "Yes Emerson. Let's start with you. Where are you from?"

County Durham, Bishop Auckland."

"And what did you do before you joined up?"

"I was training to be a mechanic sir. I like engines."

"You came straight into the Commandos?"

"I was in the Territorial Army sir. Captain Hudson, the captain of our unit, reckoned I would make a good Commando. I enjoyed the training."

"If you were a good mechanic then you could have joined a mechanized unit."

"I like the outdoors sir. I use to go walking all the time with my granda. I was always running as a kid. I like messing with engines sir but I don't like being indoors." He looked worried, "Does that sound daft sir?"

"No Emerson."

"And Hay, what about you?"

"I was in the Commandos from the start, sir. I transferred after Dunkirk. I was in the Ox and Bucks."

"A good regiment. Were you on the retreat then?"

"Aye sir. I decided there and then I wanted to hit back at Jerry and the Commandos seemed the best way to do it."

"Good. And you must have done well, you were promoted to Corporal,"

His face gave nothing away but his voice sounded bitter, "I could have been a sergeant, sir."

"But you aren't and you transferred out of Number 1 Commando which tells me there is more to your story than your service record tells me." He remained silent. "I will be honest with you Hay, my section is one of the best in the Brigade. We are always put in harm's way. I have to rely on and trust my men completely. If, during this week of training I feel that I can't rely on you then you will be shipped out to another unit. Is that clear? I like to speak plainly and have everything out in the open."

"That suits me sir. Just give me a chance and I will show you that I can be an asset to the section. I promise that I won't let you down."

"Perhaps. Right, get your gear. My section stays in digs on the sea front. Mrs Bailey. She is a good landlady. The Sergeant

Major lodges there too. She has rooms for you. I'll give you four minutes to pack and then we will double down to the town."

As I waited outside for them I wondered what his story was. Perhaps he might confide in me when we were alone. It could have been that he was unhappy about speaking in front of Emerson. At least the young lad seemed an asset to the section. His skills with vehicles and engines could prove invaluable. I set a hard pace as we ran back to the digs. I felt slightly guilty as they carried Bergens and kitbags while I had nothing. They kept up remarkably well and I was impressed. Whatever other problems Hay had fitness was not one of them.

While they got their breath back I waited for Mrs Bailey to come to the door.

"Two new lodgers Mrs Bailey, Corporal William Hay and Private Fred Emerson."

"Pleased to meet you ma'am." They both adopted the appropriate tone.

"Will Hay? Like the film star? I like him."

I saw Hay's face; he had obviously been teased about his name before, "No, Mrs. Bailey, it is Bill. I prefer Bill Hay."

She smiled, "Whatever suits you my dear. Come on then. I will show you to your rooms." She nodded to me, "Good job you brought four bunnies eh Lieutenant Harsker."

"Oh, Mrs Bailey, did you use both bottles of the elderberry wine in the stew?"

"No, Lieutenant, just the one. You are right, it is a bit strong."

"Then I will open the other after supper tonight. If you could bring it in after pudding."

"Of course. Now you two lads come with me and we will do the grand tour."

I waited in the sitting room and read the paper, depressing though it was. I wanted to catch Sergeant Poulson as soon as he arrived. He was my second in command and needed to know my fears. In the newspapers the Eighth Army was still on the defensive. Stalingrad was surrounded and the Americans had lost an aircraft carrier, *'The Wasp'*, in the far east. The war was not going well and I could see why they needed a victory, even one over Vichy France.

I heard Sergeant Poulson's cheery, "Hello Mrs B., " as he entered the hall.

I called as he passed, "Sergeant, have you got a minute?"

"You back already sir? I'll just drop my bag here."

He entered and I shut the door. "Have a seat, Sergeant."

"Problem sir?"

"Could be." I told him about Harry's promotion and our two new members of the section.

When I had finished he nodded, "It might be nothing, sir. We both know that sometimes officers and their men don't get on but I will try to have a chat with him. The problem may be the fact that you are an officer and if he had a problem with an officer in his other Brigade then he may be wary of talking to you."

I brightened, that made sense. "Good. Keep this under your hat eh, Sergeant?"

"Of course, sir.

"And I think we are going back to Africa, but with the E-Boat this time. We may be based there for some time."

"A chance to get the old knees brown then eh sir. Right, I'll go and unpack. I am pleased for Harry. He deserves it."

"I know, sergeant."

After he had gone I realised he had a far better attitude than I did. He thought of the man. I was selfish and thought of myself first.

It was a noisy dinner table. I remained silent but the two new lads were bombarded with questions. Inevitably Scouser and some of the others let slip about our exploits. I saw the eyes of the two new men widen. Corporal Hay said, "You weren't joking then, sir. In Number One Commando our section were the best trained Commandos you ever saw. I saw more action on the retreat through Belgium."

Polly said, "The Lieutenant was on that one too. He was a private then."

This time Corporal Hay's jaw actually dropped and he seemed to notice my medal ribbon for the first time, "And you have been promoted four times then sir?"

I nodded, "I am just lucky, I guess."

Sergeant Poulson laughed, "Don't you believe him, Bill. Our Lieutenant is a genuine hero and the most modest man you will ever meet."

"A pity more officers aren't like that, Sarge." Hay sounded bitter.

I caught Sergeant Poulson's eye. This was the first insight he had given us about the mysterious issue which had caused him to join us. Harry Gowland and George had been relatively quiet and I understood why. We had an extra man and an extra NCO.

I waited until Mrs Bailey came in. She had anticipated me and there were nine glasses. "Have a glass for yourself Mrs Bailey, we are celebrating tonight."

She went out and returned with a large glass and a bottle of homemade lemonade. "I hope you don't mine Lieutenant, it is a bit strong for me. This will make it more like a port and lemon."

"Whatever you wish, Mrs Bailey." When they all had a glass I said, "We have reasons to celebrate. Firstly we have two new members of the section, welcome!" Everyone raised their glasses and said something appropriate, "Secondly their arrival means we are losing one of our section, Sergeant Gowland you are moving on to bigger and better things."

He looked at me and then realised what I had said, "I am promoted! Thank you sir."

"We will miss you." I saw his friend, George, looking unhappy, "And of course we need a new Lance Sergeant and that would be you, Lance Sergeant Lowe! Cheers!"

The one glass was not enough to get anyone inebriated but somehow it enlivened the table and, soon, everyone was chattering away like magpies. Sergeant Major Dean popped his head around the door. Mrs Bailey put her hand to her mouth, "Oh I am sorry, Reg. I forgot all about you!"

He laughed, "I heard the noise and wondered what was going on."

"Just celebrating two promotions Sarn't Major."

He nodded, "And well deserved they are too. Right then Mrs B, where is this rabbit stew you promised me?"

She stood and emptied the glass. "One more thing Mrs Bailey, me and the lads will be away for a while. Perhaps a couple of months. We will make sure our rent is paid up and then... well Sergeant Major Dean will sort things out."

I saw her eyes begin to well up. Reg put his arm around her, "Come on. No more of that Lieutenant Harsker will look after your lads."

As she was led from the room she said, "But who will look after him?"

Part 4

North Africa

Chapter 15

We had three hard days of training. It was strange to be without Harry. Bill Hay also found it hard to fit in. The lads did their best but he seemed to be keeping something hidden from them. They didn't like that. They knew each other warts and all. Sergeant Poulson tried to get close to him but every time he asked him questions he clammed up. I began to think I would have to transfer him out.

On the fourth day of our training we rejoined our E-Boat. Major Foster had sent more details of our mission down to Lieutenant Jorgenson. He was going to have to work, as we did, behind enemy lines and it would necessitate creating a base where we could lie up. I was not certain how this would work but Major Foster assured me that it had all been thought through. The first thing we did was to introduce our two new members of the section to the crew of the *'Lady'*. Fred was an instant hit. Once he saw the engines he was like a pig in muck. He chatted happily to the engineer and soon had oil beneath his fingernails once more. Corporal Hay, in contrast, appeared even more withdrawn and isolated than before.

We spent the morning working on the camouflage of our boat. It would have to blend in with the African coast. To be fair to Corporal Hay he worked as hard as any but while the others bantered he remained silent. He even ate his lunch alone. Alan Jorgenson came over to speak with me. "Is he a problem, Tom?"

"I think he is. I reckon I will have to send him back to his unit, or another unit at any rate. He just doesn't fit in."

"I can see that."

"And yet he is as hard working as any of the others. He is as skilled that much is obvious. In every other respect he is a perfect Commando. Everything that is, save the most important one; he doesn't mix."

"Have you not found out the reason?"

"We have tried everything. Sergeant Poulson is really good at putting lads at their ease but he has drawn a blank too. I will give it one more day and then we will see."

He nodded and pointed below decks. "We are going to be cosy down there. We will have to spend more time in close proximity with each other. How about we have your lads sleep aboard tonight. We will take her for a tootle around the Lizard and back; a sort of working up exercise."

"Good idea. I'll send a message to Mrs B. She hates wasting food."

We had found an old bicycle and we kept it close to the boat. "Fred, hop on the bike and tell Mrs Bailey that we won't be back for dinner tonight."

"Right sir!" He cheerfully mounted the bike and set off. Considering he was like a stick insect he was remarkably fit and tough. There was not much to him but it was all muscle!

We left in the late afternoon. There were well over thirty of us on board now and that was more than the maximum compliment when she had been an E-Boat. I shared a cabin with Alan while the NCOs, Petty Officers and leading hands shared one mess. We did not race around the coast; the purpose was to see problems. We decided to pretend that we were in a combat zone. One watch in three would be below decks. We used the same system as we had before. George's section would be off duty when Sergeant Poulson and mine were on.

So it was that, by accident Bill Leslie and Bill Hay were below decks at the same time. Sometimes things happen for a reason. When the time came for the watches to be changed Bill Leslie waved me over, "Sir, can I have a word?"

"Of course."

"If we go to the bow it will be quieter."

I was intrigued. Bill looked quite serious. We got to the bow and I said, "Well, Bill, you have my attention. What is it?"

"Skipper said that you had a problem with your new Corporal." I nodded, "Well I had a chat to him. I started off saying as how we both had the same Christian name." He saw my look and said, "I know it was lame but it was a way in. Any road up we got talking about daft stuff and I found out he was a frogman. I said as how you and me had done something similar at Dieppe and then it all came out. It seems that when he was with Number 1 Commando his Captain and him hadn't got on. Something about a girl." He shrugged, "Some women, they can be poison. I reckon I am lucky with my young lady. The point is that after that this Captain had it in for Bill. Then they were at Lulworth Cove doing rock climbing. The Captain and Bill were on the rope with a young recruit at the end. The Captain hadn't checked the young lad's knots and he fell off. Bill is a good swimmer and he dived in to try to save him but the lad was dead. By the time they were rescued the captain had spread the story that it was Bill as had not tied the rope properly. That was when they transferred him. He got the blame."

"Why didn't he say something?"

"The other officers backed the captain. They stuck together and didn't believe Bill. He hates all officers. I told him you were different. When I told him how you wouldn't leave me when I got cramp he seemed to change." He shrugged, "I just thought you ought to know sir. He's alright. He was due for promotion to sergeant before all this kicked off. I might be out of line, sir, but I reckon we ought to give him a chance."

"You mean I ought to give him a chance? Thanks Bill. I appreciate this and you have given me food for thought."

I now understood Bill Hay's dilemma. He had been betrayed by an officer and it would take a long time to heal such a mistrust. I did not have the luxury of a long time. We had a few days and then the journey to Gibraltar; that was all. I could not, in all honesty, reject him. The Commandos had let him down. I was a Commando and it as up to me to right that wrong.

I had to force myself to focus on the more important issue: the operation. Hay and his problem would have to wait. As we headed back to Falmouth the next morning, Alan and I discussed how we might operate. We had yet to be given the specifics but there would be inherent problems in operating behind enemy lines and so far from help.

With his cheroot in the corner of his mouth Alan drew an imaginary line with his finger from Gibraltar to Tunis. "That is the limit of our area of operation."

"You know more than I do."

He laughed, "A friend of mine works at the Admiralty. He is the chap who recommended me for Combined Operations. I met up with him on my last leave when all of this was being planned. After a couple of whiskies he opened up. There will be an invasion and we will be hitting the length of the coast causing mayhem and generally having fun! The point is, Tom, that it is about eight hundred and fifty miles from Gib to Tunis. The *'Lady'* has a range of eight hundred and sixty. We need somewhere along the coast where we can refuel. We need a bolt hole." He looked closely at the map. "Here is Algiers; it is as near as dammit half way between the two. There is a bay here and it looks to be largely free of people."

"What is this?"

"It looks like a lake, Reghaïa."

"How would we use the bay?"

"You see here, there is a spit of land. It is like a tiny island. It is just sixty or so yards from the beach. The point is we could shelter there and use the sand to hide the diesel. We would have to

172

arrive at night and bury the drums of fuel. We just dig them up when we need them."

"Bury?"

"We have plenty of men with broad backs. We could do that."

I leaned back, "What else do you know about the operation?"

He held up his hands, "That is all I know. The Captain friend of mine just knew of the theatre of operations and our logistical needs; nothing more."

"Then we go and see Major Foster as soon as we get back. I do not like this working in the dark. This operation seems a little too vague for my liking."

Alan laughed as he threw the stub of the cheroot over the side, "Actually Tom, I thought you and your chaps were in your element when you were in the dark."

"You might be right."

Major Foster knew that something was wrong when he looked at my face. The two of us had used a car to get to the camp as soon as we had docked. As a working up exercise it had been perfect and we could now tweak various features of the boat to make life more bearable.

"This looks ominous, Tom. Is it a mutiny?"

"No, sir but we would like more information."

"Well you have pre-empted my request for a meeting. Sergeant Major!"

Sergeant Major Dean came in with a sheaf of papers and maps. "Here you are sir. I will bring a brew in. This looks like a long meeting."

"Sit down, you chaps and make yourself comfortable. I don't need to tell you that this is top secret." We nodded.

Sergeant Major Dean brought in the tea. "I'll make sure you aren't disturbed, sir."

When the door was closed Major Foster continued, "There will be three invasion forces. One will sail from the US and will land on the Atlantic coast of Africa. The other two will sail from England. You will precede all of these troop convoys. Materiel is being gathered in Gib and you and your E-Boat will be with one of

173

the smaller convoys. It will be mutually beneficial. You can hide among the merchant ships and escorts and you can be used to protect the convoy too. Once you reach Gibraltar you will work with SOE. They have agents and operatives in Spain and Africa. There is a liaison officer, Lieutenant Hugo Ferguson. He will work exclusively with you. Whatever you want then he gets for you." Major Foster smiled as he took a swallow of the tea. "Major Fleming was impressed by your work and he has made this a high priority. If you want it then you get it."

"So Major Fleming is now in command, sir?"

"Let us say he has the ear of Lord Mountbatten and has been impressed by your work thus far."

Alan nodded, "Tom and I were saying that we need somewhere on the African mainland where we can store fuel. If we have to keep coming back to Gibraltar then it will limit our theatre of operations."

"Good idea." He scribbled something on his notepad. "I will let him know you need a small, local ship to transport fuel. Now the convoy leaves Southampton five days from now. The Quartermaster and his chaps have all of your desert gear and he has plenty of ammunition for you. Whatever you need then take now for you will be a long way from a supply base."

"We will have to forage eh sir."

"That's the spirit. Oh and one more thing. This is my last operation with you chaps. I am being sent to London to work on... well you don't need to know but I wanted to thank you both for doing all that I have asked and more." He reached over and shook our hands.

"It's been almost three years sir, that I have worked with you, it will seem strange having a different superior officer."

He leaned back and put his hands behind his head, "Well until Operation Torch is over and Africa liberated you will be operating almost without an officer to give you orders. Lieutenant Ferguson will just pass on targets sent by Major Fleming and you chaps will decide how best to carry them out."

"Who will replace you here, sir?"

"I am not certain. Probably Captain Marsden. He has tired of training recruits up in Scotland."

I breathed a sigh of relief. I had dreaded them bringing in someone new. The last time they had done that, with Captain Grenville, it had been a disaster. Major Foster stood and handed the charts and maps to Alan and the smaller bundle of documents to me.

"Tom, when you have read and memorised these destroy them. Keep it all in your head. Good luck. I daresay we will be working together again. I shall be with Lord Louis and he likes to keep an eye on you pair. Regard this as a secondment to help clear the Med, eh?"

"Yes sir and it has been a pleasure."

As we headed back to the boat Alan said, "That all sounded a little final didn't it?"

"The war is moving on but I will miss Major Foster. You could trust him."

"Well the good news is that we are our own bosses! I like that!"

"Don't forget Alan, that means we might be left to hang out on the breeze; we will not have the RAF to come at our beck and call. If this is an American operation they will give help to their own chaps first!"

"Well you are a cheery fellow aren't you? I think this will be an adventure!"

"A word of warning, Alan, I don't know about the German Navy but the Afrika Korps and Rommel are the best the Germans have. Do not underestimate them."

The next five days passed in a blur. We all had new gear to collect and then find space to store it on the boat. If we thought it was cosy before then it became positively claustrophobic when the ammunition and spare weapons were added. It was little better when we returned to the digs. Mrs Bailey was perpetually tearful. Peter's death had shaken her and now we were all leaving. Reg spent more time than enough with his arm around her shoulders. I realised, as Mrs Bailey dabbed another handkerchief to her face that I needed to speak with Mum. I took the car and headed back to the camp after dark. The duty clerk vacated the office and I telephoned home.

"This is a nice surprise Tom! Are you coming home on leave again?"

"No, Mum, it is just that I am going to be unable to write or telephone for some time." I heard the hint of a sigh at the other end. "Nothing for you to worry about but I didn't want you fretting because I couldn't write you a letter."

There was a pause, "Does your Dad know?"

"No, I shall telephone him after this." There was another silence. "Are you all right Mum?"

I heard the catch in her voice, which she covered with a cough, "I am fine. Don't worry about me. I should be used to this by now. At least I get a phone call now. In the Great War I never knew what your father was up to. Thanks for telephoning."

The operator came on, "This line should be used only for important calls."

Mum snapped back, "And you shouldn't be listening!"

There was a click. "I had better ring Dad. You take care Mum. Love you."

I heard a sob and she said, brokenly, "And I love you my dear boy!"

Dad's call was easier and more businesslike. "I think I know what this is about son. You take care but I think you will be able to handle it. I'll try to keep an eye on you, from afar so to speak."

"Mum was upset."

"She always is. I will be home again this weekend. You watch out for yourself. You can't do it all on your own."

For some reason I felt empty as I headed back to the digs. The phone calls had felt like goodbye and final. Was it a sign?

Ours was a small convoy. There were ten merchant vessels. Some had tanks, some fuel and the others had the vital supplies that Malta, Gibraltar and the invasion force would need. The escorts were led by the destroyer *'Viperous'*, two corvettes, *'Jasmine'* and *'Columbine'*, a tug and us. Fifteen ships and we had to navigate the coast of France which was filled with German aeroplanes and submarines. Alan was summoned aboard the destroyer to be briefed by Captain Barraclough, the escort commander.

Alan had mixed feelings when he returned. "He seems like a good bloke. He is regular Navy and not Wavy Navy but we have orders to follow and a position in the convoy. *'Viperous'* sails at the front with the two corvettes on each flank. We are at the rear with the tug. We travel at the speed of my dowager aunt!"

I laughed, "What did you expect? Free rein to roam the seas."

"It would be nice!"

The merchant ships sailed in two parallel lines. We had Coastal Command air cover for half of the voyage. Sunderlands would take it in turns to watch for submarines. I saw why we were at the rear, even if Alan couldn't. We had no ASDIC. We could not spot submarines. Our job was to use our speed and rescue any who were torpedoed. We had scrambling nets rigged and ready to be used. I had prevailed upon Alan to have Bill Leslie and Bill Hay on the same watch. I was keen for a bond to be built there. I trusted my old comrade. He would make Corporal Hay less wary. Granddad had been a horseman and he had told me how you had to be both patient and gentle with a skittish horse which had been frightened. Perhaps it would be the same with Bill Hay.

I had done this journey twice before but that had been in a Sunderland and over with in eight hours. By the end of the first day we could still see the coast of England behind us. Admittedly it was a thin smudge on the horizon but it was a warning of our speed. We travelled with gun crews closed up. We had taken the other two MG 39/41 from the stores. It would be easier for us to replace that ammunition than .303 and we knew we might need the firepower of the powerful German guns. We had set them up on the bridge and moved the Lewis guns further aft. We bristled with weapons. We even had depth charges.

It was day two of our voyage, when we were well out to sea that we had our first scare. A Kondor circled high in the sky. The Sunderland bravely climbed to scare it away but by the time it had reached the correct altitude the German had gone. Our position was marked. Would it be a wolf pack or a flock of bombers?

We were answered three hours later. The Sunderland had just returned north and its relief had not yet arrived. We were without air cover. Despite our captain altering course the Ju 88s found us. There were five of them. The yeoman said, "Captain D orders zig zag pattern C sir."

"Righto. Let's hope the tug knows his right from his left or this could be a short voyage." The tug also had antiaircraft capabilities. This would be an early trial of our ability to defend ourselves.

I wondered if they would bomb us from a height or dive bomb us. If they had dropped their bombs above the range of our guns I am certain that they would have done some damage. Perhaps they wanted the glory of a guaranteed kill. They dived in line astern. That, in itself, helped us. They could only attack one column of merchantmen.

"Stand by lads."

Crowe and Hay were on one machine gun with Lowe and Hewitt on the other. Both crews were keen to show their skills. The pilots made a steeper dive than I expected. It increased their speed and made them a harder target to hit. At the same time it gave them a shorter time over the target and they had to be good to successfully hit a ship.

"Fire!"

The heavier sound of the Hotchkiss and Oerlikon was punctuated by the staccato German machine guns and the steady rip of the Lewis gun. The Germans fired their forward machine guns as they descended. I saw men falling from the gun emplacement on the *'MS. Corfe Castle'*. Then the bombs fell. The first bomber straddled the next ship in the line, *'SS. North Queen'*. As it pulled up it flew into the full force of the destroyer's armament. Its tail was blown off and it spiralled into the sea. Any thoughts of cheering were ended as the crew fired at the second and third bombers. This time we managed a hit on the third bomber which began to smoke. The second one, however, managed to hit *'MS. Corfe Castle'* with two of its bombs. Luckily it was carrying neither ammunition nor petrol but there was a mighty explosion. It damaged it but the blow did not appear to be mortal.

The two corvettes had closed in a little and their cross fire brought down the fifth bomber. With two shot down and one damaged the other three limped east.

"Message from *'Viperous'* sir. We are to escort the tug and see if *'MS. Corfe Castle'* needs assistance. We are to follow when the *'MS. Corfe Castle'* is repaired."

"Acknowledge." Alan turned to me. If there are any subs in the area then we will be a sitting duck. None of us have ASDIC."

The *'MS. Corfe Castle'* was on fire but I saw that the hands had it under control. Alan took the helm and he circled the tug and the merchantman as they assessed the damage. I saw the relief Sunderland to the north as the rest of the convoy disappeared south. Wacker was on the radio and he said, "The tug's captain has asked the Sunderland to land and pick up the wounded." He looked up at Alan, "They have six dead and four wounded but they reckon they can proceed under their own power. They don't need a tow."

"Good. Signal them and tell the tug's captain to lead when they are ready. We will protect the rear of our little convoy."

We had to wait until the Sunderland had landed and edged close to the *'MS. Corfe Castle'*. The wounded were transferred and the Sunderland left us. We would have four hours of daylight and no air cover. If the Ju 88s came back we would be helpless.

It was a relief when darkness fell and we were safe from aerial attack. We now had to worry about submarines. They would be able to travel on the surface and would be able to keep up with the tug and the merchantman. Alan did not zig zag. He had Symons on the radar keeping watch for the convoy. The tug and the *'MS. Corfe Castle'* used as much speed as they could. When dawn broke we were weary but all three of us were still safe and, in the distance we could see the smoke from the convoy.

I saw a light flashing from the *'Wingfield Castle'*. "Sir, message from the tug! There is a submarine on the surface. It is trailing the convoy."

179

Alan grinned, "Tell the tug to take charge. We are going after this one. Action stations!"

We had been fitted with four depth charges and they were mounted at the stern. We had both thought them a waste but now we realised they might prove their worth. Alan used every bit of horsepower at his disposal and we leapt through the water as we overtook our slower consorts. I used the binoculars and spied the deadly submarine. It appeared to be three miles astern of the convoy. No doubt it would submerge soon and attack the now unprotected rear.

"Harris, hold your fire until he starts to submerge."

"Right sir!"

"Johnson, get ready with those depth charges. Set them so that they explode deep enough not to blow off our stern."

"Aye aye skipper."

Later I wondered if the lookout on the U-Boat had seen us and thought that we were an E-boat. Whatever the reason we were five hundred yards from it before they realised that we flew the White Ensign and it began to submerge. Harris was ready and the Oerlikon pounded away. The two MG 39/41s in the tubes also opened up and I saw three men fall from the conning tower and into the sea before the submarine began to sink beneath the waves. The Oerlikon's shells continued to punch holes in the conning tower and then it was gone.

"Stand by Johnson!"

"Aye aye skipper."

Alan looked astern and shouted, "Loose depth charges!"

Johnson sent first two and then a few seconds later the last two. There were two water spouts and I felt the hull move as the underwater concussion struck us. I had experienced this from the other side and I felt pity for the crew. Alan spun the wheel and cut the revs to sail over the water we had just bombed. There was nothing save the remains of three German bodies. There would be little to examine. We circled until the tug and merchantman caught up with us.

"Do you think we got him?"

"Hard to say. The water looks a little oily but ... We have no more depth charges. Let's catch up with the convoy. Even if we didn't get him he will go deep to avoid more depth charges."

Captain Barraclough was delighted with our news. We had saved him from attack and driven off a deadly predator. For my part I was just pleased to be back with the three bigger warships.

When we finally reached Gibraltar we had survived another two desultory attacks. One was by a Kondor and did little damage. The other had been Ju 88s and *'SS. North Queen'* had been holed. She had to be towed into the harbour by the tug. The first part of our operation had been successful. Alan had done his part. The next was up to my men and me.

Chapter 16

Lieutenant Ferguson was much older than I expected. He was in his late thirties. He had a pair of wire framed glasses perched on the end of his nose; he had a habit of peering over them. I saw he had a Commando flash on his battle dress and he had a Commando dagger. As he came towards us I noticed he had a slight limp and his hand looked to have a slight shake. He was, however, the most cheerful man I had ever met. He exuded joy. He stood grinning as we stepped ashore, "My dear fellow, we have been following you on your journey. Quite an adventure. I believe it bodes well for our own particular venture. Now I am afraid that accommodation is at a premium. You will have to stay aboard your boat and berths are even more precious. Once you have loaded your stores you must anchor with the other ships. Sorry about this. Still you won't be here for long will you?" He saw my face. "Oh I am sorry, I haven't stopped talking since you arrived and I have yet to introduce myself. How rude! That's what this war does to you."

I took the pause to grab his hand, "I am Tom Harsker and this is Alan Jorgenson."

"Pleased to meet you. I am Hugo Ferguson." He nodded towards his Commando flash. "I was in the Commandoes, albeit briefly. Wounded in St. Nazaire. German grenade went off and... well I can't move quite as quickly as I once did and this damned hand shakes so much I spill more gin than I drink! Still, must be positive. I am, at least, alive. Most of my chaps are either in the bag or dead. I was grateful that I was chosen for this job. So anything you want, I am your man."

Alan took the brief pause to dive in. "Did you get the ship we asked for and fuel?"

He looked around and said, "Follow me! We shall go to my nest where we can talk a little easier."

He led us through the stores and warehouses. We went to a set of rickety stairs and we climbed them to his nest. He used three keys to unlock it, "Can't be too careful! The locals would have the pennies off a dead man's eyes!"

It was barely more than a cubby hole. If he was comfortable here then he was a born submariner. It was, however, both neat and organised. There were three chairs and a map of North Africa pinned to the wall. I also saw a radio transmitter. It looked to be powerful.

He took off his beret. He had a domed, bald pate. "Take a seat." He waited until we were comfortable. "Now I have a couple of boats in mind. They are locals. One is a Spaniard and one an Arab. Personally I would recommend the Arab. Many of the Spanish are a little too close to the Germans for my liking. I can take you to see them this afternoon. Now the diesel you wanted was a little easier to get than I would have thought. That was how I met the Spaniard; he is supplying the diesel. Many of the Spanish cars use it. It costs us a pretty penny but..."

"And we can get more?"

"Oh yes. Major Fleming made it quite clear that money was no object."

"Good. And targets?"

"The Major wanted you to get your base sorted out first and to familiarise yourself with the area." He leaned forward. "I have heard that the invasion will be in the first week of November."

"You heard?"

He laughed, "Well I worked it out. Security is very tight." He saw my expression. "Before the war I was a lecturer in logic at Manchester University. I have that sort of brain. I love crossword puzzles and all that, you know?"

"I had a place at Manchester, engineering, then the war came up."

"Well you take up that place after the war! We will need engineers to rebuild everything that we have destroyed. You know there are some philosophers who say that we need wars so that we can move our civilisation on. I mean would we have aeroplanes which can cross the Atlantic without the bombers developed in the Great War? Gives one pause for thought eh?"

Alan lit a cheroot, "It certainly does, Professor!" That was how he got his nickname. He was always Prof to us.

He pointed to the cigar in Alan's mouth. "If you get through many of those I can help you out. The Spanish are very fond of them!"

"Then you and I will be the best of friends."

"I think we should meet these two captains. Perhaps we can use them both. That way it keeps our options open."

Lieutenant Ferguson nodded, "Very logical. You would have made a good student!"

We descended the stairs and he locked up again. He led us towards an area known as Campamento. "This is where Captain Garcia can be found. His is the rather dilapidated looking boat." He then pointed further around the bay, closer to the Spanish side. There was an Arab Dhow. "That is Captain Al-Muezzin's ship. I favour that one for it is silent. His crew however..."

"Don't worry about that. Let us meet this Captain Garcia."

Captain Garcia was a tubby, barrel of a man. Like his boat he looked dirty and dilapidated but he was friendly enough. He spoke good English.

"These are the officers I told you about, captain."

"Ah and you want me to take some diesel somewhere for you?" We nodded, "Very mysterious! I am guessing that it is somewhere south of here and there may be danger along the way."

Alan said, "That might be true but you have my boat to protect you."

"Ah, you mean that converted E-Boat I saw arrive not long ago. A fine ship."

That immediately set the alarm bells ringing. If he knew then who else knew? The Spanish Captain saw my look, "I am afraid

184

that if you wished to stay hidden you should have chosen a different port. Algeciras is filled with spies and those who favour the Germans."

Alan nodded, "Then it is a good job that this will be our only visit. We need the diesel right now and we wish to leave tonight."

"Tonight? That will cost extra."

"Why?"

He looked at me as though I was stupid, "Supply and demand."

"In that case thank you, Captain, but we will find another boat."

He gave me a sly look. "And where will you get more diesel from?"

"We do not need to get any more. Our friend here has already purchased it from you has he not?"

I saw his eyes as he worked out which would be the most profitable for him. He smiled, "Let us not fall out over this. I will take it tonight for you for the price we agreed."

"Good and we may need as much again in the next weeks." It was my turn to smile. "If we are happy about your services then you will be employed again."

He did not look so cocky now. "I am certain that you will be happy."

Alan nodded to me, "We will meet you one mile east of Trinity Lighthouse at eight thirty."

"We will be there."

As we returned to our boat with Lieutenant Ferguson he said, "Well negotiated. I will speak with the Arab about the next cargo. Do you know where you will be using as a base?"

"West of Algiers. If the Germans intervene then we need to be able to interfere with their plans as much as possible."

He shook his head, "It will take too long for Captain Garcia to get that far. You need somewhere closer. That will be better for the radio too."

"We will test it on the way out. When we discover the range then we will sail back to that point when we need to report. We will arrange times and call signals."

"Good."

The '*Lady*' was bobbing in the bay and we took a Royal Navy tender out to her. The ratings were instructed to wait while we went aboard and gave Hugo a tour. It was important he knew the layout of the boat. We had found that made for better communication. We introduced him to Wacker and Scouse. We then scoured the charts for a closer base. Hugo's mind proved invaluable.

"Here, five miles east of Sidi Abderrahmane, it is a small bay. It looks quiet enough and you should be able to get there by dawn."

"It looks fine to me. We will use this one but we will still scout out the other one as well."

By the time he left, at seven thirty, we had the signals all arranged. We would return, if all went well with our patrol, in a week by which time we hoped that Major Fleming would have come up with suitable targets.

Captain Garcia was late. That worried me. However, when he hailed us he seemed quite happy that we had a night's sailing ahead of us. We did not tell him our destination. Alan fumed all the way east. The Spaniard's ship was slow and Alan fretted about us being caught at sea during daylight.

"Alan, we are going to be seen. The problem comes if someone sees us burying the diesel. If we can get there before dark then we can complete our plan. Besides the Spaniard is not as slow as you think. We have two hundred and fifty miles to go. It will be close but we should make it."

"You are right." He looked up. We had lowered the White Ensign. We would not fly under false colours but we would not advertise our nationality. If the enemy was confused then so much the better.

Alan decided to test the engines of the Spanish ship by increasing his speed. The Spaniard kept up. We passed Sidi Abderrahmane when it was still dark but it would not be for long. Captain Garcia was less than happy. "You did not tell me it was this far!"

"You did not ask! Now let us get the barrels ashore."

"And how do I do that? There is no jetty."

We had already thought this through. Our men had the dinghies already manhandled in the water. "Just back into the shallows and drop them off your stern. My men will do the rest."

"You English are mad!"

We also backed the *'Lady'* around. Alan would use the engines to make a tide and push the barrels ashore. The hard part would come once they were ashore but Hugo had found us a good beach. It was flat and we could roll them. The spit was larger than it had looked on the aerial photograph. Even better was the fact that this beach was connected to the shore by a narrow spit of sand. There was little tide here in the Mediterranean but I discovered that the connecting sand was sometimes submerged. It made it even better. There was no reason for anyone to visit it. In the dark the Spanish captain would not see that but Alan had brought us, by dead reckoning, to the perfect landing site.

Although the barrels sank a little they floated enough for them to be pushed by the engines and the ten men in the dinghies. Others waited on the beach and were already digging a hole. It was a big hole and would almost be as big as the beach. It took but fifteen minutes to off load the barrels and then the Spaniard headed west, eager to be away from the dawn and German or Vichy patrols. Once he had gone we left a skeleton crew on board our boat and went to help bury the barrels.

Dawn was now breaking. A faint glow of pink tinged sky appeared in the east. It helped us to see what we were doing but still prevented prying eyes from watching us. The seven barrels took a big hole and I worried that we would not be able to cover them. The bottom of the hole kept filling with water but we persevered. Alan pointed to the water, lapping around the spit. "This will work out fine, Tom. Don't worry. We have covered it higher than it had been and spread the surplus sand around the sides. The sea and the wind will complete our task. The wet sand mean the barrels will sink a little. Besides we will use all of this diesel in less than two weeks."

187

By the time the sun had come up we had finished. We were exhausted but the job was done and seven barrels had been buried. The eighth barrel was used to top up our tanks so that they were full again and then we headed out to sea. When we were six miles offshore we lowered the empty barrel into the sea and allowed it to fill up with water. It did not completely sink but it was harder to see. The currents would take it away from our spit.

Alan set a course for our original bay to the east of Algiers. We had a week to become familiar with the coast and it started that moment. The coastal road looked to be mercifully free of any military traffic. Our lookouts scanned the skies but saw no Luftwaffe aircraft. It was the most peaceful place we had seen. As far as I could tell the invasion would be able to walk into Algeria with no problems whatsoever.

When we passed Algiers we saw the first real military presence; part of the French fleet. Vichy were here. A couple of Vichy fighters were scrambled and they inspected us half an hour after we had passed the port. Although the gun crews stood to we did not fire. They flew over us, unable to decide what we were. When we continued east they stopped wasting fuel and returned home.

"That was easy."

Alan shook his head. "Next time it will not be so easy, my friend. Next time there will be a launch or two as well." He looked at his watch. It will be dark in an hour or two. What say we find a quiet bay and let the men have some rest."

"A good idea and we try out the radio."

We had planned on testing every three hours until midnight. Hugo would be listening then. Alan headed north east and he swung us around so that we headed back towards the coast. When Wacker tried the radio he heard nothing. The range was too far. The darkening sky behind us helped to hide us and we edged our way to Reghaïa. When we reached the beach we found our original choice had been a good one. The coastal highway had to take a mile long detour around the lake. The land between the beach and the lake was swampy and covered in mosquitoes. People would avoid it.

We pushed on while it was dark and used the night to get closer to Tunis. Radar helped us to keep close to the land without risking the rocks and shallows. When we were a few hours from Tunis we headed closer to the beach. Alan dropped an anchor.

My section and myself went to bed for a couple of hours. We would be up in the night to investigate the land and the highway. This would be the main route for the Germans to use to fight the invasion. It would be a good place for us to hold up the Germans. Just before we went to our hammocks I sought out Corporal Hay.

"Corporal, I would like you with us on this patrol."

"Certainly sir, do you mind me asking why?"

I smiled, "Let us say I wanted a different perspective on matters. Scouse and Ken are good lads but they are young and do not have your experience."

He smiled, as though relieved, "I would be delighted, sir."

We left at four a.m. I wanted to get to the coast road and see its condition. We took just hand guns and grenades. I wanted speed and not firepower. We were rowed ashore in the dinghy which then returned to the boat. We double timed it west across the rough ground. It was not as swampy as it had appeared in the aerial photographs,. Ken led. This was his element. He had the ability to find the best route.

We only had six hundred yards to run before we found the road and, at the same time, some huts with Arabs within. Dogs barked but no one came out. Had we been in France I would have turned and headed back to the boat but this was Vichy France and we had seen no signs of soldiers for many miles. We ran through the huts and found ourselves at a small cape.

"Let's explore this headland eh? It is close to the road."

There were no houses and the headland rose a little. Corporal Hay, take Fletcher and explore the beach. See what it is like. Ken you come with me." We returned to the road. "Tell me Ken, if you were going to blow the road would this be a good place?"

He went to the road surface and picked up the stones. He took out his dagger and hit the tarmac with the hilt. It crumbled a little.

Then he turned and looked at the headland where Bill and Scouse were busy looking at the sand and the shore.

He nodded, " The road surface is rubbish sir. And the road takes a ninety degree turn. If we was to wait up there in the trees then we could explode the road when something was coming this way." He smiled. "That is why you sent the Corp to check out the escape route." I nodded. "You worked this out for yourself sir."

"It is always good to get a second opinion and now we shall get a third."

Fletcher and Hay had returned, "Well?"

"No rocks sir. The beach is fairly shallow. We could wade out and there is good cover in the trees. Nice spot for an ambush."

"Ambush?"

"Yes sir. Mine the road and set off a charge when lorries or tanks come down and then have it away on our toes." He saw Ken grinning, "What? Have I said something daft, sir?"

"Don't get defensive Corporal; Private Shepherd here just came up with the self same plan. Great minds and all that! Well done. Let's get back to the boat." I saw the hint of a smile on Bill Hay's face. He was thawing.

As we passed through the huts there were villagers. They stared at us. It was only then that I remembered Arab clothes. That was something Lieutenant Ferguson could acquire for us. We boarded the boat at eight and Alan headed east. We had the gun crews closed up and all were ready for action. We were getting closer to Tunisia and that meant German patrols.

One of the hands handed me some tea as I boarded and I went to the bridge. "Well?"

"There is a headland just west of where we spent the night. It is a perfect place for an ambush." I pointed to the shore. "That is German territory."

Alan grinned, "That doesn't mean to say we can't do something there too."

I took out the map we had of Tunisia. The main road was the one we left when we took the track over the mountains. It would have to be here, Tabarka, it is a crossroads and the coastal road is just yards from the sea."

"I will take her in and have a look and then we will head west again."

It took another hour or so to reach the port and, to our dismay, we saw the German flag flying and, even worse, boats in the harbour. Alan idled the boat while we scanned the defences. A daylight attack would be out of the question but the road was clearly visible and appeared to be very close to the sea. He pointed to the jetty, "There looks to be fuel there. We might be able to nip in and steal some."

One of the lookouts said, "Eh up sir! Jerry is on the move. I can see E-boats. One has fired his engines."

Alan needed no urging, he spun the wheel around and gunned the motors. Two E-Boats raced from the harbour towards us. We had a five hundred yard start but they both had forward firing guns. They both made the mistake of firing as soon as they left the harbour. That was a major error of judgement. Both boats were heeling and the shots were wildly inaccurate. Two waterspouts appeared on our port side.

Bill Leslie shook his head, "Amateurs!"

"Are you going to show them a clean pair of heels, Alan?"

He shook his head, "A lady does not show everything on a first date, Tom. We will leave that surprise for another time. We will lose them but only slowly."

"Isn't that a risk? What if they call in air support?"

"By the time they have scrambled aeroplanes we should be losing the E-Boats already."

He was right and I remembered the time it had taken for aeroplanes to come and search for us. I stuck my head in the radio shack. "Wacker, have we been able to contact Gibraltar yet?"

"No sir. We need a better radio. This is clapped out."

"Keep trying. It would be handy to know when we can call in the cavalry!"

I took my mug of tea and went to the stern. The Germans had decided to conserve their ammunition but were using all the power at their disposal to catch us. Their captains would wonder what an enemy vessel was doing here so far from a British base. They began to increase the distance between the two boats so that they could cut off any move we made away from them. We were increasing our lead. By the time I had finished my tea they were a further fifty yards behind us. I knew our boat well enough to know that Alan still had more power available to him.

I returned to the bridge. "The problem with this speed is that we are using more juice. We will need to refuel."

"That is all right isn't it? I mean we can check out the coast from Algiers west as we head back to Gib. We have two targets already and we can report the lack of Vichy forces along the coast."

"You are probably right."

"Aeroplanes, to the east sir. Three of them. They look like FW 190s."

"It looks like we have outstayed our welcome."

"I'll get my chaps to add their firepower too." I went aft, "Sergeant Poulson, get the lads on deck with their Thompsons. We will make life difficult for these Jerries."

"Sir."

I went below decks to deposit my mug and pick up my own gun. The three aircraft were much closer when I returned. They were diving to attack. The only guns which could be not brought to bear were the two German guns in the tubes and the Oerlikon which would have to wait until they had passed the bridge. I felt the German shells as they hit our stern. I felt us slow. It was only a slight decrease in speed but a glance at Alan told me that he had felt it too. I would have to worry about that later. We opened fire. It was a wall of bullets we threw up and we got lucky. A bullet must have hit the engine for it began to smoke and, more importantly, drifted across the line of the second 190.

We, however, were still slowing. A hand raced to the bridge, "Sir, Chief says that an oil line to Number Two engine has been cut. He is repairing it but we are down to one engine for a bit."

"That means the E-Boats can begin to catch us. Do your best Tom. Keep the Luftwaffe away for a while."

"We will."

The second 190 roared overhead having failed to fire a single shot. The third flew into the firepower of the whole E-Boat and nine Thompsons. Perhaps the sudden deceleration caught him off guard or maybe we had a better gun platform but our bullets began to hit him even as his shells went over the bridge. It was the Oerlikon which made the kill. A shell hit the 190's engine as it passed overhead and the aircraft disintegrated just above us. The E-Boat was showered in falling debris.

Now that there was just one aeroplane Alan had more options. We watched the wounded bird limp home as the last FW 190 prepared to attack us.

I am going to turn to starboard when he attacks, be ready!"

A chorus of voices shouted, "Aye sir!"

His bullets struck the stern and then, suddenly, Alan yanked the wheel over and the German's bullets sliced through the water. This time the German was hit by many bullets as the full armament of the E-boat came into play. When he banked and headed east we saw smoke pouring from his engine. He would be lucky to reach land. We had no time for self congratulation. Two waterspouts appeared on either side of us. Alan threw the *'Lady'* to port. "I hope the engineer can work miracles."

Fred Emerson said, "Sir, can I go and give a hand?"

"Of course. The more the merrier." As he raced below decks I said, "Get the grenade launcher. It might come in handy!"

We had carried a grenade launcher since St. Nazaire. We had yet had a chance to use it but this was one. The two E-Boats were now six hundred yards away and closing.

Our Hotchkiss was firing in reply but he had two targets. The Germans had one. It was Alan's skill and judgement which stopped them from making a decisive hit. Some of their bullets hit the *'Lady'* and the crew were injured by splinters but there was nothing fatal. They were five hundred yards away and closing. It would be a matter of time.

Alan shouted, "Tom!"

I ran to the bridge. "Yes Alan?"

"Are they still a hundred yards apart?"

I glanced aft, "About that."

He shouted. Right lads, I am going to do a complete turn and come up on the southernmost boat. The other won't be able to fire. I want the bridge and the forrard gun decimating."

Sergeant Poulson had returned with the rifle, "This is only good for a hundred yards, sir."

"That might be all we need. Crowe, you act as loader."

Alan shouted, "Turning to port, now!"

The two Germans had closed to within three hundred yards but the savage manoeuvre caught them by surprise. Their shells hit empty water. Alan kept the full lock on as we hurtled towards their mid ships. The bigger guns did little damage but we had two guns in the tubes and every other weapon firing at the bridge and the forward gun. There were simply too many bullets for us not to hit. Then I heard the hiss as the grenade launcher fired. We were abeam of our enemy when the grenade exploded above the bridge. The concussion and debris struck the side of our boat but it made the German veer sharply to starboard towards its consort.

"Sergeant send another over!"

The second grenade exploded at the stern of the E-boat. The crew who had been about to fire were thrown from the gun. Alan gunned the motor and we headed west. The smoke from the E-boat gave us a little cover and it took some minutes for the undamaged E-Boat to continue the pursuit. We had regained our lead. There was five hundred yards of clear water.

A rating stuck his head out of the engine room hatch. "Number Two engine repaired, sir. You can have full power again,"

Within minutes the E-boat which was pursuing us began to drop back. It did not take long for him to give up his chase and go back to his damaged consort. We had survived. It had been close but that was the difference between success and failure.

Chapter 17

We reached our supply base after dark. The journey under the glare of the sun had been nerve wracking. It was only later that we realised the Germans had had to withdraw units from the western Mediterranean to support Rommel in the east. They were thinly stretched. We dug up a barrel and refilled our tanks.

The engineer could not praise Fred Emerson highly enough. "I tell you what sir, if he ever fancies transferring there is a berth for him in my engine room any day."

Fred was quite embarrassed by the attention. "If it is all the same to you, sir, I will stay with Lieutenant Harsker."

Hewitt and the SBA were kept busy with minor wounds and injuries. One of the Engineer's men had been scalded by steam from a broken steam pipe and one of the gunners had lost two fingers. It was on his left hand and not life threatening but both of our medics were keen to get him to a hospital and have it looked at by a doctor.

While we refuelled Wacker tried to contact Hugo again. "I am getting something sir but nothing I can make out."

Alan nodded and threw away the stub of his cheroot, "We will head back anyway. I'd like to get the oil line repaired properly and get the wounded seen to. Besides we did what we set out to do."

"You are right."

We left for home at eleven o'clock. We had a long night ahead of us. At twelve Wacker shouted triumphantly, "Sir, I have Gib. Lieutenant Ferguson just responded."

"Good. Tell him we are on our way home."

Bill Leslie had the boat and Alan and I joined Wacker, "What was the strength like?"

"Pretty good sir. I think that our supply base is just too far away but if he could get higher, then that might make a difference. He might be getting interference from high buildings and the like around him."

I remembered our rendezvous point. "If he could use Trinity Lighthouse that might make all the difference."

Alan nodded, "Worth a try anyway."

We reached Gibraltar just after dawn. This time there were no berths to be had. Alan took it upon himself to sail up the eastern side of the island and tie up close to the Rock. "We need somewhere for the chief to work. This will do. I will get her camouflaged. You had better report to the Professor and tell him what we discovered."

"Scouse, you come with me. Sergeant Poulson see if you can rig up some shelters ashore."

"Sir."

As we made our way through the town we noticed a buzz about the place. The word 'Alamein' was in the air. I knew better than to ask one of the locals. I would only receive rumours. Lieutenant Ferguson would be able to fill us in. As we climbed the stairs I realised that the office still had the curtains closed. The door was locked. I nodded to Scouse who took out his lock picks and had the door open in seconds. Lieutenant Ferguson was slumped over his table. I feared the worst until I saw his body rising and falling as he breathed. He had fallen asleep.

I pointed to the kettle. Scouse filled it and lit the gas. I opened the curtains so that I could see the map. Hugo slept on. He had lost that edge which Commandos on active service have. He had been on the beach too long. I would have been awake the moment Scouse's lock pick had entered the lock. Scouse was silent as he put tea in the pot and then poured the boiling water on top. I saw him wrinkle his nose as he picked up the sour milk. Lieutenant Ferguson was not as fastidious as my men.

Scouse pointed to the milk and the street, I nodded. Fletcher left.

I found some pins and I went to the map and stuck them in at the places we had found. I was sitting and looking at the map when Scouse returned with a fresh jug of milk. He poured the three teas. I tapped Hugo on the shoulder. He sat up with a jerk and a worried expression on his face. "How on earth...."

I smiled, "You were a Commando, you should know we can pick any lock."

"I was not certain if you would radio again at three. I must have fallen asleep."

"Well you have a cuppa and I will fill you in." I told him what we had done and pointed to the places on the map.

Hugo became quite excited. He leapt to his feet and stuck a pin in close to the Egyptian border, "General Montgomery is fighting a battle here at El-Alamein. It started three days ago and he appears to be winning. Germans are falling back. It is still not over but we have destroyed much of Rommel's armour." He jabbed a finger at the coast road, close to Tabarka. "If you could cut the coast road here it would mean the Germans would have to go further south to repel the Americans when they land." He leaned forward and said, "An American General landed in North Africa while you were away and made contact with some Vichy generals. It looks like not all of the landings will be opposed. Jerry will have to divert some of his forces west or he will lose the whole of North Africa."

"That is great news. The people at home will be delighted. This is the first victory in a long time. After Dieppe..."

"I know."

"Wacker and Scouse here had an idea, Hugo. If you were to move to Trinity lighthouse then you might have a better signal." I smiled, "And it might be more secure than here."

He laughed, "You are right. I should have thought of that. It is logical. I will arrange it. Do you need more fuel?"

"Just enough to fill our tanks. We still have six barrels of the stuff. Besides Alan reckons we can live off the land so to speak and get our supplies from Jerry."

"A little cheeky but I like it. Where are you berthed?"

"Hard by the Rock."

"Good. I will get a message to Major Fleming and bring your orders. How long will it take you to repair?"

"I am not certain but I would think we could leave by tonight. We can resupply if you can get the diesel."

"I have it already and I can easily get it by road to you."

We left and made our way back to the *'Lady'*. The news we brought back would give heart to the crew. This was the first chink in the German armour. Montgomery had done what had seemed impossible just a month or so earlier; he had beaten Rommel!

The word had already got out. Those who worked close to the Rock also had the news although it was somewhat more sensationalized than the reality. Many said that Montgomery had advanced to the gates of Tripoli and that Rommel himself had been killed. We knew that to be a lie. It would take many days to even reach Tripoli, let alone mop up the soldiers who would defend every inch of the desert. It showed just how much people were desperate for good news when they blew such rumours out of proportion to the reality.

The repairs were going well and, when the diesel arrived, we began to fill her up straight away. We were able to replenish all of the ammunition we had used except for the German. The four machine guns had performed better than the Lewis guns but we would have to husband our ammunition from now on. It was not until four o'clock in the afternoon that Lieutenant Ferguson arrived.

Alan gave him a cheery wave as he collected his papers from the commandeered car. "Afternoon Prof!"

Hugo was not put out by the soubriquet and waved cheerily back. "I have instructions from our lord and master!"

I shook my head. His sense of security left much to be desired! Once aboard he took over the mess and spread his maps all over it. That, in itself, was unnecessary, we had maps of our own but I saw that these maps were covered in his scribbles.

"I have permission to move into Trinity Lighthouse. The chaps there weren't that happy about it but Major Fleming has a great deal of pull, apparently. I have some REME fellows moving it over now. You were right, Tom, much more secure!" He looked at Alan. "And the repairs?"

"We can sail tomorrow if you like."

"Good. Major Fleming wants you to sail to Tunis and reconnoitre the defences there."

He shook his head, "It would be easier to get aeroplanes from Malta to do that or even a fast boat like ours. We would be on the limit of our fuel."

"Malta is still besieged. They are fighting for their lives. The LRDG can get as far as Tripoli but we need to know if they are bringing reinforcements in from Italy through Tunis."

I nodded, "And if they are then you could use the RAF to bomb Tunis harbour."

"Exactly. I am afraid that the RAF is at full stretch. The *'Lucky Lady'* is the ace in the hole. Major Fleming wants you to disguise her as an E-Boat and fly the German flag."

Alan shrugged, "It was why we were created in the first place but it will take some pulling off. We have already bloodied their noses."

An idea flashed into my head. I had a vision of the E-boat we had attacked. "We use the E-Boat's number. The one we damaged. I would bet it is still being repaired. Even if it only buys us minutes that can sometimes be enough. We just change one digit; the last one."

"What was it?"

"S-265."

"Right, I'll get the lads to painting it. We will be the S-266. Prof, any chance of getting us some coal scuttle helmets? Even two or three would be handy. It would make the gunners look

200

more realistic." He flourished his captured German hat like a conjuror. "I have mein own disguise!" He affected a German accent. Hugo laughed.

"Any other orders, Hugo?"

"When you have scouted that out Major Fleming wants you to sabotage the road from Tabarka and, if you can damage the port facilities. I know it is not a big port but as the Germans fall back such ports will become invaluable for landing reinforcements."

"And we might be able to steal some fuel and ammo." He rubbed his hands. "I, for one, have had enough of running away. It will be good to hit back."

We left the next day, just after noon. News was coming from Egypt that despite their best efforts the Afrika Korps was losing in the war of attrition. Montgomery had shorter supply lines and his losses could be made good. Rommel's were having to come from the west and the RAF was wreaking havoc with their convoys. They were having to move them at night time. It acted as a spur to us. We headed east flagless. That would change once we had refuelled. We reached our beach at eleven. We had conserved fuel and cruised economically. Our diesel drums were intact and we emptied another one. Alan then had the diesel from one barrel transferred to the empty one and we took half a barrel to allow us to refuel at sea. It was a clever idea. We could just abandon the empty barrel; it would not lead anyone to our supply base.

We left before dawn and flew under the German flag. Hugo had found four German helmets and the men on the Oerlikon wore them. Alan wore his German officer's cap rakishly slanted to the side and, with a cheroot in his mouth, he looked every inch the Teuton. Hugo had brought a box of fifty aboard when he had brought the charts. We kept well out to sea as we passed Tabarka. Even so someone must have seen us for a Fieseler flew overhead and then descended, albeit gingerly, to give us the once over. Alan waved cheerily. The spotter seemed satisfied and flew south, back to land.

201

"Well that is the first hurdle out of the way. Of course once they realise we are a Trojan Horse then they will come at us mob handed."

"Probably."

For my men the return to the coast west of Tunis brought back memories. Peter Groves still lay there. Had they buried him or just left his body for the carrion? I dismissed such morbid and redundant thoughts from my mind. We had a job to do. This part was down to Alan but once we had done it then we had our own task to complete. I took my men below decks. It stopped them remembering our last visit too.

"We have two jobs to do. First we land and mine the road; we use time charges and then we have to move into the port itself and support Lieutenant Jorgenson when he attacks. We hope that our sudden appearance behind them may well give us the edge we need. Scouse, we will be taking the radio. We need to coordinate the attacks."

He groaned, "Oh great. That's just what I need; a ton weight!"

Sergeant Poulson laughed, "You know what they say, Scouse if you can't take a joke..."

"I know, you shouldn't have volunteered."

"Our aim is twofold. First we want to get diesel and ammo but our more important job is to disable the port."

"How do we do that, sir?"

Before I could answer Bill Hay pointed to the harbour mouth. "Simple, sir, we sink something there. It looks to be about a hundred yards across. When we sailed there the first time they had two E-Boats. They are about thirty yards long. We sink an E-boat in the middle and they only have thirty yards each side. Too narrow sir."

"Good idea, Now we just need to capture the E-boat."

He smiled, "And that sir, is where you and I come in."

"We do?"

"Quite literally, sir, we come underwater. They might have sentries land side but not on the water side. We come in one way and the rest of the lads come in the other. We sail it over, open the sea cocks and Bob's your uncle."

"That might well work."

"Any other questions?"

"How big will the garrison be, sir?"

"I think, Sergeant Poulson, that General Montgomery's battle means that it will be a lot less than it was. However many there are we will have to deal with them."

"Right sir." We then pored over the maps identifying potential obstacles.

Alan shouted down, when we had largely finished, "Tunis ahead. Best keep your heads down unless I give you a shout."

I put on the German field cap which was in my Bergen and wandered up on deck. Alan said, "So you are into play acting too."

I shrugged, "I would rather see what is going on and besides my German might come in handy."

He pointed to the south, "Tunis is just beyond that headland. We'll be there in an hour. I intended to stooge around for half an hour or so and then leave when it is sunset. It will make us harder to see."

"We have planned the raid." I told him the outline.

"You are taking a lot on Tom."

"I know but Hay has had a good idea. It is the simplest way to disable the port and it prevents pursuit doesn't it?"

"I know but your luck will run out one day."

"It has run out before now. I have been left behind on at least three occasions. I always get back."

He laughed, "Those were the days when you had just twenty miles of Channel to cross. This is Africa."

"Malta isn't that far away and if push comes to shove and you and the '*Lady*' can't take us off then we will just walk back to Gibraltar!"

"Sir, German patrol boat."

"Thanks, Jameson. From now on German only."

Those who had a few words in German said, "Jawohl!"

Alan and I continued our conversation in German. "Take the binoculars, Tom, tell me what kind it is."

I focussed on the motor launch. It looked to have just a single machine gun at the bow. It was but thirty feet long and had a crew of less than ten. "Small harbour vessel. What is she doing out here?"

Alan gestured with his head to the cape behind us. "They must have an observation post up there. Probably sent a signal. It bodes well old chum. If this is the biggest thing they have in the harbour to scare us off then we are sitting pretty."

Alan steered the E-Boat towards them. He slowed the engines as they approached. Alan took the initiative, "Thank you for the welcome. We are short of fuel. Any chance of filling up here?"

"Where are you based? I do not recognise you."

He pointed to the west with his cigar, "Tabarka with the rest of the squadron."

"We heard one was damaged the other day."

Alan nodded, "Yes we ran into a Tommy. Hans was unlucky, that was all."

The officer seemed content, "There is a lighter with fuel a mile offshore. It is safer that way."

I asked, "How is it going in the desert?"

"Not good. We have truck loads of wounded every day and a constant stream of reinforcements. A freighter with tanks arrived only today." He shrugged, "It is another reason you should use the lighter. Every bit of harbour is taken up. Follow us. I will lead you in."

Once again we had been lucky. I saw that far from them not having enough warships in the harbour they had plenty. There were destroyers dotted in and amongst the merchantmen. All showed battle damage. They had run the gauntlet from Sicily and the RAF had taken their toll. The destroyers were acting as floating anti-aircraft batteries. That was a far more important job than investigating an unknown E-Boat.

When we reached the lighter there was a coaster on the other side filling up. The two lighter men shouted, "Either wait half an hour for us to finish or fill up yourselves."

"We are in a hurry, We will fill up." He then said quietly, "Dixon Armstrong, go and fill up. Wacker go with them in case the lighter men speak German."

Wacker emerged from his hack and wandered over with the two crew men. They unrolled a hose and attached it to the bowser. Harris took the end and unscrewed the inlet for the diesel tanks.

Meanwhile Alan and I scanned the ships and the defences. Rommel was, indeed being reinforced. This was important news and we needed to get back within range as soon as possible. By my reckoning it would be at least two days if we were to complete our mission. As we had recently topped up the tank it did not take long for us to fill up. We pretended that it took longer so as to avoid arousing suspicion. Then Alan said to Wacker. "We can go now!" Wacker tapped the other two on the shoulder and they returned to our boat. He waved his hand to the crew of the lighter, "Thanks." He turned to me, "Let's not outstay our welcome."

He turned the boat around and headed slowly out to sea. Once we had made the headland he opened up the engines. We had more than enough fuel now and we need not be careful with it. The sooner we reached Tabarka and finished this first task the sooner we could report back to Hugo. We went well out to sea so that we could approach Tabarka from the west. It was dark when we reached the uninhabited headland.

While we had been sailing west my section had been preparing for the raid. The explosives were in our Bergens as were the flippers and masks.

The men filled up the dinghies while I spoke with Alan. "We will set the charges for three o'clock in the morning. By that time we should be in the harbour. Scouse will send you the signal when we have the E-boat and then you can come in but if you hear firing then we will need a pick up."

"Don't worry. We will be there. We'll pick up on the seaward side."

I dropped into the dinghy and we were paddled the forty yards to the beach. It was deserted but Crowe and Ken scurried forward to check. The dinghies returned to the boat. We followed the scouts up the small hill and down the other side. From there it was just six hundred yards to the road. We had to be careful for we knew, from our voyages down the coast, that there was traffic at night in this part of the world. It avoided the RAF. Fortunately the road was empty. We made our way down to the bend which was the place we had chosen for our attack. When we reached there I set guards at the port end; the port was just over half a mile to the north east of our position but hidden from us by a rise.

Ken and George set to work, helped by Corporal Lowe. The rest of us stood watch and listened. They set charges at the side of the road and they placed some explosives in the road itself. We had chosen a spot with a pair of large palm trees. They had charges laid next to them. In all the charges covered twenty square yards. If the explosives did as we planned it would require at least two days work to repair it, longer if they wanted the road to last longer than a week of heavy traffic.

George raised his hand, "All set sir."

"Set them for three o'clock."

"Right sir."

Once set I checked my watch. It was one thirty. That left us an hour to get into the port, do some damage and then escape before the explosives went off. We fanned out and moved as silently as only Commandos can. We saw, from our elevated position, the whole of the port. There was neither barrier nor guard house at the tiny port but there was a pair of sentries patrolling. The E-boat was moored at the end of the harbour, close to the harbour mouth. Using my glasses I saw that they had a pair of sentries of their own and they were on a pair of rickety chairs on the harbour wall. It was quiet and I could faintly hear a radio playing in the E-Boat. The harbour had a dozen or so fishing boats. The houses close to the harbour looked to be those of the fishermen. I could smell the fish cooking in their homes. Most would have had a small courtyard to the rear where the families would gather.

206

Glancing to my right I saw the German flag flying from a brick building on the hill. I could just make out the black barrels of machine guns. I estimated that it was some five hundred yards from the harbour. The time it would take us to cover that would be how much time we had when the alarm was sounded. Hay and I slipped out of our uniforms. We jammed them in our Bergens. We would only have our hands and our knives but they would be enough. I gave my bag to Hewitt and Bill Hay gave his to Crowe. I nodded to Sergeant Poulson. He would command the section whilst we were underwater. We held our flippers and crawled down the sandy hill towards the harbour. I had chosen somewhere half way between the sentries. George, Ken and Scouse would take care of these patrolling sentries and the others would wait until we were aboard the boat before they surprised the two on the chairs.

We hid behind some packing cases. From the smell they had contained soap. The two sentries stopped on the other side and lit a cigarette. They spoke briefly. "These night watches are the worst."

"I know and those damned insects, always making that noise. It is unnatural."

"I get so bored I count how many steps it takes me to get to the end of my walk and turn."

I heard a hiss as the cigarette butt was thrown into the harbour and then I heard their boots as they marched off. I nodded to Hay and we slipped around the end of the cases and sat on the harbour wall. We slid in, silently and donned our flippers in the water. It was not easy. I kept my eye on the sentry to my right. He was half way along his patrol. Scouse and Ken would be stalking him. I tapped Bill on the shoulder to show him I was ready. He nodded and we slipped under water. We dived down as deep as we could go and used our flippers to propel us the one hundred and fifty yards to the E-Boat. It was remarkably easy and the hull soon hove into view.

We rose slowly so as not to make bubbles. I took off my mask and hung it around my neck. I took off my flippers. I saw that Bill had already done so. I pulled myself along the hull until I came to the stern. It was relatively easy to climb up from there. I reached up and put my flippers on the deck and then took out my dagger. I felt like a pirate as I placed it between my teeth but it was the best way to free my hands and keep it handy. I pulled myself up slowly. There was no one on the deck. I crawled forward to the hatch which led below decks. Turning I saw Bill follow me. Of the two patrolling sentries there was no sign.

I crawled to the bridge and hid behind the armoured side. The main hatch from the mess was behind me. I peered over and saw the two sentries. I waited until Bill had joined me and then I scratched my dagger down the metal side. It was not a loud noise but an unnatural one.

I heard a German voice, "What is that?"

"Just a rope. You are imagining things. Besides it came from the boat not the dock."

Silence fell and I repeated the action. "There I heard it again and it is not natural. Come we will go and wake the captain."

"He will not be happy."

"Better unhappy than without a boat."

I heard their boots as they stepped towards the boat. If they made the boat then Bill and I would kill them. If all went well then Sergeant Poulson and the other lads would subdue them. I heard a grunt and then a loud splash. I stood. One of the guards was on the harbour wall, unconscious. The other was in the water and he shouted, "Alarm!"

Sergeant Poulson shot him once with his silenced Colt. I heard movements from below decks. "Throw us some grenades."

We were each thrown two grenades. As the hatch next to me opened I pulled a pin and dropped it down. The surprised sailor looked at me and I rammed my dagger into his eye. He fell back. I dropped the second grenade down. Closing the hatch I took cover.

At the same time Bill ran to the rear hatch. As it opened and a face appeared he kicked it hard. The head disappeared and he pulled the pins on the two grenades and dropped them down. My two grenades went off in quick succession. The sound cracked across the harbour. Even if those on shore had not heard the shouts they would have heard the explosions. Then Bill's went off. The E-boat seemed to rise a little out of the water.

I ran to the gangway. "Fred, get on board. Sergeant Poulson, call the boat. We will take the E-boat and scuttle her. We will swim out from the seaward side. Get the men out. Those explosions will wake the neighbours."

"Sir. You had better get a move on." He pointed to lights coming on in the brick building.

"Bill cast off. Fred give me your Colt. Let's get down to the engines."

I opened the hatch and smoke rose. It was like stepping into an abattoir. The two grenades had scythed through men trying to get on deck. As we passed the mess a bullet cracked out from the dark. I dived to the floor and fired at the muzzle flash as someone tried a second shot. I heard a cry. I turned on the light and saw the Captain. I had hit him twice in the chest. He tried to raise his pistol again. I took it from his dying fingers. I said, in German, "Sorry, captain, such is war."

We moved down towards the engine room. I felt the hull as we moved a little. Bill had done his job. He would now be steering the boat and letting what little breeze there was carry us to the harbour entrance. When we neared the engine room I whispered, "Put your barrel around the end and give it a spray."

He nodded and did as I asked. In the confined space the Thompson sounded inordinately loud. I heard a couple of cries. As I stepped in a surviving stoker swung a wrench at me. I just reacted. I pulled the trigger on the Colt until it was empty and the man had no face. The other two had been killed by Fred.

"Get the engines started and then get on deck. We want no heroes!" I handed him the empty Colt and took the Captain's Walther.

"Sir." He pointed, "Sir the hull has been breached. The sea is coming in."

"Good then half of my work is done already! Get the engines going and get up top!"

I went to the hatch which led below deck. Alan had shown me where the sea cocks were. I had opened one when I heard the sound of the deck machine gun firing. That was Bill. I opened the second and ran back on deck. As I did so I heard the engines start. Bullets ripped into the bulkhead behind me as I stepped onto the deck. Bill was firing the machine gun. "Sorry sir. They surprised me."

I saw that he was firing at men at the far end of the harbour. Alarmingly the E-Boat was no longer aiming for the gap in the harbour. It was also lower in the water. I raced to the bridge, oblivious of the bullets around me. I pushed forward the throttles as I spun the wheel. We started to head in the right direction. Fred appeared on deck. He looked a little disorientated.

I pointed to the seaward side. "Emerson, get ready to jump. You too Bill. Mr Jorgenson will be waiting for you. Get rid of your battledress and the Thompson. They will pull you down."

He threw the Thompson into the harbour and his battledress to the deck. The boat was slowly sinking. "Sir, what about you?"

"Hay will be behind you and I will follow when we are in position and blocking the channel."

Our sudden movement had upset their aim. We sluggishly cleared one of the harbour walls, the sea was just a foot from the deck, and I felt the swell from the sea as we moved towards the gap. I cut the motors. We had enough way for us to drift towards the gap. I heard a splash as Emerson jumped over. "Ready Bill, your turn."

"Right sir."

He emptied the magazine and then ran towards the sea side of the boat. Then one of those unforeseen accidents happened. He tripped and slipped . His head cracked into the mounting of the Bofors gun and he lay still. Just then a searchlight appeared from the other side of the harbour. Another boat had come from nowhere and bullets pounded into the side of the E-Boat which was getting lower and lower in the water. We could not get out to the *'Lucky Lady'*. I would have to find another way out.

I crawled over to Hay as bits of wood were shredded from the deck. I pulled him towards the water. On the way my hand found my flippers. I grabbed them too. I found some shelter behind the torpedo tube and I pulled on my flippers. Bullets cracked and crashed all around me but I knew we were sinking for water lapped behind me.

I pulled Bill Hay backwards and our combined weight dropped us into the water. As we hit I put my left hand under Hay's neck. The German searchlight from the second boat was blinding those on the harbour wall who were firing at us and we were invisible. I lay back in the water and pulled Hay. My flippers moved us quickly through the water. I headed for the eastern side of the harbour. It lay in darkness and there were no Germans there. The E-boat was now almost completely underwater but the German gunners continued to pound her to matchwood. She would do her job and block the harbour. Hay was still alive. I felt the pulse in his neck.

The water became slightly warmer. I was nearing the wall. All I had to do was get Hay out of the water, manhandle him somehow, slip over the harbour wall and then try to swim to the *'Lucky Lady'*.

I felt something metal touch my head; it was a gun and a German voice said, in English, "Nice try, Englishman but you are now my prisoner. One move and we will shoot you now rather than wait for the firing squad in the morning."

We were prisoners!

Chapter 18

Six Germans held their guns at me as I dragged Bill Hay from the water. They made no efforts to help me with him and I had to carry him. It made sense. I could not escape with him in my arms. The night felt cold and I found myself shivering. For some reason that annoyed me; I did not want them to think I was afraid of them. When we reached the middle of the harbour wall there were two German officers, a Major and a Captain. The Captain jabbed me in the middle with his Luger, He spoke in English. "So you are some of these English Commandos we have read so much about!"

"I am only required to give you my name rank and serial number. I...

The Captain laughed and hit me backhanded across the face with his gun. I staggered and Bill, now unsupported, fell to the floor. As I lay there, wiping the blood from my face he threw Emerson's battledress at me. "We do not need to know any more than this. You are Commandos and we know what to do with such gangsters. The Fuhrer has given orders!" He flourished an official piece of paper in front of me and read from it:

"From now on all men operating against German troops in so-called Commando raids in Europe or in Africa, are to be annihilated to the last man. This is to be carried out whether they be soldiers in uniform, or saboteurs, with or without arms; and whether fighting or seeking to escape; and it is equally immaterial whether they come into action from Ships and Aircraft, or whether they land by parachute. Even if these individuals on discovery make obvious their intention of giving themselves up as prisoners, no pardon is on any account to be

given. On this matter a report is to be made on each case to
Headquarters for the information of Higher Command."

He handed the piece of paper to his sergeant, "The Major has
decided that you will be shot in the morning so that the locals can
see how we deal with such gangsters. Your fellows on the boat will
soon join you when they are captured. You have failed!"

Bill started to come to. We now had a little hope. If he was
unconscious I could not even think of escaping. Awake then we
had a chance. I tried to buy some time. "After the war is over there
will be crimes for which you will have to answer." I held my
identity disks, "I am a serving soldier and I demand to be treated as
such."

The Captain ripped my disks from around my neck and hurled
them into the harbour. "There! You are a saboteur with no
identification. You will be shot." He laughed. "You are a fool. We
will win this war and there will be no trials save those we hold for
the Jews and those war mongering leaders like Churchill and
Roosevelt. You are a paid killer and you have no rights at all in the
Third Reich." He turned to his sergeant and said, "Take them away
and lock them up. Keep two men on guard all night!"

"Are we to be shot naked? That would not impress the locals
would it? Give us a little dignity at least."

The Captain said to the Major, in German, "The man has asked
for clothes. He has a point. We will look foolish if we shoot two
men in swimming trunks."

The major snorted and waved a dismissive hand, "Find them
some trousers. One can wear the Commando jacket. Give the
other one of those Italian ones they left behind."

The captain turned and said, "We are not barbarians. We will
give you clothes but you will still be shot!"

I still supported Bill as we were led away. He said quietly,
"What's happening sir?"

"Apparently Adolph Hitler has issued an order which states that
all Commandos will be shot as soon as they are captured."

He looked up at me, terror in his eyes, "Really sir?"

I smiled, "That is their plan but let us see." I put my finger to my lips. If we were going to escape then it had to be soon, while our boat was close by. They would shoot us in the morning; of that I had no doubt. We had no weapons. We were in swimming trunks. Our only advantage lay in the fact that they did not know I spoke German. Who knew what benefits we might reap?

Despite Bill's obvious injury and my bleeding face the Germans made no concessions and the barrels of their rifles jabbed in our backs as they propelled us towards our cell. I saw that they were taking us to a building which was close to the road we had mined. They had not taken my watch. As I was supporting Bill I was able to tell the time. I could see the face. It was two thirty. The bombs would go off in thirty minutes. That was our time frame. Thirty minutes to escape. Hopes of finding our ship receded. With another German looking for them beyond the blocked harbour entrance Alan would be heading back to our supply base. I would need to come up with another plan. First we had to escape certain death at the hands of the firing squad and then we avoid the mine. After that I would think on my feet. When we reached the building the door was opened and we were thrown into it. I stubbed my toe on something sharp.

"Just hold still, Bill, until our eyes adjust. God knows what is in here."

"But sir, how do we escape?"

"Shhh, at least one of them speaks English. Say nothing. You are a Commando. Follow my lead."

"Yes sir, and thank you."

"Thank you?"

"For helping me. The last thing I knew I was running to escape and I fell. When I wake up I am on the shore. It doesn't take a genius to work out you saved me."

"We never leave anyone behind, Bill. Not in this section!" As my eyes adjusted I saw that they had thrown us into a store used by the men from the fishing boats. I reached down to feel what I had stubbed my toe on. It was a needle used to repair nets. It was as long and as thick as my finger. We had a weapon. I held it up. I

214

pointed to it, and then Bill mimed, '*Search*'. He dropped to his hands and knees and began to look. I began to feel my way around the walls. I found first one and then a second bisht hanging on hooks next to the door. They were not the normal white ones; they were dark in colour. I put one on. Bill stood triumphantly holding a second netting needle. I handed him the bisht. He put it over his head.

I reasoned that if there were needles then there would be nets. I searched around until I found one. It was damaged but it would serve a purpose. I gave one end to Bill and we went to the door and stood on either side. I had no idea how long had elapsed but I heard boots approach and a voice say, in German, "I have their uniforms. One is wet."

The guard outside laughed, "Well they cannot catch a death of cold! They are to be shot tomorrow. They only need clothes to cover their dignity. I think that these Commandos have courage. They are fools but brave fools."

"Hans, cover the door, Fritz, you open it and I will throw the clothes in."

I now had to rely on Bill Hay's training and his reactions. If there was any doubt about his ability to be a Commando it would manifest itself now and this would end in bloodshed, ours. I looked at him and held my needle and net in my right hand. He nodded and did the same.

A German voice said, in English, "Englanders, move away from door or shoot you now we will."

I said, casually, "Righto but my friend needs medical help. He is lying down again."

"What?"

"Friend, hurt!"

The door opened. To the Germans it would appear black. The German with the uniforms in his hand did not throw them but peered in.

"Now!"

We rushed forward. The German with the uniforms in his hands got in the way of the man with the gun. We pushed him to the floor and the net wrapped around him. I stabbed at the man with the gun as Bill stuck his in the eye of the German who was holding the door. I stamped down on the neck of the German wrapped in the net. I grabbed the fallen rifle and smashed the stock into the head of the man with the needle in his shoulder. He went down like a sack of potatoes. While Bill grabbed a second rifle I took the papers from two of the Germans. Who knew when they might come in handy. Bill checked that the rifle had a magazine and we ran. I looked at my watch. The explosives would go off in ten minutes. I ran towards them. I gambled that we would be fast enough to pass them and be on the other side of the road when they went off. The explosives would buy us time.

We had only killed one of the Germans and one of the others groggily raised the alarm and began to shout. Our dark cloaks hid us from sight. But it would not take them long to work out where we had gone. I saw the road we had mined. It was two hundred yards away in the dark. Suddenly a fusillade of shots rang out. They were firing blindly and the bullets zipped over our heads. They knew where we had gone. I heard a klaxon sound from the brick building. When you were running at night you did not turn around and show a white face.

I wondered about the timers. Sometimes they could go off a minute or two early or a minute or two late. As we ran over the mined road I prayed for the latter. "Head for the beach. Up and over!"

I counted on the darkness helping us. I heard engines behind us and the flash of headlights. We had turned and run up the hill not a moment too soon. The night's exertions and the blow in the face had sapped some of my energy but I found a fresh surge as I heard a machine gun fire. It was aiming down the road and not up the hill. Then I heard a sound I dreaded, a flare being fired into the air. "Keep going!" The top was tantalisingly close as the flare lit the sky above us and gently floated to earth on the parachute.

Below us I heard. "There, on the hill! After them!"

I turned and, firing from the hip emptied the magazine at the Germans I could see. It was not a Thompson and I fired single shots. Two went down, one clutching his arm. The rest took cover. I followed Bill and shouted, "Down! Dive! Down the hill."

We both dived forward and began to roll down the other side of the hill as the parabellum bullets zipped into the space where we had been and then the sky was lit, not by a flare but the light from the explosion. The charges went off almost on time. The slight delay had saved us. The explosives seemed to ripple. Stones and pieces of debris flew through the air. The sand was thrown around making a mini sandstorm. The air was ripped apart by the concussion. I had not covered my ears. I had been taken by surprise and I could hear nothing. Once the wave of concussive air had passed over us I staggered to my feet and hauled Bill to his. I pulled him down the slope. We had moments only. Soon more men would come and we had to be in the water. Our only chance was to swim back into the harbour and steal a fishing boat. It was a tall order but, as far as I could see, it was our only chance and it was one thing the Germans would not expect. What kind of fool went back into the trap from which they had just escaped?

I threw away the now useless rifle. I could hear nothing. I guessed Bill was equally stricken. I turned him to face me. I pointed to the water and mimed swimming. He nodded. I took off my bisht and rolled it up before me. Bill, curious, copied me. We had an improvised life belt. The air trapped between the layers would give us extra buoyancy. I stepped into the sea and Bill followed. It was bizarre for we were moving through an almost silent world.

Once we were deep enough I put the bisht under my hands and, leaning on it, began to kick. Now that we were in the water there was no hurry. The only splash we made came from our feet and there was little to be seen of us in the blackness of the night. To help me get a better sense of direction I led us directly out to sea. Once we were fifty yards out I would turn at ninety degrees and swim parallel to the shore.

I turned and, perhaps the sea had cleansed my ears or they were now functioning better, but whatever the reason I heard the low throb of an engine. The ship which had stopped us escaping had not followed the *'Lady'*. It was still looking for us. I stopped and trod water. Bill appeared next to me. I looked to the land. There was a slight glow behind the blob that was the hill. My hearing was returning for I could hear the sound of shouts and the motors of trucks as they started their search. Torches appeared on the hillside as they sought us.

Putting my mouth close to Bill's ear I said, "I can hear a German boat. They are looking for us. Tread water until it recedes."

"Sir."

I listened desperately for the direction of the sound of the boat's engines. It was gone. Had they shut down their engines or had they left? I could see nothing. Then I heard a voice from just behind us, "Lieutenant, grab this rope!"

I paddled around and saw Sergeant Poulson and my men. There were two ropes. I grabbed one and, after waiting until Bill had his, began to climb up the side of the hull. We were hauled up. Sergeant Poulson held his finger to his lips. With blankets draped around our shoulders I was led to the bridge. I could feel the throb of the engines beneath my feet but they were idling and could barely be heard.

Alan put his head beneath into the radar hut and stooped to see the radar screen. Symons, the radar operator, pointed to the north. I guessed that meant the ship which was hunting us was there. Alan turned the wheel. Very slowly the E-boat rotated until the bows were pointing away from the shore. He nodded and pushed the throttles forward. We were almost like a salmon leaping. My eyes had adjusted a little to the dark and I saw that the gun crews, complete with coal scuttle helmets, were closed up. We knew that every vessel we met would be an enemy. The Germans had no such luxury. Their gun crews might hesitate if they saw German helmets. On such tiny things are battles often decided.

Suddenly a searchlight appeared alarmingly ahead of us. The Oerlikon began to fire and then the two German tube machine guns. The light went out and there were shouts and cries from those struck. The Germans were using tracer and I saw where their boat was. It too was an E-Boat. It was at an angle to us and their captain was desperately trying to get away from us. Alan was aiming for the midships of the E-Boat. He had nerves of steel. I heard him say, "Ready Sergeant?"

"Yes sir!"

Just when it seemed obvious that we would tear into the other E-Boat and both of us die in a shipwreck he hurled the *'Lady'* to port. At the same time half of my men let rip with their Tommy guns while the other half threw grenades. The German sailors were too busy trying to get their vessel out of harm's way and it was desultory fire which came in our direction. As we passed I saw men falling into the sea and then, as we headed for open water, saw and heard the explosions as the grenades went off. One or two must have fallen down hatches for after the small ripples of explosions there was an enormous one as the E-Boat was blown out of the water. The night suddenly became dark once more.

Alan lit a cheroot and, as the match flared, saw my face. He hissed, "Get Mr Harsker down to the sickbay! He is wounded."

"Hay took a knock too."

"Get them both down. We are not out of this yet and we shall need them sooner rather than later."

Hewitt appeared, "Come on, sir. That looks like it will need stitches."

After the darkness of the deck the sick bay, or rather the mess they converted to a sick bay when we were in action, looked as bright as day. Johnson, the SBA asked Hay, "What happened?"

I answered for him, "He tripped and banged his head off a metal stanchion. He was out for some minutes."

"Concussion." He looked over to Hewitt. "You happy to be stitching?"

"No problem. He is my officer, I will do it."

Bill Leslie appeared with two steaming mugs of cocoa. "Captain thought you might need this sir. Stoker's cocoa. Double tot!"

"Thanks Bill and thank the captain for coming back for us."

"Don't be daft sir, we can't leave our mascot behind. You bring us good luck!"

Hewitt washed my face with alcohol. "I should really shave you but your face is still bleeding. When you have finished the cocoa sir then lie down. You must be weak from the loss of blood."

"I feel fine." It was a lie. I felt a little dizzy. I had felt so since the explosion. I had put it down to the concussion. Perhaps it was blood loss. The cocoa kicked in and I put the mug down and lay back. Hewitt had the needle ready. "Small stitches, Hewitt. Lieutenant Jorgenson is the pirate; not me."

"I'll do my best sir."

Despite my best efforts to stay awake the warmth of the sick bay and the cocoa sent me to sleep. When I awoke Hewitt was wiping his hands. He smiled, "You had a good hour sleep sir. You have a little more colour in your cheeks. I am afraid you won't be able to shave until those stitches come out."

I looked over. Hay had gone, "Where is Hay?"

"Gone to get dressed, Johnson passed him as fit."

I swung my legs off the table. "And I need to dress too."

"But sir I haven't passed you as fit yet!"

I grinned, it was a mistake, it hurt. "Rank Hewitt!"

There was a mirror on the wall and I glanced in. The stitches ran in a long line from close to my eye down to my mouth. It gave my face a lopsided look. Bill Leslie was right, I was lucky. An inch higher and I would have lost my eye. I glanced at my watch. It was four thirty. Dawn would be breaking soon. I had no doubt that Jerry would be keen to get to us. There would be aeroplanes and ships searching the Med for this rogue E-boat.

I felt better back in uniform. As I headed up on to deck I saw that the sky was lighter and Alan still had the guns closed up. I passed Emerson. He was wearing a Navy top. "Changed services, Fred?"

He laughed, "No sir. One of the stoker's gave it to me. Glad you made it out alive. I felt awful leaving you there."

"You obeyed orders and you did your job."

Sergeant Poulson came over. His face was filled with concern, "We thought we had lost you then sir. Lieutenant Jorgenson though, he kept saying as how you would get out somehow. We lost the E-boat and he waited. He said you would swim back to Gib if you had to."

"Not quite true but I am glad he waited." I remembered the Hitler order. " Sergeant, you had better tell the lads that Hitler has ordered all Commandos to be shot on sight. Even if we surrender we will be shot. They ought to know."

"But sir, that is against the Geneva convention!"

"I know but Jerry thinks he is going to win the war..."

I joined Alan to watch the dawn rise behind us. As we sipped our mug of tea and ate the corned beef sandwiches on stale bread I told him of our ordeal and the Hitler order."We shouldn't be surprised Tom. I mean you have told what the Waffen SS did. I think it is a good idea to tell your chaps. There seems little point in surrendering if they are only going to get shot. This may well backfire on the Austrian Corporal."

The sun had just risen above the horizon when Midshipman Rowe shouted, "Fighter sir! Coming low out of the sun!"

"Action stations!"

Everyone ran to their weapons. My Thompson was in my cabin. I took out my Colt. I saw that it was a 109 and he was coming low and fast. He was using the sun to blind us. The machine guns rattled and the Hotchkiss pumped shells towards the fast moving aeroplane. He opened fire at two hundred yards and I felt the shells crack into the stern. Phillips, the Hotchkiss gun layer, suddenly fell backwards with his guts spilling on the deck. The 109 roared over us as bullets flew all around him. None hit. He rolled and dived to attack us bow to stern.

"Middy, get on the Hotchkiss!"

"Sir!" The young Midshipman ran aft to be the gun layer. On a small boat everyone mucked in. The 109 opened fire again. Midshipman Rowe was torn apart by the bullets as was Taylor the gunner.

Alan pushed the throttles forward. We needed as much speed as we could. The 109 had banked and came in again hard and low. We had no Hotchkiss and we were helpless. The fighter fired one long burst and then, amazingly, banked and headed east.

Bill Leslie said, "We were bloody lucky then sir."

"I don't think Mr Rowe would agree with you Chief."

"Sorry sir, you are right. I just meant he had us dead to rights. One more pass and we would have all joined the young gentleman."

Alan was shaken. He shrugged, "He might have been out of ammo."

I shook my head, "No he had ammunition." I peered at the charts. "We have just left Tunisian waters. Perhaps he had orders not to violate Vichy France."

Alan looked at me, "The invasion?"

"They could have wind of it. Who knows?"

Just then a stoker came on deck, "Sir, the Engineer says we have been holed and we are losing fuel. He reckons you ought to get as far west as you can before we run out, sir."

"Right." He pushed the throttles forward and we surged through the sea. "What were you saying about luck, Leslie?"

"Me and my big mouth eh sir? I have jinxed us."

We discovered, as we raced west, that it was not only the fuel tanks which had been damaged. The rudder was sluggish and the transom was holed too. The only good news came from Wacker, some hours later as we headed for our supply base, "Sir, I have Lieutenant Ferguson."

"Tom get down and give him a report. Tell him we need at least a day or more to make repairs."

I went down to the radio shack and put on the spare headphones. The signal was very weak. It must have been a fluke atmosphere which enabled us to talk. I wasted no time. I told him what we had seen in the harbour at Tunis and what we had done; including the Hitler order. When I gave him the report about the *'Lady'* there was a brief silence.

"Tom, we need you to scout out the defences in Algiers. You know why."

Suddenly the signal faded. I looked at Wacker who turned dials for a while and then shrugged, "We have lost it sir."

"Keep trying to get him back eh?"

I went up top. Our supply base could be seen in the distance. Alan shook his head, "We may have to get out and push. I think we are running on fumes here! What did the Prof want?"

"We have to scout out Algiers."

He shook his head, "It will take us two days to even begin to make repairs. We will have to tell him it is a no go."

"I know the *'Lady'* can't go but my men can."

"It is over twenty miles!"

"I speak French and some of my chaps do too. We have the two bisht. Even if we had to walk then we could be there and back in a day. It isn't as though we have to contend with Jerry. They are Vichy French. There will be resistance here."

"Look, Tom, I know you have a great sense of duty. I admire you for it but we will be sitting ducks repairing the boat. It is only the fact that this is such an isolated place that gives us any chance. If you bring back Vichy French soldiers then we are as good as in the bag."

I nodded, "I know. Look Alan when we went in at Dieppe Jerry was ready for those poor sods. We left two and a half thousand of them on the beach. If I can do anything to stop that happening again then I will do." He did not look convinced, "I'll tell you what, if we get in trouble we will take to the hills and wait for the invasion. It is in seven day's time. Unless there are elite German soldiers we should manage."

"Okay. Who will you take?"

I need a couple of mechanics in case we can steal a vehicle. That will be Emerson and Lowe. Someone for explosives, Shepherd, and someone who can speak French, Poulson."

"That means you are only leaving Hay as NCO. How about a radio?"

I shook my head, "Too big and too bulky."

"Then how will you get a message back to England?" He had me stumped there. "Leave Lowe here in charge of your men and take Scouse. He is a bright lad. He might be able to do something."

223

"That is five. It is enough." I looked aft to the blanket covered bodies. "You might need my men. You are running out of crew."

"I know. We will bury them on the sand spit. They will be undisturbed there."

I shook my head, "No Alan, take them back to Gib. There should be somewhere for their families to visit when all of this over."

He nodded, "You are right."

The engine coughed and spluttered as we beached it on the spit. The crew quickly covered her with the camouflage nets and we watched as the sun began to set in the west. I gathered my men around me and explained what we would do. George said, "Sir, with due respect Emerson is just a kid. Take me. No offence Fred."

Fred shrugged.

"Fred proved himself on the boat and I need you and Hay here to help the Lieutenant. This is not up for debate, Lance Sergeant. Besides if Wacker gets through again Lieutenant Ferguson may have more orders for us. If they are different then you will have to carry them out."

"Of course sir."

"We have two bisht. Emerson and I will use them to find a vehicle and, hopefully, more cloaks. We drive into Algiers and scout out the beaches to the west of the town. We also ascertain garrison numbers. Sergeant Poulson and I can speak French. We will try to talk us out of trouble. Scouse your job is to work out how we get a signal back to Gib. I can't tell you all the details but we have a week at most. And remember if we meet Germans there is no point in giving up. They shoot Commandos."

Scouse nodded, "Suits me, sir. We know where we stand. Two can play at that game!"

"Ken, you and Scouse take Tommy guns. As for the rest of us, we use Colts. I want as many grenades as we can carry and, Ken, you need a Bergen with explosives and timers. If we can do some sabotage we will do. Get your gear. We leave in thirty minutes."

My men went to gather the gear that we would need. I donned the bisht again. I was just packing my Bergen when Bill Hay took me to one side, "Sir, I just wanted to say I am sorry for being such an idiot. I let one bad officer colour my judgement about all of the them. If you want to know my story..."

I smiled, "Later, Bill eh?"

He nodded, "Yes sir, I just wanted you to know before, you know, in case..."

"I am coming back. You should know I am hard to kill!"

Chapter 19

Our spit of land was cut off from the beach. The rest of our
section took us in on the two dinghies. Once ashore we moved
quickly across the stinking swampy area just beyond the beach. It
was messy and it smelled but it protected the boat. I turned to look
out to sea. It was so dark that I could not see the spit, let alone the
boat. Alan had all night to camouflage the *'Lady'*. He would have
to repair the boat in daylight. I put their troubles from my mind.
We needed to steal a vehicle or spend the night travelling the
twenty odd miles to Algiers.

Sergeant Poulson brought up the rear. Fred wore the bisht. It
was too large for him. He seemed to disappear into its folds.
Having explored it once we knew that we had a mile to travel
before we came to a road and then another half a mile before we
would find the first mud huts and houses. When we reached
Surcouf, Hugo had discovered its name for us, it was after
midnight. I had no idea what sort of military presence Vichy
would have in this part of the world. As we neared the small bay
with the fishing ships I spied an old dilapidated lorry. It was under
some palm trees. It would be perfect. Leaving the others to keep
watch Fred and I ran over to it. I kept watch while Fred lifted up
the bonnet. He shook his head and pointed. Even I could see that
half of the engine was missing. I waved the others over.

Rather than risking the road through the houses I led the section
to the beach. It would, hopefully, be deserted. We passed through
a garden which, mercifully, had no dog. As we crossed it I spied
four bisht. They were on the wall. Perhaps they had been drying
in the sun; I knew not. I grabbed three of them and we continued

to the beach. Once there I gave them to the other three. At least we could all blend in easier now. If we had to walk to Algiers it might not be so bad. When we had passed the huts we rejoined the road and headed west. I pointed to Ken to lead the way. I wanted to view my section. The bisht covered the Bergens well. We looked like locals. Of course our pale faces gave away our ethnic origins, especially the freckled Fred Emerson but, if he kept his hood over his face we might not be noticed.

Nothing came down the road. We walked for four miles and nothing moved either way. This was unlike the coast road we had seen near Tunis. We passed a sign to El Marsa. If we went there we would be adding to our journey. It was only a mile or so down the coast from our spit of sand. I took us to the left towards Mohammadia. Ken led the way again as I looked at the other signs. He gave a low whistle and we dropped to the ground. A Renault truck was heading for us. I had seen many such vehicles on the retreat to Dunkirk. It was a French military vehicle and I saw a kepi in the driver's cab. There were military around and they had to be avoided. The truck took the road we had just used.

I waved Ken to the left and we took a side road. We had to get off this main road. It meant moving through huts and houses again but we had no choice. The roads we took were narrow but they were silent and we made good time. I looked at my watch. We had covered about four and a half miles in an hour and a half. We still had time to be in Algiers by dawn but not if we had to keep stopping. We now no longer had the option of using the beach. There was no beach close by any more and the streets through which we moved were more densely populated. Although most were still asleep there would be many who rose early. There would be workers heading for the hotels and businesses in Algiers. That decided me. We had travelled another half a mile and I led us back to the main road. I gathered them around us.

"We aren't going to be able to steal a vehicle. We move in groups of two or three as though we aren't together. Sergeant you have some French, you go at the rear with Emerson. Ken you and Scouse in the middle. I will go ahead. If I am stopped you keep on coming. If we are asked we are going to work in an Algerian hotel." They nodded. "And we need to pick up the pace. Don't run but move quickly. Try to shuffle. It is how the locals move."

I found it much easier to lead and be alone. I had my Luger, Colt and dagger in my belt and I knew that I could speak with whomsoever I met. I would not be worrying about my companions. Just after Mohammadia I took a left. We needed to avoid the centre of Algiers if we were to reconnoitre the beaches as Hugo had requested. By my reckoning we had another twelve miles to go and it would be dawn in three hours. We were not going to make it and we needed somewhere to lay up. When the streets were busy then we would be able to blend in a little easier. I did not risk turning around and I relied on my men just following.

Soon we were not the only ones who were heading into Algiers. Although that helped us blend in I noticed that they all turned off to head north while we went steadily west. We stood out a little. The trickle became a throng as we trudged along the road. At the next road junction I followed the line of migrant workers and headed north, into the city. It took us further from our destination but we avoided close scrutiny. It worked fine for a quarter of a mile. Ahead I spied two French policemen. They were randomly examining papers. That would not do. We had no papers. To our right was a grubby cafe. Inside I saw men smoking and drinking coffee. I headed there. We had no money and I could not risk having my men spoken to but we were briefly hidden for it was busy.

Suddenly Scouse pushed passed me and bumped into a Frenchman wearing a suit. "Excusez moi!"

The Frenchman murmured, "Putain!"

Scouse bowed and backed away. As he passed me he slipped me the wallet he had stolen. He shrugged and pulled the hood of his bisht over his face once more. I examined the wallet. We had papers and we had money. I walked over to Sergeant Poulson and gave him some notes. I nodded to Scouse. He went inside with Scouse. I waited a moment or two and followed. Emerson and Shepherd came with me. We did not go inside but sat outside at a table. I did not mind if no one came. We looked like customers and I could observe the French policemen. After ten minutes an Arab came over and looked at us, "Trois café, s'il vous plait."

He grunted and wandered off.

The policemen were still examining one in three of those who came by. There was a pattern. That was no good. There were five of us. The coffee came and I paid with a note. We were supposed to be poor and I did not leave a tip. Emerson and Shepherd picked up the strong black coffee. I shook my head and put a couple of sugar lumps in each. They drank the thick, viscous liquid and wrinkled their noses but I knew that had they not added the sugar they would have given themselves away. I glanced inside and saw that Sergeant Poulson and Scouse had been served.

I had finished my coffee and wondered how long we could stay when suddenly one of those approaching the French policemen ran. Perhaps he had no papers or he could have been resistance. It did not matter. The two policemen ran after him. This was our chance. I murmured, "Let's go!"

We headed into Algiers. Sergeant Poulson and Scouse were soon behind me. When we reached the next junction we headed left, out of the city. There was another road block at the end of the road some three hundred yards away. Dawn had broken and we could see further ahead. I saw that they were not bothering with those leaving, only those entering. I would worry how to get back through later. We walked through the checkpoint with scarcely a look. The traffic heading towards us was much less than that leaving. No one gave us a second glance.

I could smell the sea ahead. We were almost at the beaches. We were tired but we had evaded capture; so far. It was gone ten when we finally sat on the edge of the road which ran along the beach. There was little vehicular traffic and we were alone. I risked speaking.

"Well done chaps."

"Sir, that coffee was bloody awful! Next time order tea!"

I smiled, "Right, Emerson. Now we need to scout out the beach and the defences. As far as I can see it is not mined and there is no wire. Sergeant Poulson I will take Shepherd and Emerson. We will walk the length of the beach and look for defences. You two see if you can find a transmitter or radio we can use. If you see a vehicle we can steal don't take it but let me know. We will meet back here at noon and Scouse..."

"Yes sir?"

"Nice lift. If you can get another set, without getting caught..."

"Will do. By the way what did he say to me?"

"The nearest translation is *'Fuck You* or *Fuck Off'*, fairly offensive anyway."

"I'll remember that, sir!"

As we headed to the western end of the beach I said, "If anyone comes near you holdout your hand and say, 'Baksheesh'." Emerson looked confused, "You are begging for money. If they give you any just say 'merci effendi'."

"Right sir."

I made sure we shuffled and were hunched over. Beggars were common and would be avoided. I kept my head down, only glancing up to see where we were going. As we neared the headland at the end of the beach I smelled cigarette smoke. There was a battery there. It was not in a bunker but the six guns were protected by both sand bags and barbed wire. I saw French soldiers who viewed us with suspicion. I headed for the beach. My two companions played their part well and shuffled after me. Once at the water's edge I relieved myself. The sound of the surf covered our voices and I said, "Go on relieve yourself."

"But I don't need to go sir."

"Then pretend Shepherd. It will make the guards at the guns less suspicious."

When I had finished I turned and glanced up at the guns. I saw there were three German soldiers there. That was news; we had thought it was just Vicky French. We began to walk down the beach. Hugo had told me before we left Gib that the invasion would be at a beach west of the city centre. This was the only beach we had seen. I stopped occasionally to bend down and pick up flotsam and jetsam. It was what beggars might do. It gave me the chance to examine the sand. This was not shingle as we had had at Dieppe. It was firmer. Tanks would have no problem here. I saw that the road was only protected from the sand by a high kerb. A car could get over it. A tank would have no problems whatsoever. Although the beach was well over a mile long there was a narrow section in the middle where it was only thirty yards wide. Here was a second battery. This time there were just three guns there. I saw no German uniforms. The far end also had a battery of six guns but this time there was a German lorry and ten Germans.

As we headed back to the rendezvous I wondered what to make of this. Was there a connection here between Vichy and the Third Reich? If so then it could herald problems for the invasion. We reached the rendezvous early. "You two stay here. I am going back to the last battery we saw. Stay here until the Sergeant comes. If anything happens to me then get back to the boat."

"Sir?"

"I will be fine, Shepherd."

I shuffled back and sat on the rocks some ten yards from the barbed wire and the Germans. After a few moments I curled up in a ball and lay down pretending to be asleep. I had chosen the part of the barbed wire which was closest to the Germans. I knew they were close for I could smell them. One spoke French with a German accent.

"What is he doing?"

A Frenchman answered him. "He is a beggar there are many of them. They will steal anything but do not worry he is on the other side of the barbed wire. All he can steal there are sea shells." He laughed at his own joke. The other German did not reply, "Look, there are four more down the beach. Keep your eye on them. They would steal your truck if you didn't watch them like hawks."

"If we ran this town they would all be locked up."

"Well perhaps soon they will. It is time for my lunch. If you need me I shall be in the brasserie across the street."

There was silence and then the German spoke to his companion in German. "No wonder the allies plan to invade. These Vichy French are no better than the ones we thrashed in France."

"We do not have long to wait, Heine. In two days the column will leave Tunis and be here within five days. Then we will tell these Frenchmen what to do! We will be the masters!"

There was silence again. "God but this beggar stinks."

"All beggars stink." Suddenly a rock hit me on the back of the head and the German said, in bad French, "Go away before I shoot you!"

I jumped up and held out my hands in supplication, "Baksheesh, effendi, baksheesh!"

In answer he threw another stone at me and shouted, "Go away!"

I backed away. The other one said, "Did you see the scar on his face? He must have been in a knife fight."

"These damned Arabs make my flesh creep."

I heard no more as I turned around and headed for the road. When I was twenty yards from my companion I said, "Follow me, in ones and twos."

We had all the information we needed. The problem was getting that information out. I did not want to head back down the road we had just used for there were the checkpoints to contend with. I led them to a stand of palm trees. There was no one nearby.

"Well sergeant?"

"We found at least two transmitters sir but they had four or five guards around them. They were just too public."

I nodded, "And vehicles?"

"The same."

"Then it is Shanks' pony for us."

Scouse's mouth dropped open, "Walk back sir? It was over twenty miles to get here. We have had no food and no sleep. Can't we get our heads down for a bit?"

"Listen, lads, the Germans are sending a flying column. It will be here in five days. Six days from now... well let us say that if we don't get the information back this will end up like another Dieppe."

Sergeant Poulson nodded, "Then we had best get to it, sir. Same arrangements?"

"Yes, Sergeant. I will try to avoid checkpoints. Unless, of course, Fletcher here has lifted another wallet?"

"No sir, not yet."

"Then keep your eyes open for a vehicle."

I used the streets themselves to avoid roadblocks and checkpoints. It took us longer but was infinitely safer. It was as we came around a corner in a quiet suburb that an opportunity presented itself. An old beat up French truck pulled up outside a shabby looking apartment building on the south side of the city. The driver, a young man dressed in western clothes jumped out and looked around furtively. He went to the back and, opening it up took a carton of cigarettes from a large cardboard container. He closed and locked the tailgate and then rang the bell at the apartment entrance. A middle aged, blousy looking woman wearing too much makeup opened the door. She peered around and then dragged him in. I saw a light illuminate a window on the third floor and then the curtains were closed.

"Fred, can you get this thing started?"

"I reckon so."

He opened the bonnet and fiddled with some wires.

"Scouse, open the back."

Sergeant Poulson said, "Don't bother messing about there, Fred. It has a starting handle. Ken sit behind the wheel and pump the accelerator when the engine turns."

The roller door slid open; a little too noisily for my liking. Then the engine fired. "Ken, Fred, get in the back with Scouse."

The window on the third floor opened and the young man shouted down. All he saw was two Arabs stealing his lorry. With Sergeant Poulson on my right with his Colt in his lap I sped off south. We could afford to take a long detour now and throw off any pursuit. We used the roads well to the south of Algiers and I only headed east once we had passed Saoula. We went north at

Reghaïa and reached the edge of the swampy scrubland as darkness began to fall.

Sergeant Poulson said, "What do we do with the lorry sir? If we leave it here then it is a dead giveaway."

"We drive it to El-Marsa and leave the back open. I am betting the locals will be on it like ants on sugar."

We went to the back and opened it.

Scouse shook his head, "The bloke we nicked it from won't be going to the police sir. This is black market stuff. Fags, stockings, chocolate. There's even some false papers here."

"Right, the papers we keep."

"Could we not keep the chocolate, sir?"

"Okay, Fred, you can keep some chocolate and a couple of cartons of cigarettes. They may come in handy. Sergeant Poulson, you go and dump the lorry and we will wait here for you."

"Right sir."

Emerson, who had a sweet tooth, took charge of the chocolate while I held on to the papers. El Marsa was just a mile or so down the road and half an hour later my two Commandos ran down to meet us. "Right, let's head to the *'Lady'* and see if Wacker is in touch with Gib."

We moved quickly across the scrubland to the beach. Scouse took out his torch and flashed the signal to the boat. He had to repeat it a number of times but eventually he received a reply. "They are sending the dinghies for us, sir."

It was gratifying that we could not see the boat. When Scouse had flashed the reply had come from the inky blackness of the night.

"Sorry we took so long, Lieutenant, we have been busy pumping and bailing. The holes were worse than we thought."

"Never mind, Symons. Is everything going well now?"

As we were paddled out he said, "Not really sir. We are on battery power and that will run out by morning."

"How about the radio?"

"Lieutenant Jorgenson does not want to risk draining the battery."

That was a problem. It was no wonder we had seen nothing. The E-boat was in darkness. The crew were using torches. Alan shook his head, "Sorry about this Tom. We spent too long repairing the hole in the hull. We did not even start to repair the fuel tank. We used all the juice we had on the pump. Still we are dry now." He saw my face. "Is that a problem?"

I nodded and told him what we had discovered. "We need to get the information to Hugo. If they invaded today or tomorrow then there would not be a problem but if the Germans arrive then it will be a different story."

"You say they are leaving Tunisia in two day's time?"

"That is what I heard. It could just be rumour."

"Then we need to get the boat repaired and radio the Prof. I have a feeling he will ask us to stop the column before it leaves Tunis."

"You mean go back."

He nodded. "We still have plenty of explosives on board. If we could ambush them while they were still in Tunisia then we could obviate the problem."

"Is there anything we can do?"

"I reckon we all need a good night's sleep. At first light we can start to weld patches on the holes in the fuel tank and get men over the side to sort out the rudder. Once we have filled the tanks and started the engines then we can radio the Prof."

"If the atmospheric conditions are right."

He laughed, "Be positive. Think good thoughts! We are due a little bit of luck."

Alan could see how exhausted we were and he allowed us a full night's sleep. We were all up before dawn, however, for we had already pushed our luck to the very limit. We had been here for a couple of days and no one had yet investigated. It could not last. With George and Fred helping the engineer I had the rest of my men except for Hewitt who was helping Johnson, don the bisht and we became sentries. To cover ourselves I had the men hunt for eggs and shellfish in the swamp and the scrubland. After half an hour of fruitless searching Scouse came over and said, quietly, "There's bugger all here, sir."

"I know Fletcher, it is just cover in case anyone comes."

Alan had told me that it would take all morning at the very least to effect repairs. It was mid morning when we had visitors. A delegation of men wandered from the north. Sergeant Poulson gave a low whistle. I, surreptitiously, headed towards them. I heard them speak to Crowe. He, of course, said nothing. He could not speak French.

There were four of them and one was an older man with a white beard. I gave a slight bow, "How can I help you elder?"

"You are not from around here. You and the others work on the boat. Who are you? Do you bring danger to my people?"

I put my hood back so that he could see my face, "Perhaps we do. Although we mean you no harm. It might be better if you walk away and pretend you have never seen us."

"We cannot do that. Yesterday the police came and said to report any strangers in the area. You are strangers."

"But we mean you no harm and we shall be gone in a very short time."

He spread his arms, "Some of my people wish to tell the police. Good may come to us if we do the police a favour. We owe you nothing."

I realised at that point the difference between us and those who had captured us the other day. They would not have hesitated to kill these four out of hand. I would not do that. I turned and waved over Scouse. When he was next to me I said, "Take Crowe. Fetch those cigarette cartons and half of the chocolate from the boat."

He ran off. It would take some time they had to paddle the dinghy out to the boat and then return. The elder smiled, "Do you send for more men, Englishman? Will they bring guns?"

I gave a slight bow and smiled. I opened my bisht and patted the Luger, "I do not need more weapons and I told you, we mean you no harm. By this evening we will be but a memory."

"The men who run our country do not like the English. They speak with the Germans."

"And have you seen Germans in your village?"

He shook his head, "No, but we have seen Germans." He smiled, "Perhaps they would pay for information about a boat load of Englishmen."

I shook my head, "They have other ways of getting what they need. If the Germans come, my friend then I would hide."

He looked beyond me, "Your two men return."

"I sent them for some gifts for you. They are little enough."

I turned as Scouse neared me. He put his head close to mine and said, "The Lieutenant says we can be at sea in two hours."

I nodded and said, "Give the cigarettes and chocolate to these men." I smiled at the elder, "Take these with our blessing. I promise you that we will be gone by the morning and then you can tell the French that we were here. They may reward you too."

"Thank you. We will do so. May God be with you."

"And with you."

The four of them began to trudge to the north west and the huts we had seen. "Right lads, back to the boat."

"Trouble sir?"

"I reckon so."

When we got back to the boat I told Alan what had happened. "You have got two hours at the most. I didn't see either a vehicle or a telephone. They will have to send someone to inform on us."

"Then this is finished as a supply base."

"I guess so. How many barrels will it take to fill her up?"

"A barrel and a half."

Then we will need to take another barrel and a half and fill up when we are close to our target."

"You mean you don't think we ought to go home?"

"I am guessing that Hugo will tell us to stop the column. You know that." He nodded. "Besides the French may know there was a strange warship off the coast but they won't know what we were up to."

237

"There was an urgent air to the repairs. My men manned the guns in case we were attacked and the three barrels we would use were manhandled close to the boat. As soon as the rudder was repaired one barrel was lashed to the stern. An hour and a half after we had returned the engineer said, triumphantly, "She's ready. She might leak a bit. We need a new tank really but we can fill her up."

It took slightly under a barrel and a half to fill her. He lashed the half empty barrel close to the stern. We would jettison that one half way to our target. As soon as the engines were started we dismantled the camouflage nets and Wacker got on the radio. It took him half an hour, by which time we had left the coast behind, but he got through.

Alan was at the bridge and I spoke with Hugo. I told him as succinctly as I could what we had discovered and what had happened. He had a quick mind. "Stop the column, Tom, or slow it down. We can't afford to have Germans spoiling the party."

"You know that we will be out of touch now for some time."

"I know. Just do your best eh?"

I returned to the bridge. "We go."

"I thought as much." He turned the wheel and we headed east. We were going to poke the bear and hope that he was slow!

Chapter 20

Alan was conserving fuel as we cruised east. We had not rigged the radar yet. It gained us a knot or two. We relied on human eyes to spot danger. Martindale, the lookout, shouted, "Sir, patrol boat astern of us!"

We both swung around and raised our binoculars. It was a fast French patrol boat and was flying the Vichy flag. "The chocolate and cigarettes didn't work then Tom."

"I knew they wouldn't. I was just playing a game."

"Well we will have to outrun him." He shouted, "Hold on!" He gave her all that he had. Soon we had a lead on the Frenchman. He tried one desultory shot from his forward gun but the waterspout was half a mile astern of us. He gave up. When he disappeared from view Alan slowed down. "Well it looks like we shall have those to contend with all the way back to Gibraltar after we have completed our mission."

"One problem at a time eh, Alan?"

Fate, was not on our side. We were delayed when we refuelled with the half empty barrel. Rather than discard it we retained it. It was too useful to waste. It was dark as we closed with the coast. We passed the town of Annaba and kept a good watch on the road. We were still many miles from Tabarka when Martindale, who had sharp eyes and an even sharper sense of smell, said, "Sir, to the south. I can hear lorries."

Alan turned the E-boat and cut the speed. He headed slowly towards the land. I ducked into the chart shack and used the torch to look at the map. The closest place to us was Lac Tonga. It was in Algeria. I returned to the bridge. We could now hear the rumble of vehicles and see the tiny glow from dipped headlights. We moved ever closet to the shore. Alan turned us slowly so that we were heading west and every eye peered at the land.

Martindale, the lookout, had glasses. He said, "It is a convoy of German lorries sir. And there are a couple of tanks."

Alan cut the engines and we floated. The rumble of vehicles was now deafening. "Alan, they have crossed the border. They are in Algeria."

He started the engines again, "Leslie take us west by north. When we have lost the convoy give it full speed. Try not to hit the cape!"

"I'll do my best sir," He said, cheerfully.

We went to the charts. "We need somewhere to ambush where the road is close to the sea."

Alan jabbed his finger at El Kala. "There is El Kala but it is a big place and is less than ten miles from the convoy. How long would you and your chaps need?"

"Longer than that." I traced a line along the road, "Here, ten miles from Annaba. There is nothing close by and the road is just a few yards from the sea. It is forty miles away. They will be there by dawn."

"I thought you wanted to attack at night."

"Beggars can't be choosers. If we are going to do what Major Fleming asks then we have to compromise. How long for us to get there?"

"Less than two hours."

He was as good as his word and we edged close to shore one hour and forty eight minutes later. We had not been idle on the voyage. We had been preparing the charges we would use and coming up with a plan. The odds were it would be daylight when the convoy passed over the charges. We could not use timers. We had to stop the convoy while destroying as much of it as possible. Shepherd had heard tanks. That changed everything. We would have to detonate them at the right time. Human eyes would be needed and not a clock.

We went ashore in two dinghies. Alan dropped Shepherd, Fletcher and me four hundred yards east of the main ambush site. Shepherd and Fletcher would have the hardest job. We paddled the dinghy ashore and hurried across the scrubland to the road some four hundred yards away. We had the grenade launcher and the last five grenades as well as spare hand grenades for booby traps. We would be much lighter as we raced for safety when the operation was over.

The road passed close to a lake and there was plenty of cover. We only had four hundred yards or so to go. The road appeared empty. It was not the best of roads but it had tarmac over ancient cobbles. I kept watch while the two of them buried charges at the side of the road as well as in the actual surface in some of the potholes. They covered the charges in the potholes with gravel.. We would not have the luxury of burying them all in the road. All that we were doing was blocking their retreat. When Shepherd was satisfied I left them to make booby traps to cover their escape and I ran down the road to the bridge over the Oued Bou Nammousa. It was just three quarters of a mile. As the crow flies it was just over four hundred yards but the road curves around a rocky outcrop. This was the bridge and the spot where we would halt the convoy.

When I arrived Poulson and Lowe had already manhandled the empty diesel barrel beneath the centre of the bridge. That in itself was impressive. The rest of my men were laying charges at both ends of the bridge. Our aim was to blow the bridge once the convoy was on it. I saw the sun begin to peer over the eastern horizon. We could see *'Lady'*, she was as close to the river as we could get and she now had her radar arrayed. We had eyes once more. A light flashed from the bridge. Hewitt said, "Message from the boat sir. The convoy is five miles away."

They had made good time. "How long, George?"

"All done sir!"

"Good then you know what to do, Sergeant."

"Yes sir. And you watch out for yourself, eh sir? We have the *'Lady'* to protect us. You have a few hundred yards to cover."

"I will get back. Good luck."

I ran back to the others. I ran along the road. I knew roughly where they were but I was impressed that I could not see them. A voice came from the scrub. "Walk towards my voice sir." I began walking. "Stop. Turn left. Stop. Straight on, sir. We have laid as many tripwires and traps as we could."

I kept going for forty yards and Fletcher and Shepherd rose from the ground. They had been hidden by their bisht. The three of us wore them. "The convoy is coming. Everything set?"

"Yes sir."

"Then let us get to ground." I took out my Thompson and lay on the ground next to my two men. I was confident we would not be seen. The little thorny bushes would hide our outline and there were plenty of rocks too. In the distance I heard the rumble of vehicles. They were coming. I risked a glance to my left. A mile down the road they turned the bend that had been our first choice of ambush site. We had decided it was too far from the bridge. This was the most secure place. The ground was vibrating with the weight of vehicles. I could see them as they negotiated the sharp ninety degree bend. They came closer.

I had been looking for my men and not seen them. The Germans would be tired. They had been driving all night and they would not even think of danger. We were in the middle of nowhere. They would not see us. I did not have to turn my head to see them now. A Kubelwagen led the convoy followed by a Panzer Mark IV with the 75mm gun. They had thirty yards between vehicles. I saw that there were eight lorries and a couple of Kubelwagens. I wondered if we had underestimated the size of the convoy. Another Kubelwagen and a second Panzer brought up the rear. It was too late to worry. We were now in the hands of Lance Sergeant George Lowe. He would begin the ambush when he blew the bridge. I saw that there were just the two tanks. If they could blow one at the bridge then that left one for us to disable.

It was hard not to press closer into the ground beneath the scrubby brush before us but any movement would give us away. We had stained our faces and hands. The bisht blended in as well as camouflage nets. We just needed to hold our nerve. The

Kubelwagen passed and then the panzer. Germans liked to have a gunner outside the turret with the machine gun and these were no exception. He gave our position a cursory glance but we were far enough from the road to evade detection. The trucks had tarpaulin over them and it was hard to estimate numbers. The third one towed an 88mm anti-tank gun. I realised the column was bigger than we had expected. The last tank would not have passed before the bridge was blown. Shepherd would wait for my order. The decision to blow would be mine.

The penultimate truck was just passing when I heard the explosion from ahead. The column did not stop immediately and the last truck was next to us when they did. The last Kubelwagen pulled alongside the truck and I saw the two drivers talking. Then I heard the rattle of machine gun fire and the sound of grenades as my section, at the bridge, fought off the Germans. The officer in the Kubelwagen shouted something and the column began to move once more. I saw smoke in the distance. The Kubelwagen raced along the side of the road.

"Ready Shepherd?"

"Yes sir."

I held the grenade rifle ready to spring into action.

As the tank reached the charges Shepherd set them off. They were well placed and the tank rose in the air and came down with one track ripped off and smoke coming from inside. I aimed the grenade rifle like a rifle and sent a grenade into the back of the nearest truck. It ripped it apart. I heard the rattle of Fletcher's Thompson as he shot the driver of the tank. As the rest of the crew emerged they, too, were shot. I fitted another grenade and launched it high in the air. It exploded on the cab of the next lorry along and flames ripped along the tarpaulin. I saw that the Kubelwagen had turned and was coming back towards us.

"Kubelwagen!"

I sent the third grenade as far as I could down the road and did the same with the fourth and the fifth. The three grenades caused carnage as they exploded in the air. The officer in the Kubelwagen fell clutching his head. The machine gun on the Kubelwagen

243

rattled but it was bumping along so unsteadily that any hit would have been pure luck. Shepherd and Fletcher aimed for the tyres and, as they shredded, the light car rolled over and over killing the crew.

"Fletcher, Shepherd, move back, Light Infantry style. I will cover!"

"Yes sir."

Light Infantry style meant one covered while one moved back.

Someone was now giving orders to the men who had survived our first attack. They were spreading out and coming for us. I heard their rifles as they cracked away. I wanted to draw them on to me and the labyrinth of booby traps which lay adjacent to the road. I half stood and fired a long burst. It was more in hope than expectation but a couple of my bullets found flesh and the wounded men dropped to the ground. I emptied the magazine at the tardy ones. One fell clutching his shoulder. I changed my magazine as there was another fusillade. I heard a cry from behind me, "Sir, Scouse is hit!"

"Get him to the dinghy. I will be right behind you." Of course I wouldn't. I had to buy them at least five minutes. The best laid plans.... I wriggled back and right through the scrubby bushes. Bullets zipped above me. The bisht proved remarkably tough. I heard the sound of the MG 42 as it shredded the bushes I had just vacated. I heard a German voice shout, "Advance!"

I raised myself on to one knee and, supporting the Thompson on my knee, I gave a burst. I saw the officer and two men fall. A sergeant shouted, "He is one man! Get him!"

I had their attention and I fired again. I had just turned to find a different spot when the first of the booby traps was triggered. The blast threw me to the ground. Two more went off in quick succession. The sergeant shouted, "Mines! Stay where you are!"

I risked rising and emptying my second magazine. I had two left. I caught them by surprise and four men fell. To my horror I saw the other surviving trucks had disgorged their men and they were coming towards my flank. There were no booby traps there. They were three hundred yards away. I changed magazines as I ran after Fletcher and Shepherd. Fletcher was slowing down Shepherd and they had only covered two hundred odd yards. I ran after them. I wanted to get to a new defensive position.

Bullets zipped around me. I heard another explosion as another grenade was set off. Then there was an enormous explosion as something in the tank ignited the ammunition. This time I was thrown to the ground. When I rose, somewhat groggily, I saw that there were no Germans left in the vicinity of the tank. There were, however, forty others eager for vengeance. I ran on and ignored the bullets. They were fired more in hope than expectation. I reached the edge of the scrub and saw *'Lady Luck'* heading towards the surf. Shepherd was dragging Fletcher. I could see the blood on his bisht. I lay down, protected by sand and thin wispy grass. I held my fire.

The keen, fitter Germans had outrun their fellows. They could not see me but they could see, on the beach, Shepherd as he tried to get Fletcher in the dinghy. They were to my right. I waited until they stood at the edge of the sand and raised their rifles. I rose like a wraith and emptied my magazine into them. I was less than twenty feet from them and I could not miss. I took a grenade and hurled it high, quickly followed by a second. Once again bullets zipped around me but I concentrated on getting height with the grenades. Then I turned, picked up my Thompson and ran for the dinghy which was now in the water. The two explosions were followed by cries and screams as the shrapnel fell through the air.

"Paddle, Ken, I will swim!"

He began to paddle. *'Lady Luck'* was just forty yards from shore but it might have been four hundred. Paddling a dinghy with one paddle is hard. I reached the water and began to wade through it. Suddenly I heard the unmistakeable *'whump'* of a German mortar. A huge water spout erupted just ten feet from the dinghy. Shepherd lost the paddle as the rubber boat rose and fell. I kept forcing my way through the water. A second shell landed between me and the dinghy, knocking me into the sea. I rose, spluttering. I turned and, changing my magazine took a bead on the Germans. I could not see the mortar but the Oerlikon on our boat was pumping

245

shell after shell into the scrub. I fired at the Germans I could see and then turned to half wade, half swim towards the dinghy.

The next shell exploded next to the dinghy I saw it rise into the air and the two Commandos' bodies thrown high into the air. I found myself falling to the side and the last thing I remember before it all went black was Bill Hay diving into the water and then the sea and darkness washed over me.

Chapter 21

When I awoke I was looking up at the sky and I could hear the guns on *'Lady Luck'* firing. We were under attack. Sergeant Poulson held his hand out. Come on sir, let's get you below decks."

I shook my head, "I am fine." I pulled on his hand to raise myself. I saw that Lieutenant Jorgenson was turning the boat and the beach was filled with angry Germans firing everything they had. I saw the 88mm as it was traversed to enable it to fire at us. "Alan, they have an anti-tank gun!"

"Thanks. Hang on." He had turned the boat sufficiently and he gave it full power. I saw the muzzle flash from the anti-tank gun. I felt sure it was going to hit. I know it is impossible but I swear I saw something whizz by and miss the stern by inches. By the time they had reloaded and realigned it we would be well out to sea.

I looked for Shepherd and Fletcher. "Where are Scouse and Ken?"

"In the sick bay. Bill Hay saved them. He dived in and pulled them out. He is a damned strong swimmer."

"And how did I get out?"

He pointed to the bridge where there was a dripping Bill Leslie. "He dived in straight after Bill Hay. When he got you out he just said, *'That makes us even.'* "

"How did the bridge go?"

He laughed, "Boom! George did a cracking job. A Kubelwagen, a tank and the cab of a lorry were on it when it blew. All three went in. The booby traps we set stopped them pursuing us and *'Lady Luck'* used her guns to cover us. When we reached your beach we could see that you had hit trouble."

"We did our job, The column is stopped. They have no tanks left and only three or four trucks. They will go no further."

"Aircraft, sir, from the south!"

I looked up and saw the two Messerschmitt 109's as they dived to attack us. I took my last magazine and fitted it to the Thompson. We had been attacked by so many aeroplanes that Alan's crew knew what to expect and how to repel such an attack. That, and the added firepower of my men meant a hailstorm of lead through which they had to fly. The lead 109 pulled up a little but, in doing so, his bullets tore through the radar array and the radio antennae. We were now blind and out of touch with anyone. The Hotchkiss gunners were new but the dead Midshipman was on their minds as they opened fire. The second 109 was hit squarely in the belly as it pulled its nose up. We were showered with glycol and pieces of aluminium. The first 109 came around for a second pass but one of us must have got lucky. I saw holes stitched along the fuselage. He turned and headed for home.

I went up to the bridge. Alan grinned at me, "I don't think we will escape as easily as all that. You had best get your chaps fed and watered. This is going to be a long journey back to Gib." He shook his head, "God but you are lucky!"

"What do you mean?"

In answer Sergeant Poulson took off my bisht. It looked like moths had been at it. None of the bullets had stuck me but I saw nicks and holes in my battle dress and tunic. He was right; I had been lucky

"I had best go and see to my men. Sergeant Poulson, arrange for food and tea. I will be in sick bay." As I passed him I said, "Thanks Bill."

Petty Officer Leslie nodded, "It seemed only right sir!"

I descended through the hatch to the mess we used as a sick bay. I saw Ken Shepherd sitting up with a mug of tea. He had a bandage over his head but he was grinning. Bill Hay was next to him smoking his pipe. "Well done Corporal Hay. Welcome to the section."

"They are good lads. I am proud to be one of them sir."

"How are you Shepherd?"

"Just hit by a bit of shrapnel but I was lucky. An inch lower and I would have lost an eye."

I looked at the table where Johnson, the SBA and Hewitt were working on Fletcher. "How is he lads?"

"Touch and go, sir, he has lost a lot of blood. It was just the one bullet and it went through his thigh but it was damned close to the artery. He has a chunk of shrapnel in his cheek. We are trying to get it out without damaging his eye."

"I'll leave you lads to it." I took the mug of tea Poulson had for me and went on deck. I spoke to all of my section as I passed them. Everyone was a hero and they needed to know that. It would be a long way back.

I joined Alan on the bridge. He had his cheroot going. He used it to point to the last barrel at the stern. "As soon as it is dark we will refill from the barrel. That way if we have to we can dump it. It is a ton weight."

"And we have no means of communicating with anyone."

"We have almost eight hundred miles to travel. Allowing for the time to refuel that is twenty four hours. I think it will prove to be an interesting time."

Without the radar we were blind. It had saved us before, when were off Dieppe. Here it meant we would have no warning whatsoever of enemy vessels. It would be down to the skill of Lieutenant Jorgenson and his look outs. The Lieutenant kept us well away from the coast. That way we had sea room and we avoided being observed from the land.

At noon I returned to the sick bay. Fletcher was sleeping. "We got it, sir." Hewitt rattled a piece of metal the size of a threepenny bit.

"He was lucky."

"I reckon it is because he was in the water, sir. The water cushioned the force. He is a lucky chap."

During the afternoon we watched. We cleaned our guns and refilled our magazines. Alan managed to get a little sleep. I could not. I was still filled with the proximity of death. It had been close, once more, on my very shoulder. The bullet ridden bisht was a reminder of just how close we had come.

Alan came back on deck at six. He had a mug of tea and an enormous corned beef sandwich. "Any sign of Jerry?"

I shook my head. "The lookouts saw German aeroplanes all afternoon but they were high up and far away. None investigated."

"Then we might be lucky and get away with it. How is the fuel, Leslie?"

"We have a quarter of a tank left."

"Then as soon as it is dark we will stop and refuel. I shall be glad to get rid of the barrel on the stern. It makes the *'Lady'* look damned ugly!"

Seamen and their ships. They say that most sailors are married to the sea; Alan proved my point. I went below deck for some food and tea. Darkness always came quickly in the Mediterranean. I had only been below deck for half an hour and it went from day to night. Half an hour later we stopped. With no engines the silence was eerie. It took time to refuel and it was a nervous time. All of us were on deck keeping watch. If we were attacked while refuelling then the game would be up.

The night was pitch black. The clouds which had been rolling in all afternoon obscured any light that might have remained. It made the whole process really difficult. We relied on gravity to move the viscous diesel from the barrel down to the engines. The motion of the sea made the flow less smooth than it might have been. We had just finished when Martindale said, "Sir, I can hear diesel engines. They are coming from the south."

"Silent routine!" everyone stopped moving and listened.

Soon I could hear it too and then I heard from a second lookout, "Sir, there is another engine coming from the north."

"Bugger!"

I went close to Alan so that we could speak. "Is it Jerry?"

"If it is diesel engines it sure as shooting isn't our lads. I think we can safely assume it is Jerry."

"They are coming from astern aren't they?"

"Yes why? Have you got a devious plan up your sleeve."

"I have an idea. Look if they come closer then you and I talk in German. It will throw them. I will go and see my lads."

The engines we could hear appeared to move closer and then further away. I guessed that they were looking for us. The aeroplanes we assumed hadn't seen us must have alerted them and they had a rough idea of our course and position.

I went below deck and took Lowe and Poulson with me. The hull would muffle our words. I saw Shepherd, "You three, I need advice. Have we any explosives left?"

"Yes sir. About ten pounds. We kept it back in case of an emergency."

"We have an emergency now. Sergeant go and get the top off that drum of diesel. I want as much rope as we can get attaching to it." Not certain what I intended he left. "We are going to make the empty drum into a bomb. I intend to tow it behind us and explode it when the two German boats are close."

"You will have to use a timer, sir." George was ever practical.

"That makes things difficult. Still if there is no other way."

Ken said, "Sir they keep all the old shells after we fire them. When we get back to port they are melted down. Scrap metal is valuable."

"And?"

"It we packed them around the explosives and put in some of the oily rags from the engine room then it would make a better explosive."

George suddenly said, "Sir! They have white spirit. They use it to clean up their oily hands. We can soak a rag in it and use that as a fuse. If we put detonators in the explosive then the burning rags should set them off."

Ken said, "We could still use a timer in case that didn't work but it is worth a shot. We could use a flare gun to ignite it."

"Right get on with it. I leave it to you two to decide when to blow up the bomb. The Lieutenant and I will get their attention. I will tell the Lieutenant what we have planned."

I picked up two helmets from the Hotchkiss and went to the bridge. The engines were much louder now. Alan spoke in German. "If you have a plan then let me know. They are almost on us. Do we cut and run?"

I switched to English. "They would catch us, right?"

"Right."

"I have my lads making the diesel drum into a bomb. We will run it astern. It will barely be visible as we are going to pack it with explosives and scrap metal." He looked at me curiously, "I will tell you later. We need to entice them in. We need to pretend we are German." I took out of my pocket the papers we had stolen from the dead Germans. I handed one lot to Alan. Use this name and identity. We say that we have captured the Tommies and their boat but we don't know how to sail it."

"Would they buy that?"

"I doubt it but in the time it takes to investigate it gives my lads time to explode the bomb." Sergeant Poulson came up to us and gave the thumbs up. I nodded. "The rest of you lie down as though you are dead or just hide." A few minutes later there was a slight splash as the drum hit the water. As I expected it had immediate results. I handed a helmet to Alan and donned one myself. The engines became louder and then two searchlights played across the water. They picked us out. The two E-Boats were over a hundred yards away. A German voice shouted, "Halt! We have our guns trained on you! If you move we will shoot."

I cupped my hands and shouted, in German, "Thank goodness you have come. I am Feldwebel Gert Muller of the 302nd infantry battalion. We were captured at Tabarka. We have overcome the crew but we cannot start the engines."

The two boats were closer now.

"And who is that with you?"

"Private Hans Gruber of the 302nd infantry battalion. We thought we were stuck here."

The two boats could now be seen as they closed with us and I had to shade my eyes from the powerful light. I said, out of the side of my mouth, in English, "Get ready." I saw that they were now twenty yards astern of us. They were a few yards apart. They had slowed their boats but every gun was trained on us. I saw that Poulson, Shepherd and Lowe were lying over the rope at the stern as though they were dead. Ken's bandage was very convincing. Suddenly Sergeant Poulson raised his hand and the flare flew to the barrel. It was so close he could not miss.

Alan shouted, "Open fire!" as he started the engines. The flare was so bright it blinded, temporarily, the German gunners. My men's Thompsons were deadly at such close range and the immediate danger, the two forrard guns on the two E-Boats had their crews slaughtered.

A German voice shouted, "Open fire!" as Alan pushed the throttles and we moved away. Suddenly it became daylight as the explosives went off in the drum. The two E-boats were less than thirty yards apart; their bows gave us some protection from the blast. That added to the quick thinking Lieutenant Jorgenson meant that we were not damaged as much as we might have been. The two E-boats were rocked. Our Hotchkiss crew began pumping shell after shell into the boat on our port side. Alan threw the *'Lady'* around so that we could bring the Oerlikon to bear on the second one. As we raked it I saw, by the light of the shells, that we had killed many of the crew. We swept around in a circle and then headed west. The two E-boats were still afloat but their crews had been decimated by our attack.

Alan used every ounce of speed at his disposal. He turned to me, "Nice trick Tom. Better check on injuries."

We had not escaped unscathed. Sergeant Poulson and George Lowe both had slight bullet wounds. At least six of our own crew had been hit by flying debris. Able Seaman Martin had lost an eye. I found the SBA and Hewitt tending to him. "He'll live sir but his days as a sailor are long gone."

Ken had tied tourniquets to Lowe and Poulson. "Come on lads. Let's get the two sergeants below decks."

The young recruit of a few months ago had grown up. He was now taking charge. I helped Sergeant Poulson down the hatch, "Sorry about this Sergeant."

"It was a good plan sir. You know what they say, you can't make an omelette without breaking eggs. We were as good as in the bag but for the bomb idea, sir."

"And that was a nice shot too."

He snorted as we entered the mess, "If I couldn't hit the barrel at that range I ought to give up and become an ARP."

He was right, of course; it had been a risk but we had escaped. We kept watch for the rest of the night but, as dawn broke we saw the Spanish coast ahead and the rock that was Gibraltar. We had escaped once more. We had pushed our luck but it had paid off.

Epilogue

Major Fleming let us know, through Hugo, how pleased he was with our efforts. On the eighth of November the invasion of North Africa, Operation Torch took place from Casablanca to Algiers. It was a huge success. Apart from two pockets of resistance from the Vichy French it mostly took place with minimal casualties. Bill Hay's old brigade was involved too. This was no Dieppe. This was not a disaster. This was a huge success. The Americans had not suffered as the Canadians had. Perhaps Dieppe had been necessary. The lessons learned had saved lives. Our efforts, while seemingly small, had stopped German reinforcements reaching Algiers. German E-boat activity had been curtailed and the French who sided with the Germans had been busy searching our old haunts trying to find us. While we had been busy at Tabarka General Montgomery had finally won the battle of El-Alamein and the Germans were in full retreat. We had only played a small part in the victory but we had helped.

The damage to the E-boat and the wounds our men had suffered meant that we spent the rest of November on Gibraltar. All of us needed healing for our success meant that we would not be going home any time soon. Major Fleming had more plans for us. He even flew down, at the end of November, to brief us. Not content with North Africa, Churchill and Roosevelt now wanted a second front. Sicily beckoned. When our replacements arrived we would move to Malta. We would have a new base and a new war. Our fight continued.

The End

Glossary

Abwehr- German Intelligence

Bisht- Arab cloak

Butchers- Look (Cockney slang Butcher's Hook- Look)

Butties- sandwiches (slang)

Chah- tea (slang)

Comforter- the lining for the helmet; a sort of woollen hat

Corned dog- Corned Beef (slang)

Fruit salad- medal ribbons (slang)

Gash- spare (slang)

Gauloise- French cigarette

Gib- Gibraltar (slang)

Glasshouse- Military prison

Goon- Guard in a POW camp (slang)- comes from a 1930s Popeye cartoon

Jankers- field punishment

Jimmy the One- First Lieutenant on a warship

LRDG- Long Range Desert group (Commandoes operating from the desert behind enemy lines.)

MGB- Motor Gun Boat

Mickey- *'taking the mickey'*, making fun of (slang)

MTB- Motor Torpedo Boat

ML- Motor Launch

Killick- leading hand (Navy) (slang)

Oik- worthless person (slang)

Oppo/oppos- pals/comrades (slang)

Pom-pom- Quick Firing 2lb (40mm) Maxim cannon

Pongo (es)- soldier (slang)

Potato mashers- German Hand Grenades (slang)

PTI- Physical Training Instructor

QM- Quarter Master (stores)

Recce- Reconnoitre (slang)

SBA- Sick Bay Attendant

Schnellboote -German for E-boat (literally translated as fast boat)

Schtum -keep quiet (German)

Scragging - roughing someone up (slang)

Scrumpy- farm cider

Shooting brake- an estate car

SP- Starting price (slang)- what's going on

Snug- a small lounge in a pub (slang)

Sprogs- children or young soldiers (slang)

Squaddy- ordinary soldier (slang)

Stag- sentry duty (slang)

Stand your corner- get a round of drinks in (slang)

Subbie- Sub-lieutenant (slang)

Tatties- potatoes (slang)

Thobe- Arab garment

Tommy (Atkins)- Ordinary British soldier

Two penn'orth- two pennies worth (slang for opinion)

Wavy Navy- Royal Naval Reserve (slang)

WVS- Women's Voluntary Service

Maps

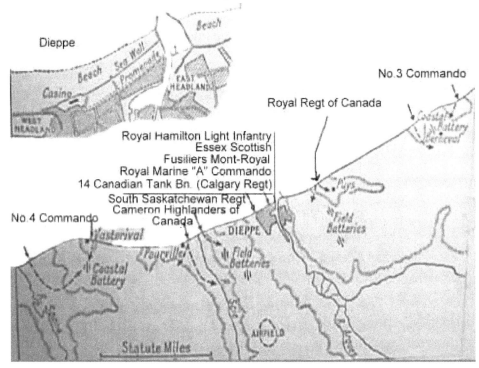

Map courtesy of Geoff Slee and his Dieppe web page. An excellent resource for anyone who wants to know about the real battle.

Operation Torch November 1942

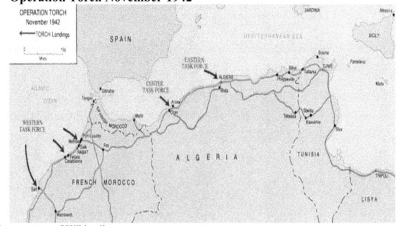

259

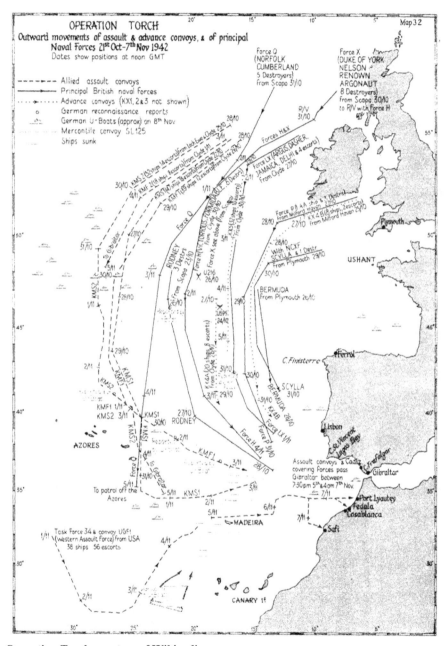

Operation Torch-courtesy of Wikipedia

Historical note

The first person I would like to thank for this particular book and series is my Dad. He was in the Royal Navy but served in Combined Operations. He was at Dieppe, D-Day and Walcheren. His boat: LCA 523 was the one which took in the French Commandos on D-Day. He was proud that his ships had taken in Bill Millens and Lord Lovat. I wish that, before he died I had learned more in detail about life in Combined Operations but like many heroes he was reluctant to speak of the war. He is the character in the book called Bill Leslie. Dad ended the war as Leading Seaman- I promoted him! I reckon he deserved it.

I went to Normandy in 1994, with my Dad, to Sword beach and he took me through that day on June 6th 1944. He also told me about the raid on Dieppe. He had taken the Canadians in. We even found the grave of his cousin George Hogan who died on D-Day. As far as I know we were the only members of the family ever to do so. Sadly that was Dad's only visit but we planted forget-me-nots on the grave of George. Wally Friedmann is a real Canadian who served in WW2 with my Uncle Ted. The description is perfect- I lived with Wally and his family for three months in 1972. He was a real gentleman. As far as I know he did not serve with the Saskatchewan regiment, he came from Ontario. As I keep saying, it is my story and my imagination. God bless, Wally.

I would also like to thank Roger who is my railway expert. The train Tom and the Major catch from Paddington to Oswestry ran until 1961. The details of the livery, the compartments and the engine are all, hopefully accurate. I would certainly not argue with Roger! Thanks also to John Dinsdale, another railway buff and a scientist. It was he who advised on the use of explosives . Not the sort of thing to Google these days!

I used a number of books in the research. The list is at the end of this historical section. However the best book, by far, was the actual Commando handbook which was reprinted in 2012. All of the details about hand to hand, explosives, esprit de corps etc were taken directly from it. The advice about salt, oatmeal and water is taken from the book. It even says that taking too much salt is not a

261

bad thing! I shall use the book as a Bible for the rest of the series. The Commandos were expected to find their own accommodation. Some even saved the money for lodgings and slept rough. That did not mean that standards of discipline and presentation were neglected; they were not.

German Panzer Mk. 2 used in the Low Countries. 20 mm gun and machine gun in rotating turret. Photograph courtesy of Wikipedia.

The 1st Loyal Lancashire existed as a regiment. They were in the BEF and they were the rearguard. All the rest is the work of the author's imagination. The use of booby traps using grenades was common. The details of the German potato masher grenade are also accurate. The Germans used the grenade as an early warning system by hanging them from fences so that an intruder would move the grenade and it would explode. The Mills bomb had first been used in the Great War. It threw shrapnel for up to one hundred yards. When thrown the thrower had to take cover too. However my Uncle Norman, who survived Dunkirk was demonstrating a grenade with an instructor kneeling next to him. It was a faulty grenade and exploded in my uncle's hand. Both he and the Sergeant survived. My uncle just lost his hand. I am guessing that my uncle's hand prevented the grenade fragmenting as much as it was intended. Rifle grenades were used from 1915 onwards and enabled a grenade to be thrown much further than by hand

During the retreat the British tank, the Matilda was superior to the German Panzers. It was slow but it was so heavily armoured that it could only be stopped by using the 88 anti aircraft guns. Had there been more of them and had they been used in greater numbers then who knows what the outcome might have been. What they did succeed in doing, however, was making the German High Command believe that we had more tanks than they actually encountered. The Germans thought that the 17 Matildas they fought were many times that number. They halted at Arras for reinforcements. That enabled the Navy to take off over 300,000 men from the beaches.

Although we view Dunkirk as a disaster now, at the time it was seen as a setback. An invasion force set off to reinforce the French a week after Dunkirk. It was recalled. Equally there were many units cut off behind enemy lines. The Highland Division was one such force. 10,000 men were captured. The fate of many of those captured in the early days of the war was to be sent to work in factories making weapons which would be used against England.

Germany had radar stations and they were accurate. They also had large naval guns at Cape Gris Nez as well as railway guns. They made the Channel dangerous although they only actually sank a handful of ships during the whole of the war. They did however make Southend and Kent dangerous places to live.

Commando dagger

The first Commando raids were a shambles. Churchill himself took action and appointed Sir Roger Keyes to bring some order to what the Germans called thugs and killers. Major Foster and his troop reflect that change.

The parachute training for Commandos was taken from this link http://www.bbc.co.uk/history/ww2peopleswar/stories/72/a3530972 .shtml.

Thank you to Thomas Davies. The Number 2 Commandos were trained as a battalion and became the Airborne Division eventually. The SOE also trained at Ringway but they were secreted away at an Edwardian House, Bowden. As a vaguely related fact 43 out of 57 SOE agents sent to France between June 1942 and Autumn 1943 were captured, 36 were executed!

The details about the Commando equipment are also accurate. They were issued with American weapons although some did use the Lee Enfield. When large numbers attacked the Lofoten Islands they used regular army issue. The Commandos appeared in dribs and drabs but 1940 was the year when they began their training. It was Lord Lovat who gave them a home in Scotland but that was not until 1941. I wanted my hero, Tom, to begin to fight early. His adventures will continue throughout the war.

The raid on German Headquarters is based on an attempt by Number 3 Commando to kill General Erwin Rommel. In a real life version of *'The Eagle Has Landed'* they almost succeeded. They went in by lorry. Commandos were used extensively in the early desert war but, sadly, many of them perished in Greece and Cyprus and Crete. Of 800 sent to Crete only 200 returned to Egypt. Churchill also compounded his mistake of supporting Greece by sending all 300 British tanks to the Western Desert and the Balkans. The map shows the area where Tom and the others fled. The Green Howards were not in that part of the desert at that time. The Germans did begin to reinforce their allies at the start of 1941.

Motor launch Courtesy of Wikipedia

Motor Gun Boat Courtesy of Wikipedia

E-Boat

Short Sunderland

Messerschmitt 110s over France
Aeroplane photographs courtesy of Wikipedia

Fieseler Fi 156 Storch

The Dieppe raid was deemed, at the time, to be a fiasco. Many of the new Churchill tanks were lost and out of the 6000 men who were used on the raid only 2078 returned to England. 3,367 Canadians were killed. wounded or captured. On the face of it the words disaster and fiasco were rightly used. However the losses at Dieppe meant that the planners for D-Day changed their approach.

Instead of capturing a port, which would be too costly they would build their own port. Mulberry was born out of the blood of the Canadians. In the long run it saved thousands of lives. Three of the beaches on D-Day were assaulted with a fraction of the casualties from Dieppe. The Canadians made a sacrifice but it was not in vain.

S-160 Courtesy of Wikipedia

The E-Boats were far superior to the early MTBs and Motor Launches. It was not until the Fairmile boats were developed that the tide swung in the favour of the Royal Navy. Some MTBs were fitted with depth charges. Bill's improvisation is the sort of thing Combined Operations did. It could have ended in disaster but in this case it did not. There were stories of captured E-Boats being used by covert forces in World War II. I took the inspiration from S-160 which was used to land agents in the Low Countries and, after the war, was used against the Soviet Bloc. They were very fast, powerful and sturdy ships.

Sherman Tank- courtesy of Wikipedia

The first Sherman Tanks to be used in combat were in North Africa. 300 M4A1 and M4A2 tanks arrived in Egypt in September 1942. The war was not going well in the desert at that point and Rommel was on the point of breaking through to Suez. The battle of El Alamein did not take place until the end of October.

The Hitler order

Top Secret

Fuhrer H.Q. 18.10.42

1. For a long time now our opponents have been employing in their conduct of the war, methods which contravene the International Convention of Geneva. The members of the so-called Commandos behave in a particularly brutal and underhanded manner; and it has been established that those units recruit criminals not only from their own country but even former convicts set free in enemy territories. From captured orders it emerges that they are instructed not only to tie up prisoners, but also to kill out-of-hand unarmed captives who they think might prove an encumbrance to them, or hinder them in successfully

carrying out their aims. Orders have indeed been found in which the killing of prisoners has positively been demanded of them.

2. In this connection it has already been notified in an Appendix to Army Orders of 7.10.1942. that in future, Germany will adopt the same methods against these Sabotage units of the British and their Allies; i.e. that, whenever they appear, they shall be ruthlessly destroyed by the German troops.

3. I order, therefore:— From now on all men operating against German troops in so-called Commando raids in Europe or in Africa, are to be annihilated to the last man. This is to be carried out whether they be soldiers in uniform, or saboteurs, with or without arms; and whether fighting or seeking to escape; and it is equally immaterial whether they come into action from Ships and Aircraft, or whether they land by parachute. Even if these individuals on discovery make obvious their intention of giving themselves up as prisoners, no pardon is on any account to be given. On this matter a report is to be made on each case to Headquarters for the information of Higher Command.

4. Should individual members of these Commandos, such as agents, saboteurs etc., fall into the hands of the Armed Forces through any means – as, for example, through the Police in one of the Occupied Territories – they are to be instantly handed over to the SD

To hold them in military custody – for example in P.O.W. Camps, etc., – even if only as a temporary measure, is strictly forbidden.

5. This order does not apply to the treatment of those enemy soldiers who are taken prisoner or give themselves up in open battle, in the course of normal operations, large scale attacks; or in major assault landings or airborne operations. Neither does it apply to those who fall into our hands after a sea fight, nor to those enemy soldiers who, after air battle, seek to save their lives by parachute.

6. I will hold all Commanders and Officers responsible under Military Law for any omission to carry out this order, whether by

failure in their duty to instruct their units accordingly, or if they themselves act contrary to it.

The order was accompanied by this letter from Field Marshal Jodl

The enclosed Order from the Fuhrer is forwarded in connection with destruction of enemy Terror and Sabotage-troops.

This order is intended for Commanders only and is in no circumstances to fall into Enemy hands.

Further distribution by receiving Headquarters is to be most strictly limited.

The Headquarters mentioned in the Distribution list are responsible that all parts of the Order, or extracts taken from it, which are issued are again withdrawn and, together with this copy, destroyed.

Chief of Staff of the Army
Jodl

Reference Books used

- The Commando Pocket Manual 1949-45- Christopher Westhorp
- The Second World War Miscellany- Norman Ferguson
- Army Commandos 1940-45- Mike Chappell
- Military Slang- Lee Pemberton
- World War II- Donald Sommerville
- St Nazaire 1942-Ken Ford
- Dieppe 1942- Ken Ford
- The Historical Atlas of World War II-Swanston and Swanston
- The Battle of Britain- Hough and Richards
- The Hardest Day- Price

Griff Hosker January 2016

Other books

by

Griff Hosker

If you enjoyed reading this book, then why not read another one by the author?

Ancient History

The Sword of Cartimandua Series (Germania and Britannia 50A.D. – 128 A.D.)

Ulpius Felix- Roman Warrior (prequel)
Book 1 The Sword of Cartimandua
Book 2 The Horse Warriors
Book 3 Invasion Caledonia
Book 4 Roman Retreat
Book 5 Revolt of the Red Witch
Book 6 Druid's Gold
Book 7 Trajan's Hunters
Book 8 The Last Frontier
Book 9 Hero of Rome
Book 10 Roman Hawk
Book 11 Roman Treachery
Book 12 Roman Wall

The Aelfraed Series (Britain and Byzantium 1050 A.D. - 1085 A.D.

Book 1 Housecarl
Book 2 Outlaw
Book 3 Varangian

The Wolf Warrior series (Britain in the late 6th Century)
Book 1 Saxon Dawn

Book 2 Saxon Revenge
Book 3 Saxon England
Book 4 Saxon Blood
Book 5 Saxon Slayer
Book 6 Saxon Slaughter
Book 7 Saxon Bane
Book 8 Saxon Fall: Rise of the Warlord
Book 9 Saxon Throne

The Dragon Heart Series
Book 1 Viking Slave
Book 2 Viking Warrior
Book 3 Viking Jarl
Book 4 Viking Kingdom
Book 5 Viking Wolf
Book 6 Viking War
Book 7 Viking Sword
Book 8 Viking Wrath
Book 9 Viking Raid
Book 10 Viking Legend
Book 11 Viking Vengeance
Book 12 Viking Dragon
Book 13 Viking Treasure
Book 14 Viking Enemy
Book 15 Viking Witch
Bool 16 Viking Blood
Book 17 Viking Weregeld
Book 18 Viking Storm
Book 19 Viking Warband

The Norman Genesis Series
Rolf
Horseman
The Battle for a Home
Revenge of the Franks
The Land of the Northmen

Ragnvald Hrolfsson
Brothers in Blood

The Anarchy Series England 1120-1180
English Knight
Knight of the Empress
Northern Knight
Baron of the North
Earl
King Henry's Champion
The King is Dead
Warlord of the North
Enemy at the Gate
Warlord's War
Kingmaker
Henry II
Crusader
The Welsh Marches
Irish War

Border Knight 1190-1300
Sword for Hire

Modern History
The Napoleonic Horseman Series
Book 1 Chasseur a Cheval
Book 2 Napoleon's Guard
Book 3 British Light Dragoon
Book 4 Soldier Spy
Book 5 1808: The Road to Corunna
Waterloo

The Lucky Jack American Civil War series
Rebel Raiders
Confederate Rangers
The Road to Gettysburg

The British Ace Series
1914
1915 Fokker Scourge
1916 Angels over the Somme
1917 Eagles Fall
1918 We will remember them
From Arctic Snow to Desert Sand
Wings over Persia

Combined Operations series 1940-1945
Commando
Raider
Behind Enemy Lines
Dieppe
Toehold in Europe
Sword Beach
Breakout
The Battle for Antwerp
King Tiger
Beyond the Rhine

Other Books
Carnage at Cannes (a thriller)
Great Granny's Ghost (Aimed at 9-14-year-old young people)
Adventure at 63-Backpacking to Istanbul

For more information on all of the books then please visit the author's web site at http://www.griffhosker.com where there is a link to contact him.

CPSIA information can be obtained
at www.ICGtesting.com
Printed in the USA
BVHW041255121119
563595BV00009B/42/P